lieu

science fiction short stories

edited by Lafcadio Adams

Idle Winter Press
Portland, Oregon

The Big Trip Up Yonder by Kurt Vonnegut, Jr. was published in *Galaxy Science Fiction* January 1954.
The Judas Valley by Randall Garrett and Robert Silverberg was published under the name "Gerald Vance" in *Amazing Stories* October 1956.
The Moon is Green by Fritz Leiber was published in *Galaxy Science Fiction* April 1952.
Old Rambling House by Frank Herbert was published in *Galaxy Science Fiction* April 1958.
Piper in the Woods by Philip K. Dick was published in *Imagination: Stories of Science and Fantasy* February 1953.
Sentiment, Inc. by Poul Anderson was published in *Science Fiction Stories* 1953.
The Tunnel Under the World by Frederik Pohl was published in *Galaxy Science Fiction* January 1955.
Year of the Big Thaw by Marion Zimmer Bradley was published in *Fantastic Universe* May 1954.
Youth by Isaac Asimov was published in *Space Science Fiction* May 1952.

All of the above are in the public domain.

Idle Winter Press
Portland, Oregon
http://IdleWinter.com

This collection published 2015
Printed in the United States of America

The text of this book is in Adobe Caslon Pro

ISBN-13: 978-0692385029 (Idle Winter Press)
ISBN-10: 0692385029

INTRODUCTION

Lieu. Place. Stead.

Each story in this collection by some of science fiction's greatest minds features *something* in lieu of *something else*: replacing names on a will, exchanging medicinal tonic for water (or water for medicine), seeking beauty over safety, trading responsibilities for a great dirt nap, smuggling false data in exchange for Soviet secrets, rebuilding a regular-sized world in miniature, finding the most effective marketing strategy, and weighing the advantages of future business prospects against defending oneself.

These short stories and novelettes, originally published between 1952 and 1958, have elements that are clearly products of their time, like telephones that still need to be *dialed* and the aforementioned Soviet secrets. But, like all science fiction, the era in which it was written matters only superficially, and dated details can be ignored to delve deep into these worlds.

TABLE OF CONTENTS

THE BIG TRIP
UP YONDER

by KURT VONNEGUT, JR.

If it was good enough for your grandfather,
forget it... it is much too good for anyone else!

G RAMPS FORD, his chin resting on his hands, his hands on the crook of his cane, was staring irascibly at the five-foot television screen that dominated the tiny room. On the screen, a news commentator was summarizing the day's happenings. Every thirty seconds or so, Gramps would jab the floor with his cane-tip and shout, "Hell, we did that a hundred years ago!"

Emerald and Lou, coming in from the balcony, where they had been seeking that 2185 A.D. rarity—privacy—were obliged to take the seats in the back row, behind Lou's father and mother, brother and sister-in-law, son and daughter-in-law, grandson and wife, granddaughter and husband, great-grandson and wife, nephew and wife, grandnephew and wife, great-grandniece and husband, great-grandnephew and wife—and, of course, Gramps, who was in front of everybody. All save Gramps, who was somewhat withered and bent, seemed, by pre-anti-gerasone standards, to be about the same age—somewhere in their late twenties or early thirties. Gramps looked older because he had already reached 70 when anti-gerasone was invented. He had not aged in the 102 years since.

"Meanwhile," the commentator was saying, "Council Bluffs, Iowa, was still threatened by stark tragedy. But 200 weary rescue workers have refused to give up hope, and continue to dig in an effort to save Elbert Haggedorn, 183, who has been wedged for two days in a..."

"I wish he'd get something more cheerful," Emerald whispered to Lou.

"SILENCE!" cried Gramps. "Next one shoots off his big bazoo while the TV's on is gonna find hisself cut off without a dollar—" his voice suddenly softened and sweetened—"when they wave that checkered flag at the Indianapolis Speedway, and old Gramps gets ready for the Big Trip Up Yonder."

He sniffed sentimentally, while his wary heirs concentrated desperately on not making the slightest sound. For them, the poignancy of the prospective Big Trip had been dulled somewhat, through having been mentioned by Gramps about once a day for fifty years.

"Dr. Brainard Keyes Bullard," continued the commentator, "President of Wyandotte College, said in an address tonight that most of the world's ills can be traced to the fact that Man's knowledge of himself has not kept pace with his knowledge of the physical world."

"*Hell!*" snorted Gramps. "We said *that* a hundred years ago!"

"In Chicago tonight," the commentator went on, "a special celebration is taking place in the Chicago Lying-in Hospital. The guest of honor is Lowell W. Hitz, age zero. Hitz, born this morning, is the twenty-five-millionth child to be born in the hospital." The commentator faded, and was replaced on the screen by young Hitz, who squalled furiously.

"Hell!" whispered Lou to Emerald. "We said that a hundred years ago."

"I heard that!" shouted Gramps. He snapped off the television set and his petrified descendants stared silently at the screen. "You, there, boy—"

"I didn't mean anything by it, sir," said Lou, aged 103.

"Get me my will. You know where it is. You kids *all* know where it is. Fetch, boy!" Gramps snapped his gnarled fingers sharply.

Lou nodded dully and found himself going down the hall, picking his way over bedding to Gramps' room, the only private room in the Ford apartment. The other rooms were the bathroom, the living room and the wide windowless hallway, which was originally intended to serve as a dining area, and which had a kitchenette in one end. Six mattresses and four sleeping bags were dispersed in the hallway and living room, and the daybed, in the living room, accommodated the eleventh couple, the favorites of the moment.

On Gramps' bureau was his will, smeared, dog-eared, perforated and blotched with hundreds of additions, deletions, accusations, conditions, warnings, advice and homely philosophy. The document was, Lou reflected, a fifty-year diary, all jammed onto two sheets—a garbled, illegible log of day after day of strife. This day, Lou would be disinherited for the eleventh time, and it would take him perhaps six months of impeccable behavior to regain the promise of a share in the estate. To say nothing of the daybed in the living room for Em and himself.

"Boy!" called Gramps.

"Coming, sir." Lou hurried back into the living room and handed Gramps the will.

"Pen!" said Gramps.

HE WAS instantly offered eleven pens, one from each couple.

"Not *that* leaky thing," he said, brushing Lou's pen aside. "Ah, *there's* a nice one. Good boy, Willy." He accepted Willy's pen. That was the tip they had all been waiting for. Willy, then—Lou's father—was the new favorite.

Willy, who looked almost as young as Lou, though he was 142, did a poor job of concealing his pleasure. He glanced shyly at the daybed, which would become his, and from which Lou and Emerald would have to move back into the hall, back to the worst spot of all by the bathroom door.

Gramps missed none of the high drama he had authored and he gave his own familiar role everything he had. Frowning and running his finger along each line, as though he were seeing the will for the first time, he read aloud in a deep portentous monotone, like a bass note on a cathedral organ.

"I, Harold D. Ford, residing in Building 257 of Alden Village, New York City, Connecticut, do hereby make, publish and declare this to be my last Will and Testament, revoking any and all former wills and codicils by me at any time heretofore made." He blew his nose importantly and went on, not missing a word, and repeating many for emphasis—repeating in particular his ever-more-elaborate specifications for a funeral.

At the end of these specifications, Gramps was so choked with emotion that Lou thought he might have forgotten why he'd brought out the will in the first place. But Gramps heroically brought his powerful emotions under control and, after erasing for a full minute, began to write and speak at the same time. Lou could have spoken his lines for him, he had heard them so often.

"I have had many heartbreaks ere leaving this vale of tears for a better land," Gramps said and wrote. "But the deepest hurt of all has been dealt me by—" He looked around the group, trying to remember who the malefactor was.

Everyone looked helpfully at Lou, who held up his hand resignedly.

Gramps nodded, remembering, and completed the sentence—"my great-grandson, Louis J. Ford."

"Grandson, sir," said Lou.

"Don't quibble. You're in deep enough now, young man," said Gramps, but he made the change. And, from there, he went without a misstep through the phrasing of the disinheritance, causes for which were disrespectfulness and quibbling.

I N THE paragraph following, the paragraph that had belonged to everyone in the room at one time or another, Lou's name was scratched out and Willy's substituted as heir to the apartment and, the biggest plum of all, the double bed in the private bedroom.

"So!" said Gramps, beaming. He erased the date at the foot of the will and substituted a new one, including the time of day. "Well—time to watch the McGarvey Family." The McGarvey Family was a television serial that Gramps had been following since he was 60, or for a total of 112 years. "I can't wait to see what's going to happen next," he said.

Lou detached himself from the group and lay down on his bed of pain by the bathroom door. Wishing Em would join him, he wondered where she was.

He dozed for a few moments, until he was disturbed by someone stepping over him to get into the bathroom. A moment later, he heard a faint gurgling sound, as though something were being poured down the washbasin drain. Suddenly, it entered his mind that Em had cracked up, that she was in there doing something drastic about Gramps.

"Em?" he whispered through the panel. There was no reply, and Lou pressed against the door. The worn lock, whose bolt barely engaged its socket, held for a second, then let the door swing inward.

"Morty!" gasped Lou.

KURT VONNEGUT, JR.

Lou's great-grandnephew, Mortimer, who had just married and brought his wife home to the Ford menage, looked at Lou with consternation and surprise. Morty kicked the door shut, but not before Lou had glimpsed what was in his hand—Gramps' enormous economy-size bottle of anti-gerasone, which had apparently been half-emptied, and which Morty was refilling with tap water.

A moment later, Morty came out, glared defiantly at Lou and brushed past him wordlessly to rejoin his pretty bride.

Shocked, Lou didn't know what to do. He couldn't let Gramps take the mousetrapped anti-gerasone—but, if he warned Gramps about it, Gramps would certainly make life in the apartment, which was merely insufferable now, harrowing.

Lou glanced into the living room and saw that the Fords, Emerald among them, were momentarily at rest, relishing the botches that the McGarveys had made of *their* lives. Stealthily, he went into the bathroom, locked the door as well as he could and began to pour the contents of Gramps' bottle down the drain. He was going to refill it with full-strength anti-gerasone from the 22 smaller bottles on the shelf.

The bottle contained a half-gallon, and its neck was small, so it seemed to Lou that the emptying would take forever. And the almost imperceptible smell of anti-gerasone, like Worcestershire sauce, now seemed to Lou, in his nervousness, to be pouring out into the rest of the apartment, through the keyhole and under the door.

THE BOTTLE gurgled monotonously. Suddenly, up came the sound of music from the living room and there were murmurs and the scraping of chair-legs on the floor. "Thus ends," said the television announcer, "the 29,121st chapter in the life of your neighbors and mine, the McGarveys." Footsteps were coming down the hall. There was a knock on the bathroom door.

"Just a sec," Lou cheerily called out. Desperately, he shook the big bottle, trying to speed up the flow. His palms slipped on the wet glass, and the heavy bottle smashed on the tile floor.

The door was pushed open, and Gramps, dumbfounded, stared at the incriminating mess.

Lou felt a hideous prickling sensation on his scalp and the back of his neck. He grinned engagingly through his nausea and, for want of anything remotely resembling a thought, waited for Gramps to speak.

"Well, boy," said Gramps at last, "looks like you've got a little tidying up to do."

And that was all he said. He turned around, elbowed his way through the crowd and locked himself in his bedroom.

The Fords contemplated Lou in incredulous silence a moment longer, and then hurried back to the living room, as though some of his horrible guilt would taint them, too, if they looked too long. Morty stayed behind long enough to give Lou a quizzical, annoyed glance. Then he also went into the living room, leaving only Emerald standing in the doorway.

Tears streamed over her cheeks. "Oh, you poor lamb—*please* don't look so awful! It was my fault. I put you up to this with my nagging about Gramps."

"No," said Lou, finding his voice, "really you didn't. Honest, Em, I was just—"

"You don't have to explain anything to me, hon. I'm on your side, no matter what." She kissed him on one cheek and whispered in his ear, "It wouldn't have been murder, hon. It wouldn't have killed him. It wasn't such a terrible thing to do. It just would have fixed him up so he'd be able to go any time God decided He wanted him."

"What's going to happen next, Em?" said Lou hollowly. "What's he going to do?"

L OU AND Emerald stayed fearfully awake almost all night, waiting to see what Gramps was going to do. But not a sound came from the sacred bedroom. Two hours before dawn, they finally dropped off to sleep.

At six o'clock, they arose again, for it was time for their generation to eat breakfast in the kitchenette. No one spoke to them. They had twenty minutes in which to eat, but their reflexes were so dulled by the bad night that they had hardly swallowed two mouthfuls of egg-type processed seaweed before it was time to surrender their places to their son's generation.

Then, as was the custom for whoever had been most recently disinherited, they began preparing Gramps' breakfast, which would presently be served to him in bed, on a tray. They tried to be cheerful about it. The toughest part of the job was having to handle the honest-to-God eggs and bacon and oleomargarine, on which Gramps spent so much of the income from his fortune.

"Well," said Emerald, "I'm not going to get all panicky until I'm sure there's something to be panicky about."

"Maybe he doesn't know what it was I busted," Lou said hopefully.

"Probably thinks it was your watch crystal," offered Eddie, their son, who was toying apathetically with his buckwheat-type processed sawdust cakes.

"Don't get sarcastic with your father," said Em, "and don't talk with your mouth full, either."

"I'd like to see anybody take a mouthful of this stuff and *not* say something," complained Eddie, who was 73. He glanced at the clock. "It's time to take Gramps his breakfast, you know."

"Yeah, it is, isn't it?" said Lou weakly. He shrugged. "Let's have the tray, Em."

"We'll both go."

Walking slowly, smiling bravely, they found a large semi-circle of long-faced Fords standing around the bedroom door.

Em knocked. "Gramps," she called brightly, "*break*-fast is *rea*-dy."

There was no reply and she knocked again, harder.

The door swung open before her fist. In the middle of the room, the soft, deep, wide, canopied bed, the symbol of the sweet by-and-by to every Ford, was empty.

A sense of death, as unfamiliar to the Fords as Zoroastrianism or the causes of the Sepoy Mutiny, stilled every voice, slowed every heart. Awed, the heirs began to search gingerly, under the furniture and behind the drapes, for all that was mortal of Gramps, father of the clan.

BUT GRAMPS had left not his Earthly husk but a note, which Lou finally found on the dresser, under a paperweight which was a treasured souvenir from the World's Fair of 2000. Unsteadily, Lou read it aloud:

"'Somebody who I have sheltered and protected and taught the best I know how all these years last night turned on me like a mad dog and diluted my anti-gerasone, or tried to. I am no longer a young man. I can no longer bear the crushing burden of life as I once could. So, after last night's bitter experience, I say good-by. The cares of this world will soon drop away like a cloak of thorns and I shall know peace. By the time you find this, I will be gone.'"

"Gosh," said Willy brokenly, "he didn't even get to see how the 5000-mile Speedway Race was going to come out."

"Or the Solar Series," Eddie said, with large mournful eyes.

"Or whether Mrs. McGarvey got her eyesight back," added Morty.

"There's more," said Lou, and he began reading aloud again: "'I, Harold D. Ford, etc., do hereby make, publish and declare this to be my last Will and Testament, revoking any and all former wills and codicils by me at any time heretofore made.'"

"No!" cried Willy. "Not another one!"

"'I do stipulate,'" read Lou, "'that all of my property, of whatsoever kind and nature, not be divided, but do devise and bequeath it to be held in common by my issue, without regard for generation, equally, share and share alike.'"

"Issue?" said Emerald.

Lou included the multitude in a sweep of his hand. "It means we all own the whole damn shootin' match."

Each eye turned instantly to the bed.

"Share and share alike?" asked Morty.

"Actually," said Willy, who was the oldest one present, "it's just like the old system, where the oldest people head up things with their headquarters in here and—"

"I like *that*!" exclaimed Em. "Lou owns as much of it as you do, and I say it ought to be for the oldest one who's still working. You can snooze around here all day, waiting for your pension check, while poor Lou stumbles in here after work, all tuckered out, and—"

"How about letting somebody who's never had *any* privacy get a little crack at it?" Eddie demanded hotly. "Hell, you old people had plenty of privacy back when you were kids. I was born and raised in the middle of that goddamn barracks in the hall! How about—"

"Yeah?" challenged Morty. "Sure, you've all had it pretty tough, and my heart bleeds for you. But try honeymooning in the hall for a real kick."

"*Silence!*" shouted Willy imperiously. "The next person who opens his mouth spends the next sixth months by the bathroom. Now clear out of my room. I want to think."

A vase shattered against the wall, inches above his head.

I N THE next moment, a free-for-all was under way, with each couple battling to eject every other couple from the room. Fighting coalitions formed and dissolved with the lightning changes of the tactical situation. Em and Lou were thrown into the hall, where they organized others in the same situation, and stormed back into the room.

After two hours of struggle, with nothing like a decision in sight, the cops broke in, followed by television cameramen from mobile units.

For the next half-hour, patrol wagons and ambulances hauled away Fords, and then the apartment was still and spacious.

An hour later, films of the last stages of the riot were being televised to 500,000,000 delighted viewers on the Eastern Seaboard.

In the stillness of the three-room Ford apartment on the 76th floor of Building 257, the television set had been left on. Once more the air was filled with the cries and grunts and crashes of the fray, coming harmlessly now from the loudspeaker.

The battle also appeared on the screen of the television set in the police station, where the Fords and their captors watched with professional interest.

Em and Lou, in adjacent four-by-eight cells, were stretched out peacefully on their cots.

"Em," called Lou through the partition, "you got a washbasin all your own, too?"

"Sure. Washbasin, bed, light—the works. And we thought *Gramps'* room was something. How long has this been going on?" She held out her hand. "For the first time in forty years, hon, I haven't got the shakes—look at me!"

"Cross your fingers," said Lou. "The lawyer's going to try to get us a year."

"Gee!" Em said dreamily. "I wonder what kind of wires you'd have to pull to get put away in solitary?"

"All right, pipe down," said the turnkey, "or I'll toss the whole kit and caboodle of you right out. And first one who lets on to anybody outside how good jail is ain't never getting back in!"

The prisoners instantly fell silent.

THE LIVING room of the apartment darkened for a moment as the riot scenes faded on the television screen, and then the face of the announcer appeared, like the Sun coming from behind a cloud. "And now, friends," he said, "I have a special message from the makers of anti-gerasone, a message for all you folks over 150. Are you hampered socially by wrinkles, by stiffness of joints and discoloration or loss of hair, all because these things came upon you before anti-gerasone was developed? Well, if you are, you need no longer suffer, need no longer feel different and out of things.

"After years of research, medical science has now developed *Super*-anti-gerasone! In weeks—yes, weeks—you can look, feel and act as young as your great-great-grandchildren! Wouldn't you pay $5,000 to be indistinguishable from everybody else? Well, you don't have to. Safe, tested *Super*-anti-gerasone costs you only a few dollars a day.

"Write now for your free trial carton. Just put your name and address on a dollar postcard, and mail it to '*Super*,' Box 500,000, Schenectady, N. Y. Have you got that? I'll repeat it. '*Super*,' Box 500,000..."

Underlining the announcer's words was the scratching of Gramps' pen, the one Willy had given him the night before. He had come in, a few minutes earlier, from the Idle Hour Tavern, which commanded a view of Building 257 from across the square of asphalt known as the Alden Village Green. He had called a cleaning woman to come straighten the place up, then had hired the best lawyer in town to get his descendants a conviction, a genius who had never gotten a client less than a year and a day. Gramps had then moved the daybed before the television screen, so that he could watch from a reclining position. It was something he'd dreamed of doing for years.

"Schen-*ec*-ta-dy," murmured Gramps. "Got it!" His face had changed remarkably. His facial muscles seemed to have relaxed, revealing kindness and equanimity under what had been taut lines of bad temper. It was almost as though his trial package of *Super*-anti-gerasone had already arrived. When something amused him on television, he smiled easily, rather than barely managing to lengthen the thin line of his mouth a millimeter.

Life was good. He could hardly wait to see what was going to happen next.

THE JUDAS VALLEY
by RANDALL GARRETT
and ROBERT SILVERBERG

Why did everybody step off the ship in this strange valley and promptly drop dead? How could a well-equipped corps of tough spacemen become a field of rotting skeletons in this quiet world of peace and contentment? It was a mystery Peter and Sherri had to solve. If they could live long enough!

P ETER WAYNE took the letter out of the machine, broke the seal, and examined it curiously. It was an official communication from the Interstellar Exploration Service. It read:

FROM: Lieutenant General Martin Scarborough, I.E.S.
TO: Captain Peter Wayne, Preliminary Survey Corps

Report immediately to this office for assignment to I.E.S. *Lord Nelson*. Full briefing will be held at 2200 hours, 14 April 2103.

By order of the Fleet Commandant.

It was short, brief, and to the point. And it gave no information whatsoever. Peter Wayne shrugged resignedly, put the letter down on his bed, walked over to the phone, and dialed a number.

A moment later, a girl's face appeared—blonde-haired, with high cheekbones, deep blue-green eyes, and an expression of the lips that intriguingly combined desirability and crisp military bearing.

"Lieutenant James speaking," she said formally. Then, as Wayne's image appeared on her screen, she grinned. "Hi, Pete. What's up?"

"Listen, Sherri," Wayne said quickly. "I'm going to have to cancel that date we had for tomorrow night. I just got my orders."

The girl laughed. "I was just going to call *you*, I got a fac-sheet too. Looks as though we won't see each other for a while, Pete."

"What ship are you getting?"

"The *Lord Nelson*."

It was Wayne's turn to laugh. "It looks as though we *will* be seeing each other. That's my ship too. We can keep our date in the briefing room."

Her face brightened. "Good! I'll see you there, then," she said. "I've got to get my gear packed."

"Okay," Wayne said. "Let's be on time, you know how General Scarborough is."

She smiled. "Don't worry, Peter. I'll be there. So long for now."

"Bye, Sherri." He cut the connection, watched the girl's face melt away into a rainbow-colored diamond of light, and turned away. There were a lot of things to do before he would be ready to leave Earth for an interstellar tour of duty.

He wondered briefly as he started to pack just what was going on. There was usually much more notice on any big jump of this order. Something special was up, he thought, as he dragged his dufflebag out of the closet.

H E WAS at the briefing room at 2158 on the nose. The Interstellar Exploration Service didn't much go for tardiness, but they didn't pay extra if you got there a half-hour early. Captain Peter Wayne made it a point of being at any appointment two minutes early—no more, no less.

The room was starting to fill up, with men and women Wayne knew well, had worked with on other expeditions, had lived with since he'd joined the IES. They looked just as puzzled as he probably did, he saw; they knew they were being called in on something big, and in the IES big meant *big*.

At precisely 2200, Lieutenant General Scarborough emerged from the inner office, strode briskly up the aisle of the briefing room, and took his customary stance on the platform in front. His face looked stern, and he held his hands clasped behind his back. His royal blue uniform was neat and trim. Over his head, the second hand of the big clock whirled endlessly. In the silence of the briefing room, it seemed to be ticking much too loudly.

The general nodded curtly and said, "Some of you are probably wondering why the order to report here wasn't more specific. There are two reasons for that. In the first place, we have reason to believe that we have found a substantial deposit of double-nucleus beryllium."

There was a murmur of sound in the briefing room. Wayne felt his heart starting to pound; D-N beryllium *was* big. So big that a whole fleet of IES ships did nothing but search the galaxy for it, full time.

"Naturally," the general continued, "we don't want any of this information to leak out, just in case it should prove false. The prospect of enough D-N beryllium to make fusion power really cheap could cause a panic if we didn't handle it properly. The Economics Board has warned us that we'll have to proceed carefully if there actually is a big deposit on this planet."

Captain Wayne stared uneasily at Sherri James, who frowned and chewed her lip. To his left, a short, stubby private named Manetti murmured worriedly, "That means trouble. D-N beryllium always means trouble. There's a catch somewhere."

General Scarborough, on the platform, said, "There's a second reason for secrecy. I think it can better be explained by a man who has the evidence firsthand."

He paused and looked around the room. "Four weeks ago, the Scout Ship *Mavis* came back from Fomalhaut V." There was a dead silence in the briefing room.

"Lieutenant Jervis, will you tell the crew exactly what happened on Fomalhaut V?"

L IEUTENANT JERVIS stepped forward and took his place on the platform. He was small and wiry, with a hawk nose and piercingly intense eyes. He cleared his throat and smiled a little sheepishly.

"I've told this story so many times that it doesn't even sound real to me any more. I've told it to the Supreme Senate Space Committee, to half the top brass in the IES, and to a Board of Physicians from the Medical Department.

"As well as I can remember it, it goes something like this."

Laughter rippled through the room.

"We orbited around Fomalhaut V for a Scouting Survey," Jervis said. "The planet is hot and rocky, but it has a breathable atmosphere. The detectors showed various kinds of metals in the crust, some of them in commercially feasible concentration. But the crust is so mountainous and rocky that there aren't very many places to land a ship.

"Then we picked up the double-nucleus beryllium deposit on our detectors. Nearby, there was a small, fairly level valley, so we brought the ship down for a closer check. We wanted to make absolutely positive that it was double-nucleus beryllium before we made our report."

He paused, as if arranging the story he wanted to tell in his mind, and went on. "The D-N beryllium deposit lies at the top of a fairly low mountain about five miles from the valley. We triangulated it first, and then we decided we ought to send up a party to get samples of the ore if it were at all possible.

"I was chosen to go, along with another member of the crew, a man named Lee Bellows. We left the ship at about five in the morning, and spent most of the day climbing up to the spot where we had detected the beryllium. We couldn't get a sample; the main deposit is located several feet beneath the surface of the mountaintop, and the mountain is too rough and rocky to climb without special equipment. We got less than halfway before we had to stop."

Wayne felt Sherri nudge him, and turned to nod. He knew what she was thinking. This was where he came in; it was a job that called for a specialist, a trained mountaineer—such as Captain Peter Wayne. He frowned and turned his attention back to the man on the platform.

"We made all the readings we could," Jervis continued. "Then we headed back to our temporary base."

His face looked troubled. "When we got back, every man at the base was dead."

Silence in the room. Complete, utter, deafening silence.

"There were only nine of us in the ship," Jervis said. He was obviously still greatly affected by whatever had taken place on Fomalhaut V. "With seven of us dead, that left only Bellows and myself. We couldn't find out what had killed them. They were lying scattered over the valley floor for several yards around the ship. They looked as though they had suddenly dropped dead at whatever they were doing."

Peter Wayne made use of his extra few inches of height to glance around the briefing room. He saw row on row of tense faces—faces that reflected the same emotions he was feeling. Space exploration was something still new and mostly unknown, and even the experienced men of IES still knew fear occasionally. The galaxy was a big place; unknown terrors lurked on planets unimaginably distant. Every now and then, something like this would come up—something to give you pause, before you ventured into space again.

"We couldn't find out what had killed them," Jervis said again. "They were lying scattered every which way, with no clues at all." The small man's fingers were trembling from relived fright. "Bellows and I were pretty scared, I'll have to admit. We couldn't find a sign of what had killed the men—they'd just—just *died*."

There was a quiver in his voice. It was obvious he could never take the story lightly, no matter how many times he had to tell it.

Wayne heard Private Manetti mutter, "There's always a price for D-N beryllium."

"The Scout Ship hadn't been molested," Jervis went on. "I went inside and checked it over. It was untouched, undisturbed in every way. I checked the control panel, the cabins, everything. All unbothered. The ship was empty and dead. And—outside—

"When I came out, Bellows was dead too." He took a deep breath. "I'm afraid I panicked then. I locked myself inside the ship, set the autocontrols, and headed back to Earth at top velocity. I set the ship in an orbit around the moon and notified headquarters. I was quarantined immediately, of course, to make sure

I wasn't carrying anything. The medics checked me over carefully. I wasn't and am not now carrying any virus or bacteria unknown to Terrestrial medicine.

"Since I'm the only one who knows exactly where this valley is, the general has asked me to guide the *Lord Nelson* to the exact spot. Actually, it could be found eventually with the D-N beryllium as a guide. But the *Mavis* was in orbit around Fomalhaut V for two weeks before we found the D-N beryllium deposit, and the Service feels that we shouldn't waste any time."

The lieutenant sat, and General Scarborough resumed his place on the platform.

"THAT'S the situation," Scarborough said bluntly. "You know the setup, now—and I think some of you see how your specialities are going to fit into the operation. As Lieutenant Jervis pointed out, we don't know what killed the crew of the *Mavis*; therefore, we are going to take every possible precaution. As far as we know, there are no inimical life forms on Fomalhaut V—but it's possible that there are things we don't know about, such as airborne viruses that kill in a very short time. If so, then Lieutenant Jervis is immune to the virus and is not a transmitter or carrier of it.

"However, to guard against such a possibility, no one will leave the *Lord Nelson*, once it has landed, without wearing a spacesuit. The air is breathable, but we're taking no chances. Also, no one will go out alone; scouting parties will always be in pairs, with wide open communication with the ship. And at no time will more than ten percent of the ship's company be outside at any one time."

Wayne made a rough mental computation. *The Lord Nelson holds sixty. That means no more than six out at any single time. They really must be worried.*

"Aside from those orders, which were decided by the Service Command, you'll be under the direct orders of Colonel Nels Petersen. Colonel Petersen."

Petersen was a tall, hard-faced man with a touch of gray at his temples. He stepped forward and stared intently at the assembled crew.

"OUR JOB is to make the preliminary preparations for getting D-N beryllium out of the crust of Fomalhaut V. We're supposed to stay alive while we do it. Therefore, our secondary job is to find out what it was that killed the scouting expedition of the *Mavis.* There are sixty of us going aboard the *Lord Nelson* tomorrow, and I'd like to have sixty aboard when we come back. Got that?"

He leaned forward, stretched upward on his toes, and smiled mechanically. "Fine. Now, you all know your jobs, but we're going to have to work together as a team. We're going to have to correlate our work so that we'll know what we're doing. So don't think we won't have anything to do during the two weeks it will take us to get to Fomalhaut V. We're going to work it as though it were a shakedown cruise. If anyone doesn't work out, he'll be replaced, even if we have to turn around and come back to Earth. On a planet which has wiped out a whole scouting expedition, we can't afford to have any slip-ups. And that means we can't afford to have anyone aboard who doesn't know what he's doing or doesn't care. Is that clear?"

It was.

"All right," said the colonel. "Let's go out and get acquainted with the *Lord Nelson*."

T HE BRIEFING session broke up well past midnight, and the group that shortly would become the crew of the *Lord Nelson* filtered out of the building and into the cool spring air. Each man had a fairly good idea of his job and each man knew the dangers involved. No one had backed out.

"What d'ye think of it, Pete?" Sherri James asked, as they left together. "Sounds pretty mean."

"I wish we knew what the answers were beforehand," Wayne said. He glanced down at Sherri. The moon was full, and its rays glinted brightly off her golden hair. "It's a risky deal, as Petersen said. Nine men go out, and eight die—of what? Just dead, that's all."

"It's the way the game goes," Sherri said. "You knew that when you joined the corps." They turned down the main road of the IES compound and headed for the snack bar.

Wayne nodded. "I know, kid. It's a job, and it has to be done. But nobody likes to walk into an empty planet like that knowing that eight of the last nine guys who did didn't come back."

He put his arm around her and they entered the snack bar that way. Most of the other crew-members were there already; Wayne sensed the heightening tenseness on their faces.

"Two nuclear fizzes," he said to the pfc at the bar. "With all the trimmings."

"What's the matter, Captain?" said a balding, potbellied major a few stools down, who was nursing a beer. "How come the soft drinks tonight, Wayne?"

Peter grinned. "I'm in training now, Major Osborne. Gotta kill the evil green horde from Rigel Seven, and I don't dare drink anything stronger than sarsaparilla."

"How about the amazon, then?" Osborne said, gesturing at Sherri. "Her too?"

"Me too," Sherri said.

Osborne stared at his beer. "You two must be in Scarborough's new project, then." He squinted at Peter, who nodded almost imperceptibly.

"You'll need luck," Osborne said.

"No we won't," Wayne said. "Not luck. We'll need more than just luck to pull us through."

The nuclear fizzes arrived. He began to sip it quietly. A few more members of the crew entered the snack bar. Their faces were drawn tensely.

He guzzled the drink and looked up at Sherri, who was sucking down the last of the soda. "Let's get going, Lieutenant James. The noncoms are coming, and we don't want them to make nasty remarks about us."

THE *LORD NELSON* blasted off the next evening, after a frenzied day of hurried preparations. The crew of sixty filed solemnly aboard, Colonel Petersen last, and the great hatch swung closed.

There was the usual routine loudspeaker-business while everyone quickly and efficiently strapped into his acceleration cradle, and then the ship leaped skyward. It climbed rapidly, broke free of Earth's grasp, and, out past the moon, abruptly winked out of normal space into overdrive. It would spend the next two weeks in hyperspace, short-cutting across the galaxy to Fomalhaut V.

It was a busy two weeks for everyone involved. Captain Peter Wayne, as a central part of the team, spent much of his time planning his attack. His job would be the actual climbing of the mountain where the double-nucleus beryllium was located. It wasn't going to be an easy job; the terrain was rough, the wind, according to Jervis, whipped ragingly through the hills, and the jagged peaks thrust into the air like the teeth of some mythical dragon.

Study of the three-dimensional aerial photographs taken from the *Mavis* showed that the best route was probably up through one end of the valley, through a narrow pass that led around the mountain, and up the west slope, which appeared to offer better handholds and was less perpendicular than the other sides of the mountain.

This time, the expedition would have the equipment to make the climb. There were ropes, picks, and crampons, and sets of metamagnetic boots and grapples. With metamagnetic boots, Wayne thought, they'd be able to walk up the side of the mountain almost as easily as if it were flat.

He studied the thick, heavy soles of the boots for a moment, then set to work polishing. Wayne liked to keep his boots mirror-bright; it wasn't required, but it was a habit of his nonetheless.

He set to work vigorously. Everyone aboard the ship was working that way. Sherri James, who was in charge of the Correlation Section, had noticed the same thing the day before. Her job was to co-ordinate all the information from various members of the expedition, run them through the computers, and record them. She had been busy since blastoff, testing the computers, checking and rechecking them, being overly efficient.

"I know why we're doing it," she said. "It keeps our mind off the end of the trip. When we spend the whole day working out complicated circuits for the computers, or polishing mountain boots, or cleaning the jet tubes, it's just so we don't have to think about Fomalhaut V. It helps to concentrate on details."

Wayne nodded and said nothing. Sherri was right. There was one thought in everyone's mind: what was the deadly secret of the valley?

There was another thought, after that:

Will we find it out in time?

AFTER two weeks of flight through the vast blackness of interstellar space, the *Lord Nelson* came out of overdrive and set itself in an orbit around Fomalhaut V. Lieutenant Jervis, the sole survivor of the ill-fated

Mavis, located the small valley between the giant crags that covered the planet, and the huge spherical bulk of the spaceship settled gently to the floor of the valley.

They were gathered in the central room of the ship ten minutes after the *all-clear* rang through the corridors, informing everyone that the landing had been safely accomplished. From the portholes they could see the white bones of the *Mavis's* crew lying on the reddish sand of the valley bottom.

"There they are," Jervis said quietly. "Just bones. Those were my shipmates."

Wayne saw Sherri repress a shudder. Little heaps of bones lay here and there on the sand, shining brightly in the hot sun. That was the crew of the *Mavis* —or what was left of them.

Colonel Petersen entered the room and confronted the crew. "We're here," he said. "You know the schedule from now on. No one's to leave the ship until we've made a check outside, and after that—assuming it's OK to go out—no more than six are to leave the ship at any one time."

He pointed to a row of metal magnetic tabs clinging to the wall nearest the corridor that led to the airlock. "When you go out, take one of those tabs and touch it on your suit. There are exactly six tabs. If none are there, don't go out. It's as simple as that."

Four men in spacesuits entered the room, followed by two others. The leader of the group saluted. "We're ready, sir," he said.

"Go out and get a look at the bodies," the colonel told the men, who were Medical Corpsmen. "You know the procedure. Air and sand samples too, of course."

The leader saluted again, turned, and left. Wayne watched the six spacesuited figures step one at a time to the wall, withdraw one of the metal tabs, and affix it to the outer skin of his suit. Then they went outside.

CAPTAIN WAYNE and Sherri James stood by one of the portholes and watched the six medics as they bent over the corpses outside. "I don't get it, I just don't understand," Wayne said quietly.

"What don't you get?" Sherri asked.

"Those skeletons. Those men have only been dead for two months, and they've been reduced to nothing but bones already. Even the fabric of their clothing is gone. Why? There must be something here that causes human flesh to deteriorate much faster than normal."

"It does look pretty gruesome," Sherri agreed. "I'm glad we've been ordered to keep our spacesuits on. I wouldn't want to be exposed to anything that might be out there."

"I wonder—" Wayne muttered.

"What? What's the matter?"

Wayne pointed to one figure lying on the sand. "See that? What's that over his head?"

"Why—it's a space helmet!"

"Yeah," said Wayne. "The question is: was he wearing just the helmet, or the whole suit? If he was wearing the whole suit, we're not going to be as well protected as we thought, even with our fancy suits."

Fifteen minutes passed slowly before the medics returned, and five minutes more before they had passed through the decontamination chambers and were allowed into the ship proper. A ring of tense faces surrounded them as they made their report.

THE LEADER, a tall, bespectacled doctor named Stevelman, was the spokesman. He shrugged when Colonel Petersen put forth the question whose answer everyone waited for.

"I don't know," the medic replied. "I don't know what killed them. There's dry bones out there, but no sign of anything that might have done it. It's pretty hard to make a quick diagnosis on a skeleton, Colonel."

"What about the one skeleton with the bubble helmet?" Peter Wayne asked. "Did you see any sign of a full suit on him?"

Stevelman shook his head. "Not a sign, sir."

Colonel Petersen turned and glanced at Lieutenant Jervis. "Do you remember what the circumstances were, Lieutenant?"

Jervis shrugged. "I don't recall it very clearly, sir. I honestly couldn't tell you whether they were wearing suits or bubble-helmets or anything. I was too upset at the time to make careful observations."

"I understand," Petersen said.

But the medic had a different theory. He pointed at Jervis and said, "That's a point I've meant to make, Lieutenant. You're a trained space scout. Your psychological records show that you're not the sort of man given to panic or to become confused."

"Are you implying that there's something improper about my statement, Dr. Stevelman?"

The medic held up a hand. "Nothing of the sort, Lieutenant. But since you're not the sort to panic, even in such a crisis as the complete destruction of the entire crew of your scout ship, you must have been ill—partly delirious from fever. Not delirious enough to cause hallucinations, but just enough to impair your judgment."

Jervis nodded. "That is possible," he said.

"Good," said Stevelman. "I have two tentative hypotheses, then." He turned to the colonel. "Should I state them now, Colonel Petersen?"

"There's to be no secrecy aboard this ship, Doctor. I want every man and woman on the ship to know all the facts at all times."

"Very well," the medic said. "I'd suggest the deaths were caused by some unknown virus—or, perhaps, by some virulent poison that occurred occasionally, a poisonous smog of some kind that had settled in the valley for a time and then dissipated."

Wayne frowned and shook his head. Both hypotheses made sense.

"Do you have any suggestions, Doctor?" Petersen said.

"Since we don't have any direct information about why those men died, Colonel, I can't make any definite statements. But I can offer one bit of advice to everyone: *wear your suits and be alert.*"

D URING the week that followed, several groups went out without suffering any ill effects. A short service was held for the eight of the *Mavis* and then the skeletons were buried in the valley.

They ran a check on the double-nucleus beryllium toward the end of the week, after it had been fairly safely established that no apparent harm was going to come to them. Wayne and Sherri were both in the crew that went outside to set up the detector.

"You man the detector plate," said Major MacDougal, who was in charge of the group, turning to Wayne.

He put his hand on the plate and waited for the guide coordinates to be set. MacDougal fumbled at the base of the detector for a moment, and the machine began picking up eloptic radiations.

Wayne now looked down at the detector plate. "Here we are," he said. "The dial's oscillating between four and eight, all right. The stuff's here."

MacDougal whistled gently. "It's really sending, isn't it!" He pointed toward the mountaintop. "From up there, too. It's going to be a nice climb. Okay, pack the detector up and let's get back inside."

They entered the airlock and passed on into the ship.

"The D-N beryllium up there, sir," Major MacDougal said. "It's going to be a devil of a job to get up to find the stuff."

"That's what Captain Wayne's here for," Petersen said. "Captain, what do you think? Can you get up here?"

"It would have been easier to bring along a helicopter," Wayne said wryly. "Pity the things don't fit into spaceships. But I think I can get up there. I'd like to try surveying the lay of the land, first. I want to know all the possible routes before I start climbing."

"Good idea," Petersen said. "I'll send you out with three men to do some preliminary exploring. Boggs! Manetti! MacPherson! Suit up and get with it!"

W AYNE strode toward the spacesuit locker, took out his suit, and donned it. Instead of the normal space boots, he put on the special metamagnetic boots for mountain climbing. The little reactors in the back of the calf activated the thick metal sole of each boot so that it would cling tightly to the metallic rock of the mountain. Unlike ordinary magnetism, the metamagnetic field acted on all metals, even when they were in combination with other elements.

His team of three stood before him in the air-lock room. He knew all three of them fairly well from Earthside; they were capable, level-headed men, and at least one—Boggs—had already been out in the valley surveying once, and so knew the area pretty well.

He pulled on the boots and looked up. "We're not going to climb the mountain this time, men. We'll just take a look around it to decide which is the best way."

"You have any ideas, sir?" Sergeant Boggs asked.

"From looking at the photographs, I'd guess that the western approach is the best. But I may be wrong. Little details are hard to see from five hundred miles up, even with the best of instruments, and there may be things in our way that will make the west slope impassible. If so, we'll try the southern side. It looks pretty steep, but it also seems rough enough to offer plenty of handholds."

"Too bad we couldn't have had that helicopter you were talking about," said Boggs.

Wayne grinned. "With these winds? They'd smash us against the side of the mountain before we'd get up fifty feet. You ought to know, Sergeant—you've been out in them once already."

"They're not so bad down in this valley, sir," Boggs said. "The only time you really notice them is when you climb the escarpment at the northern end. They get pretty rough up there."

Wayne nodded. "You can see what kind of a job we'll have. Even with metamagnetic boots and grapples, we'll still have to use the old standbys." He looked at the men. "Okay; we're all ready. Let's go."

They unhooked four of the six tabs from the wall and donned them. Then they moved on into the airlock and closed the inner door. The air was pumped out, just as though the ship were in space or on a planet with a poisonous atmosphere. As far as anyone knew, the atmosphere of Fomalhaut V actually was poisonous. Some of the tension had relaxed after a week spent in safety, but there was always the first expedition to consider; no one took chances.

When all the air had been removed, a bleeder valve allowed the outer air to come into the chamber. Then the outer door opened, and the four men went down the ladder to the valley floor.

WAYNE led the way across the sand in silence. The four men made their way toward the slope on the western side of the valley. Overhead, the bright globe of Fomalhaut shed its orange light over the rugged landscape.

When they reached the beginning of the slope, Wayne stopped and looked upwards. "Doesn't look easy," he grunted. "Damned rough hill, matter of fact. MacPherson, do you think you could make it to the top?"

Corporal MacPherson was a small, wiry man who had the reputation of being a first-rank mountaineer. He had been a member of the eighteenth Mount Everest Party, and had been the second of that party to reach the summit of the towering peak.

"Sure I can, sir," he said confidently. "Shall I take the rope?"

"Go ahead. You and Manetti get the rope to the top, and Sergeant Boggs and I will follow up."

"Righto, sir."

Corporal MacPherson reached his gloved hands forward and contracted his fingers. The tiny microswitches in his gloves actuated the relays, and his hands clung to the rock. Then he put his boots against the wall and began to move up the steep escarpment.

Private Manetti followed after him. The two men were lashed together by the light plastisteel cable. The sergeant held the end of the cable in his hands, waiting for the coil to be paid out.

Wayne watched the two men climb, while a chill wind whipped down out of the mountains and raised the sand in the valley. It was less than eighty feet to the precipice edge above, but it was almost perpendicular, and as they climbed, the buffeting winds began to press against their bodies with ever increasing force.

They reached the top and secured the rope, and then they peered over the edge and signaled that Wayne and the sergeant should start up.

"We're coming," Wayne shouted, and returned the signal. It was at that instant that he felt something slam against the sole of his heavy metamagnetic boot. It was as though something had kicked him savagely on the sole of his right foot.

He winced sharply at the impact. Then, somewhat puzzled he looked down at the boot. He felt something move under the sand. He tried to step back, and almost tripped. It was as though his right foot were stuck firmly to the sand!

He pushed himself back, and with a tremendous heave managed to pull himself free. He braced his body against the cliff, lifted his foot, and looked at it.

Hanging from his boot sole was one of the ugliest monstrosities he had ever seen; it was unusually grotesque.

I T WAS about the size and shape of a regulation football, and was covered with a wrinkled, reddish hide. At one end was a bright red gash of a mouth studded with greenish, gnashing teeth. From the other end of the creature's body protruded a long, needle-like projection which had imbedded itself in the metal sole of Wayne's boot.

"Good God! If I'd been wearing ordinary boots, that thing would have stuck clear into my foot!"

He hefted the weighted pick with one hand and swung, catching the monster with the point. It sank in and ripped through the creature, spilling red-orange blood over the sand. Shuddering a little, Wayne put his other foot on the dead thing and pulled his right boot free of the needle beak.

He started to say something, but he had a sudden premonition that made him look up in time. Sergeant Boggs put both hands against the Captain's shoulder and pushed.

"What the hell?" Wayne asked in surprise as he felt the shove. He almost fell to the sand, but he had had just enough warning to allow him to keep his balance. He put out a foot and staggered wildly.

A sudden strange noise caused him to turn and look back. Five needles were jabbing viciously up out of the sand in the spot where he would have fallen.

"You out of your head, Boggs?" he started to ask—but before the last word was out of his mouth, the sergeant charged in madly and tried to push him over again. He was fighting like a man gone berserk—which he was.

Wayne grabbed him by the wrist and flipped him desperately aside. The sergeant fell, sprawled out for a moment on the sand, then bounced to his feet again. His eyes were alight with a strange, terrifying flame.

Silently, he leaped for Wayne. The captain slammed his fist forward, sending it crashing into Boggs's midsection. The sergeant came back with a jab to the stomach that pushed Wayne backward. Again the deadly needles flicked up from the ground, but they did not strike home.

Wayne gasped for breath and reached out for Boggs. Boggs leaped on him, trying to push Wayne down where the beaks could get to him. Wayne side-stepped, threw Boggs off balance, and clubbed down hard with his fist.

Boggs wandered dizzily for a second before Wayne's other fist came blasting in, knocking the breath out of him. A third blow, and the sergeant collapsed on the sand.

Wayne paused and caught his breath. The sergeant remained unconscious. Wayne shook his head uncertainly, wondering what had come over the mild-mannered Boggs. A chilling thought struck him: *was this what happened to the crew of the Mavis?*

H E LOOKED up the cliff, where the other two men were still peering over the edge.

"MacPherson! Manetti! Come down! We're going back to the ship!"

He heaved the unconscious body of Sergeant Boggs over his shoulder like a potato-sack, and waited for the two men to come down. They drew near.

"Boggs must have gone out of his head," Wayne said. "He jumped me like a madman."

They had nothing to say, so he turned and began to trudge back to the *Lord Nelson*, trying to assemble the facts in his mind. They followed alongside.

What was behind the attack? After seeing the monster, why had Boggs tried to push his superior officer over into the sand? There were other little beasts under that sand; why would Boggs want one of them—there seemed to be dozens—to jab him with its needle of a beak?

And what were the beastly little animals, anyway?

There were no answers. But the answers would have to come, soon.

He tossed Boggs into the airlock and waited for the others to catch up. They climbed up the ladder and said nothing as the airlock went through its cycle and the antibacterial spray covered them.

C OLONEL PETERSEN looked at him across the desk and put the palms of his hands together. "Then, as I understand it, Captain, Sergeant Boggs tried to push you over into the sand when this—ah—*monster* jabbed you in the foot?"

"That's right, sir," Wayne said. He felt uncomfortable. This wasn't a formal court-martial; it was simply an inquiry into the sergeant's actions. Charges would be preferred later, if there were any to be preferred.

Sergeant Boggs stood stolidly on the far side of the room. A livid bruise along his jaw testified to the struggle that had taken place. One eye was puffed, and his expression was an unhappy one. Near him, MacPherson and Private Manetti stood stiffly at attention.

The colonel looked at Boggs. "What's your side of the story, Sergeant?"

The non-com's face didn't change. "Sir, the captain's statement isn't true."

"*What's that?*" Wayne asked angrily.

"Quiet, Captain," Petersen said. "Go ahead, Boggs."

The sergeant licked his bruised lips. "I was about to start up the rope when, for no reason at all, he struck me in the stomach. Then he hit me again a few more times, and I passed out."

"Did he say anything when he did this?" the Colonel asked.

"No, sir."

Wayne frowned. What was the sergeant trying to do? What the devil was he up to?

"Corporal MacPherson," the colonel said, "Did you witness the fight?"

"Yes, sir," the small man said, stepping a pace forward.

"Describe it."

"Well, sir, we were up on top of the cliff, and we called—or rather, *I* called for the captain and the sergeant to come on up. Sergeant Boggs took a hold of the rope and then the captain hit him in the belly, sir. He hit him twice more and the sergeant fell down. Then the captain told us to come down, which we did, sir. That was all." He gestured with his hands to indicate he had no more to say.

Wayne could hardly believe his ears. Making an effort, he managed to restrain himself.

"Private Manetti, do you have anything to add to that?" the colonel asked.

"No, sir. It happened just like that, sir. We both seen the entire thing. That's the way it happened. The captain hauled off and let him have it."

The colonel swiveled around and let his cold eyes rest on Wayne. "Captain, you have stated that Sergeant Boggs did not talk to either of these two men after you struck him. That eliminates any collusion."

"Yes, sir," Wayne said stonily.

"I talked to both men separately, and they tell substantially the same story. The records of all three of these men are excellent. The sergeant claims he never saw any monster of the type you describe, and the group I sent out to check says that there is no body of any alien animal anywhere near the spot. How do you explain the discrepancies between your story and theirs?"

W AYNE glared angrily at the three men. "They're lying, sir," he said evenly. "I don't know why they're doing it. The whole thing took place exactly as I told you."

"I find that very difficult to believe, Captain."

"Is that a formal accusation, sir?"

Petersen shrugged and rubbed his hands against his iron-grey temples. "Captain," he said finally, "you have a very fine record. You have never before been known to strike an enlisted man for any cause whatever. I hold that in your favor."

"Thank you, sir."

"On the other hand, the evidence here definitely indicates that your story is not quite true. Now, we know that Lieutenant Jervis acted peculiarly after the crew of the *Mavis* met its mysterious end, and the

Medical Corps thinks that whatever is causing the deaths could also cause mental confusion. Therefore, I am remanding you to the custody of the Medical Corps for observation. You'll be kept in close confinement until this thing is cleared up."

Wayne frowned bitterly. "Yes, sir," he said.

P ETER WAYNE sat in his cell in the hospital sector and stared at the wall in confusion. What in blazes was going on? What possible motive would three enlisted men have to frame him in this way? It didn't make any sense.

Was it possible that he really *had* gone off his rocker? Had he imagined the little beast under the sand?

He lifted his foot and looked again at the sole. There it was: a little pit about an eighth of an inch deep.

The colonel had explained it away easily enough, saying that he might possibly have stepped on a sharp rock. Wayne shook his head. He knew he wasn't nuts. But what the hell was going on?

There were no answers. But he knew that the eventual answer, when it came, would have something to do with the mystery of the *Mavis's* eight corpses.

It was late that afternoon when Sherri James came storming into the hospital sector. She was wearing a spacesuit, and she was brandishing a pass countersigned by Colonel Petersen himself. She was determined to enter.

"The medics didn't want to let me in," she explained. "But I told them I'd wear a spacesuit if it would make them any happier."

"Sherri! What the devil are you doing here?"

"I just wanted to check on you," she said. Her voice sounded oddly distorted coming over the speaker in the helmet. "You're supposed to have blown your wig or something. Did you?"

"No. Of course not."

"I didn't think so." She unscrewed her helmet quickly. "Listen, Peter, there's something funny going on aboard this ship."

"I've known that a long time," he said.

"I think Boggs and those other two are trying to frame you," she said, her voice low. "Do you know of anyone aboard named Masters?"

"Masters?" Wayne repeated. "Not that I know of—why?"

"Well, I overheard Boggs talking to one of the other men. I didn't hear very clearly, but it sounded as though he said: 'We've got to get Moore out and turn him over to Masters.' Bill Moore is one of my computermen—tall, skinny fellow."

Wayne nodded, frowning. "Yeah, but who is Masters? This is the queerest thing I ever heard of."

Footsteps sounded in the corridor outside.

"Better put your helmet on," Wayne advised. "Whoever's coming might not like to see you this way."

Quickly, she slipped the helmet back on. "I don't know what's going on," she said. "But I intend to find out."

ONE OF the medics entered the cell without knocking and came up to Sherri. "You'll have to go now, Lieutenant," he said. "We're going to perform some tests on the captain now."

Sherri bristled. "Tests? What kind of tests?"

"Nothing very serious," the medic said. "Just a routine checkup to clarify some points we're interested in."

"All right," Sherri said. "You won't find anything the matter with him." She left.

"Come with me, Captain," said the medic politely. He unlocked the cell door and, equally politely, drew a needle-beam pistol. "Don't try anything, please, sir. I have my orders."

Silently, Wayne followed the medic into the lab. Several other medics were standing around watching him, with Stevelman, the head man, in the back.

"Over this way, Captain," Stevelman called.

There was a box sitting on a table in the middle of the room. It was full of sand.

"Give me your hand, please, Captain," the medic said tonelessly.

In a sudden flash of insight, Wayne realized what was in the box. He thought fast but moved slowly. He held out his hand, but just as the medic took it, he twisted suddenly away.

His hand flashed out and grasped the other's wrist in a steely grip. The medic's fingers tightened on the needle-beam, and managed to pull the trigger. A bright beam flared briefly against the lab's plastalloy floor, doing nothing but scorching it slightly. Wayne's other hand balled into a fist and came up hard against the medic's jaw.

He grabbed the needle-beam pistol from the collapsing man's limp hand and had the other three men covered before the slugged medic had finished sagging to the floor.

"All of you! Raise your hands!"

They paid no attention to him. Instead of standing where they were, they began to move toward him. Wayne swore and, with a quick flip of his thumb, turned the beam down to low power and pulled the trigger three times in quick succession.

The three men fell as though they'd been pole-axed, knocked out by the low-power beam.

"The whole ship's gone crazy," he murmured softly, looking at the three men slumped together on the lab floor. "Stark, staring, raving nuts."

He took one step and someone jumped him from behind. The needle-beam pistol spun from his hand and slithered across the floor as Wayne fell under the impact of the heavy body. Apparently the whole Medical Corps was out to knock him down today.

He twisted rapidly as an arm encircled his neck, and rammed an elbow into the newcomer's mid-section. Then he jerked his head back, smashing the back of his skull into his opponent's nose.

The hold around his neck weakened, and Wayne tore himself loose from the other's grasp. He jumped to his feet, but the other man was a long way from being unconscious. A stinging right smashed into Wayne's mouth, and he felt the taste of blood. Hastily he wiped the trickle away with the back of his hand.

With his nose pouring blood, Wayne's antagonist charged in. His eyes burned with the strange flame that had been gleaming in Boggs's face out on the desert in the valley. He ploughed into Wayne's stomach with a savage blow that rocked Wayne back.

He grunted and drove back with a flurry of blows. The other aimed a wild blow at Wayne's head; Wayne seized the wrist as the arm flew past his ear, and twisted, hard. The medic flipped through the air and came to rest against the wall with a brief crunching impact. He moaned and then lapsed into silence.

QUICKLY, Wayne grabbed the gun off the floor and planted his back to the wall, looking around for new antagonists. But there was evidently no one left who cared to tangle with him, and the four medics strewn out on the floor didn't seem to have much fight left in them.

Wayne crossed the room in a couple of strides and bolted the door. Then he walked over to the box of sand. If it contained what he suspected—

He stepped over to the lab bench and picked out a long steel support rod from the equipment drawer. He placed the rod gently against the sand, and pushed downward, hard. There was a tinny scream, and a six-inch needle shot up instantly through the surface.

"Just what I thought," Wayne murmured. "Can you talk, you nasty little brute?" He prodded into the sand—more viciously this time. There was a flurry of sand, and the football-shaped thing came to the surface, clashing its teeth and screaming shrilly.

Wayne cursed. Then he turned the needle gun back up to full power and calmly burned the thing to a crisp. An odor of singed flesh drifted up from the ashes on the sand.

H E BENT and fumbled in Stevelman's pocket, pulling out a ring of keys.

"They better be the right ones," he told the unconscious medic. Holstering the needle gun, he walked over to the medical stores cabinet, hoping that the things he needed would be inside. He knew exactly what he was facing now, and what he would have to do.

He checked over the labels, peering through the neatly-arranged racks for the substance he was searching for.

Finally he picked a large plastine container filled with a white, crystalline powder. Then he selected a couple of bottles filled with a clear, faintly yellow liquid, and took a hypodermic gun from the rack. He relocked the cabinet.

Suddenly a knock sounded. He stiffened, sucked in his breath, and turned to face the door.

"Who's there?" he asked cautiously, trying to counterfeit Stevelman's voice.

"Harrenburg," said a rumbling voice. "I'm on guard duty. Heard some noise coming from in there a while back, and thought I'd look in. Everything all right, Dr. Stevelman? I mean—"

"Everything's fine, Harrenburg," Wayne said, imitating the medic's thin, dry voice. "We're running some tests on Captain Wayne. They're pretty complicated affairs, and I'd appreciate it if you didn't interrupt again."

"Sure, sir," the guard said through the door. "Just a routine check, sir. Colonel Petersen's orders. Sorry if I've caused any trouble, sir."

"That's all right," Wayne said. "Just go away and let us continue, will you?"

There was the sound of the guard's footsteps retreating down the corridor. Wayne counted to ten and turned back to the things he had taken from the cabinet.

The bottles of liquid and the hypo gun went into his belt pouch. He tucked the big bottle of white powder under his left arm and cautiously unbolted and opened the door. There was no sign of anyone in the corridor. *Good*, he thought. It was a lucky thing Harrenburg had blundered along just then, and not two minutes later.

He stepped outside the Medic Section and locked the door behind him with the key he'd taken from Stevelman. After turning the needle gun back to low power again in order to keep from killing anyone, he started on tiptoe toward the stairway that led into the bowels of the ship.

After about ten paces, he saw a shadow on the stairway, and cowered in a dark recess while two crewmen passed, talking volubly. Once they were gone, he came out and continued on his way.

It took quite a while to get where he was going, since it involved hiding and ducking two or three more times along the way, but he finally reached the big compartment where the water repurifiers were. He climbed up the ladder to the top of the reserve tank, opened the hatch, and emptied the contents of the jar into the ship's water supply.

"That ought to do it," he said to himself. Smiling, he carefully smashed the jar and dropped the fragments down the waste chute. He surveyed his handiwork for a moment, then turned and headed back.

He hadn't been seen going down, and he didn't want to be seen going out. If anyone even suspected that he had tampered with the water supply, all they would have to do would be to run the water through the purifiers. That would undo everything Wayne had been carefully preparing.

H E MADE his way safely back up to the main deck and headed through the quiet ship toward the airlock. He wasn't so lucky this time; a guard saw him.

"Where you goin', Captain?" the guard demanded, starting to lift his gun. "Seems to me you ought to be in the brig, and—"

Wayne made no reply. He brought his gun up in a rapid motion and beamed the man down. The guard toppled, a hurt expression on his face.

Wayne raced to the airlock. He didn't bother with a spacesuit—not *now*, when he knew that the air was perfectly harmless outside. He opened the inner door, closed it, and opened the outer door.

Then, grinning gleefully, he pressed the button that would start the pumping cycle. The outer door started to close automatically, and Wayne just barely managed to get outside and onto the ladder before it clanged shut. As soon as the great hatch had sealed itself, the pumps started exhausting the air from the airlock. No one could open the doors until the pumping cycle was over.

He climbed down the ladder and began walking over toward the western wall. He would have to keep away from the ship for a while, and the rocks were as good a place as any to hide out.

I T WAS dark. Fomalhaut had set, leaving the moonless planet in utter blackness, broken only by the cold gleam of the stars. The interior lights streaming from the portholes of the *Lord Nelson* gave a small degree of illumination to the dark valley.

The valley. It was spread out before him, calm and peaceful, rippling dunes of sand curling out toward the mountains. The valley, he knew, was a betrayer—calm and quiet above, alive with an army of hideous vermin a few feet below its surface.

He started to walk, and moistened his lips. He knew he was going to get awfully thirsty in the next few hours, but there was not the slightest help for it. There hadn't been any way to carry water from the ship.

"I can wait," he told himself. He stared back at the circular bulk of the *Lord Nelson* behind him, and his fingers trembled a little. He had known, when he joined the Corps, that space was full of traps like this one—but this was the first time he had actually experienced anything like this. It was foul.

Something slammed into his boot sole, and this time Wayne knew what it was.

"Persistent, aren't you!" He jerked his foot up. This monster hadn't stuck as the other one had, but he saw the tip of the needle-beak thrashing around wildly in the loose sand. Wayne thumbed the gun up to full power, and there was a piercing shriek as the gun burned into the sand. There was a sharp shrill sound, and the odor of something burning. He spat.

The little beasts must be all over the floor of the valley! Scurrying frantically, like blood-red giant crabs, sidling up and down beneath the valley, searching upward for things to strike at. How they must hate his metamagnetic boots, he thought!

He kept on walking, expecting to feel the impact of another thrust momentarily, but he was not molested again. *They must be getting wise*, he thought. *They know they can't get through my boots, and so they're leaving me alone. That way they don't call attention to themselves.*

A new, more chilling question struck him:
Just how smart are they?

He had made it to the wall and was climbing up the treacherous slope when the airlock door opened, and someone stood outlined in the bright circle of light that cut into the inky blackness. An amplified voice filled the valley and ricocheted back off the walls of the mountains, casting eerie echoes down on the lone man on the desert.

"CAPTAIN WAYNE! THIS IS COLONEL PETERSEN SPEAKING. DON'T YOU REALIZE THAT YOU'RE A SICK MAN? YOU MAY

DIE OUT THERE. COME BACK. THAT'S AN ORDER, CAPTAIN. REPEAT: COME BACK. THAT'S AN ORDER!"

"I'm afraid an order from you just doesn't hold much weight for me right now, Colonel," Wayne said quietly, to himself. Silently he went on climbing the escarpment, digging into the rough rock.

He kept on climbing until he found the niche for which he had been heading. He dragged himself in and sat down, as comfortably as possible. He began to wait.

D AWN CAME in less than three hours, as Fomalhaut burst up over the horizon and exploded in radiance over the valley. With dawn came a patrol of men, slinking surreptitiously across the valley, probably with orders to bring him in. Wayne was ensconced comfortably in his little rock niche, hidden from the men in the valley below, but with a perfect view of everything that went on. The wind whistled around the cliffs, ceaselessly moaning a tuneless song. He felt like standing up and shouting wildly, "Here I am! Here I am!" but he repressed the perverse urge.

The patrol group stood in a small clump in the valley below, seemingly waiting for something. Moments passed, and then it became apparent what that something was. Hollingwood, the metallurgist, appeared, dragging with him the detector. They were going to look for Captain Wayne with it, just as they had searched out the double-nucleus beryllium.

Wayne frowned. It was a possibility he hadn't thought about. They could easily detect the metal in his boots! And he didn't dare take them off; he'd never make it back across that hellish stretch of sand without them. He glanced uneasily at his watch. *How much longer do I have to keep evading them?* he wondered. It was a wearing task.

It looked as though it would be much too long.

The muzzle of the detector began to swing back and forth slowly and precisely, covering the valley floor inch by inch. He heard their whispered consultations drifting up from below, though he couldn't make out what they were saying.

THEY FINISHED with the valley, evidently concluding he wasn't there, and started searching the walls. Wayne decided it was time to get out while the getting was good. He crawled slowly out of the niche and wriggled along the escarpment, heading south, keeping low so the men in the valley wouldn't see him.

Unfortunately, he couldn't see them either. He kept moving, hoping they wouldn't spot him with the detector. He wished he had the metamagnetic hand grapples with him. For one thing, the sharp rock outcroppings sliced his hands like so much meat. For another, he could have dropped the grapples somewhere as a decoy.

Oh, well, you can't think of everything, Wayne told himself. He glanced at his watch. How long was it going to take?

He heard the scrape of boot leather on a rock somewhere ahead of him. He glanced up sharply, seeing nothing, and scowled. They had spotted him.

They were laying a trap.

Cautiously, he climbed over a huge boulder, making no sound. There was one man standing behind it, waiting, apparently, for Wayne to step around into view. He peered down, trying to see who it was. It seemed to be Hollingwood, the dignified, austere metallurgist.

Wayne smiled grimly, picked up a heavy rock, and dropped it straight down, square on the man's helmet. The plexalloy rang like a bell through the clear early-morning air, and the man dropped to his knees, dazed by the shock.

KNOWING he had just a moment to finish the job, Wayne pushed off against the side of the rock and plummeted down, landing neatly on the metallurgist's shoulders. The man reeled and fell flat. Wayne spun him over and delivered a hard punch to the solar plexus. "Sorry, Dave," he said softly. The metallurgist gasped and curled up in a tight ball. Wayne stood up. It was brutal, but it was the only place you could hit a man wearing a space helmet.

One down, Wayne thought. *Fifty-eight to go.* He was alone against the crew—and, for all he knew, against all fifty-nine of them.

Hollingwood groaned and stretched. Wayne bent and, for good measure, took off the man's helmet and tapped him none too gently on the skull.

There was the sound of footsteps, the harsh *chitch-chitch* of feet against the rock. "He's up that way," he heard a deep voice boom.

That meant the others had heard the rock hitting Hollingwood's plexalloy helmet. They were coming toward him.

Wayne sprang back defensively and glanced around. He hoped there were only five of them, that the rule of six was still being maintained. Otherwise things could become really complicated, as they hunted him relentlessly through the twisted gullies.

He hated to have to knock out too many of the men; it just meant more trouble later. Still, there was no help for it, if he wanted there to be any later. He thought of the bleached bones of the crew of the *Mavis*, and shuddered.

It was something of an advantage not to be wearing a helmet. Even with the best of acoustical systems, hearing inside a helmet tended to be distorted and dimmed. The men couldn't hear him as well as he could hear them. And since they couldn't hear themselves too well, they made a little more noise than he did.

A space boot came into view around a big rock, and Wayne aimed his needle-beam at the spot where the man's head would appear.

When the head came around the rock, Wayne fired. The man dropped instantly. *Sorry, friend,* Wayne apologized mentally. *Two down. Fifty-seven to go.* The odds were still pretty heavy.

He knew he had to move quickly now; the others had seen the man drop, and by now they should have a pretty good idea exactly where Wayne was.

He picked up a rock and lobbed it over a nearby boulder, then started moving cat-like in the other direction. He climbed up onto another boulder and watched two men move away from him. They were stepping warily, their beam guns in their hands. Wayne wiped away a bead of perspiration, aimed carefully, and squeezed the firing stud twice.

Four down. Fifty-five to go.

A MOMENT later, something hissed near his ear. Without waiting, he spun and rolled off the boulder, landing cat-like on his feet. Another crewman was standing on top of a nearby boulder. Wayne began to sweat; this pursuit seemed to be indefinitely prolonged, and it was beginning to look unlikely that he could avoid them forever.

He had dropped his pistol during the fall; it was wedged between a couple of rocks several feet away.

He heard someone call: "I got him. He fell off the rock. We'll take him back down below."

Then another voice—ominously. "He won't mind. He'll be glad we did it for him—afterwards."

"I'll go get him," said the first voice. The man stepped around the side of the boulder—just in time to have a hard-pitched rock come thunking into his midsection.

"Oof!" he grunted, then took a couple of steps backwards, and collapsed.

Five down. Fifty-four to go. It could go on forever this way.

"What's the matter?" asked the man who had replied to the first one with those chilling words.

"Nothing," said Wayne, in a fair imitation of the prostrate crewman's voice. "He's heavy. Come help me."

Then he reached down and picked up the fallen man's beam gun. He took careful aim.

When the sixth man stepped around the rock, he fired. The beam went wide of the mark, slowing the other down, and Wayne charged forward. He pounded two swift punches into the amazed crewman, who responded with a woozy, wild blow. Wayne ducked and let the fist glide past his ear, then came in hard with a solid body-blow and let the man sag to the ground. He took a deep breath.

Six down and only fifty-three to go.

H E CRAWLED back to the edge of the precipice and peered down into the valley. There was no one to be seen. It was obvious that Colonel Petersen was still enforcing the six-man rule.

As he watched, he saw the airlock door open. A spacesuited figure scrambled down the ladder and sprinted across the deadly sand of the valley floor.

It was Sherri! Wayne held his breath, expecting at any moment that one of the little monsters beneath the sand would sink its vicious needle upward into Sherri's foot. But her stride never faltered.

As she neared the precipice, another figure appeared at the airlock door and took aim with a gun.

Wayne thumbed his own needle-beam pistol up to full and fired hastily at the distant figure. At that distance, even the full beam would only stun. The distant figure collapsed backwards into the airlock, and Wayne grinned in satisfaction.

Seven down. Fifty-two to go.

He kept an eye on the airlock door and a finger on his firing stud, waiting to see if anyone else would come out. No one else did.

As soon as Sherri was safely up to the top of the precipice, Wayne ran to meet her.

"Sherri! What the devil did you come out here for?"

"I had to see you," she said, panting for breath. "If you'll come back to the ship before they beam you down, we can prove to Colonel Petersen that you're all right. We can show them that the Masters—"

She realized suddenly what she said and uttered a little gasp. She had her pistol out before the surprised Wayne could move.

He stared coldly at the pistol, thinking bitterly that this was a hell of a way for it all to finish. "So they got you too," he said. "That little display at the airlock was a phony. You were sent out here to lure me back into the ship. Just another Judas."

She nodded slowly. "That's right," she said. "We all have to go to the Masters. It is—it—is—is—"

Her eyes glazed, and she swayed on her feet. The pistol wavered and swung in a feeble spiral, no longer pointed at Wayne. Gently, he took it from her nerveless fingers and caught her supple body as she fell.

He wiped his forehead dry. Up above, the sun was climbing toward the top of the sky, and its beams raked the planet below, pouring down heat.

H E GLANCED at his wristwatch while waiting for his nerves to stop tingling. Sherri must have been the last one—the drug must have taken effect at last, and not a moment too soon. He decided to wait another half hour before he tried to get into the spaceship, just the same.

The huge globe of the *Lord Nelson* stood forlornly in the center of the valley. The airlock door stayed open; no one tried to close it.

Wayne's mouth was growing dry; his tongue felt like sandpaper. Nevertheless, he forced himself to sit quietly, watching the ship closely for the full half hour, before he picked up Sherri, tied his rope around her waist, and lowered her to the valley floor. Then he wandered around the rocks, collecting the six unconscious men, and did the same for them.

He carried them all, one by one, across the sand, burning a path before him with the needle beam.

Long before he had finished his task, the sand was churning loathsomely with the needles of hundreds and thousands of the monstrous little beasts. They were trying frantically to bring down the being that was so effectively thwarting their plans, jabbing viciously with their upthrust beaks. The expanse of sand that was the valley looked like a pincushion, with the writhing needles ploughing through the ground one after another. Wayne kept the orifice of his beam pistol hot as he cut his way back and forth from the base of the cliff to the ship.

When he had dumped the seven unconscious ones all inside the airlock, he closed the outer door and opened the inner one. There was not a sound from within.

Fifty-nine down, he thought, *and none to go.*

He entered the ship and dashed down the winding staircase to the water purifiers to change the water in the reservoir tanks. Thirsty as he was, he was not going to take a drink until the water had been cleared of the knockout drug he had dropped into the tanks.

After that came the laborious job of getting everyone in the ship strapped into their bunks for the takeoff. It took the better part of an hour to get all sixty of them up—they had fallen all over the ship— and nestled in the acceleration cradles. When the job was done, he went to the main control room and set the autopilot to lift the spaceship into the ionosphere.

Then, sighting carefully on the valley far below, he dropped a flare bomb.

"Goodbye, little monsters," he said exultantly.

For a short space of time, nothing happened. Then the viewplate was filled with a deadly blue-white glare. Unlike an ordinary atomic bomb, the flare bomb would not explode violently; it simply burned, sending out a brilliant flare of deadly radiation that would crisp all life dozens of feet below the ground.

He watched the radiation blazing below. Then it began to die down, and when the glare cleared away, all was quiet below.

The valley was dead.

When it was all over, Wayne took the hypodermic gun from his pouch, filled it with the anti-hypnotic drug that he had taken from the medical cabinet, and began to make his rounds. He fired a shot into each and every one aboard. He had no way of knowing who had been injected by the small monsters and who had not, so he was taking no chances.

Then he went to the colonel's room. He wanted to be there when the Commanding Officer awoke.

T HE ENTIRE crew of the *Lord Nelson* was gathered in the big mess hall. Wayne stared down at the tired, frightened faces of the puzzled people looking up at him, and continued his explanation.

"Those of you who were under the control of the monsters know what it was like. They had the ability to inject a hypnotic drug into a human being through a normal space boot with those stingers of theirs. The drug takes effect so fast that the victim hardly has any idea of what has happened to him."

"But why do they do it?" It was Hollingwood, the metallurgist, looking unhappy with a tremendous bruise on his head where Wayne had clobbered him.

"Why does a wasp sting a spider? It doesn't kill the spider, it simply stuns it. That way, the spider remains alive and fresh so that young wasps can feed upon it at their leisure."

Wayne glanced over to his right. "Lieutenant Jervis, you've been under the effect of the drug longer than any of us. Would you explain what *really* happened when the *Mavis* landed?"

The young officer stood up. He was pale and shaken, but his voice was clear and steady.

"Just about the same thing that almost happened here," Jervis said. "We all walked around the valley floor and got stung one at a time. The things did it so quietly that none of us knew what was going on until we got hit ourselves. When we had all been enslaved, we were ready to do their bidding. They can't talk, but they can communicate by means of nerve messages when that needle is stuck into you."

Nearly half the crew nodded in sympathy. Wayne studied them, wondering what it must have been like. They *knew*; he could only guess.

"Naturally," Jervis went on, "those who have already been injected with the drug try to get others injected. When everyone aboard the *Mavis* had been stung, they ordered me to take the ship home and get another load of Earthmen. Apparently they like our taste. I had to obey; I was completely under their power. You know what it's like."

"And what happened to the others—the eight men you left behind?" asked Colonel Petersen.

Jervis clenched his teeth bitterly. "They just laid down on the sand—and waited."

"Horrible!" Sherri said.

J ERVIS fell silent. Wayne was picturing the sight, and knew everyone else was, too—the sight of hordes of carnivorous little aliens burrowing up through the valley's sand and approaching the eight Earthmen who lay there, alive but helpless. Approaching them—and beginning to feed.

Just when the atmosphere began to grow too depressing, Wayne decided to break the spell. "I'd like to point out that the valley's been completely cauterized," he said. "The aliens have been wiped out. And I propose to lead a mission out to reconnoitre for the double-nucleus beryllium."

He looked around. "MacPherson? Boggs? Manetti? You three want to start over where we left off the last time?"

Sergeant Boggs came up to him. "Sir, I want you to understand that—"

"I know, Boggs," Wayne said. "Let's forget all about it. There's work to be done."

"I'm sorry I misjudged you, Wayne. If it hadn't been for your quick action, this crew would have gone the way of the *Mavis*."

"Just luck, Colonel," Wayne said. "If it hadn't been for the heavy-soled climbing boots, I'd probably be lying out there with the rest of you right now."

Colonel Petersen grinned. "Thanks to your boots, then."

Wayne turned to his team of three. "Let's get moving, fellows. We've wasted enough time already."

"Do we need spacesuits, sir?" Manetti asked.

"No, Manetti. The air's perfectly fine out there," Wayne said. "But I'd suggest you wear your climbing boots." He grinned. "You never can tell when they'll come in handy."

THE MOON IS GREEN

by FRITZ LEIBER

*Anybody who wanted to escape death could,
by paying a very simple price—denial of life!*

"**E**FFIE! What the devil are you up to?"

Her husband's voice, chopping through her mood of terrified rapture, made her heart jump like a startled cat, yet by some miracle of feminine self-control her body did not show a tremor.

Dear God, she thought, *he mustn't see it. It's so beautiful, and he always kills beauty.*

"I'm just looking at the Moon," she said listlessly. "It's green."

Mustn't, mustn't see it. And now, with luck, he wouldn't. For the face, as if it also heard and sensed the menace in the voice, was moving back from the window's glow into the outside dark, but slowly, reluctantly, and still faunlike, pleading, cajoling, tempting, and incredibly beautiful.

"Close the shutters at once, you little fool, and come away from the window!"

"Green as a beer bottle," she went on dreamily, "green as emeralds, green as leaves with sunshine striking through them and green grass to lie on." She couldn't help saying those last words. They were her token to the face, even though it couldn't hear.

"Effie!"

She knew what that last tone meant. Wearily she swung shut the ponderous lead inner shutters and drove home the heavy bolts. That hurt her fingers; it always did, but he mustn't know that.

"You know that those shutters are not to be touched! Not for five more years at least!"

"I only wanted to look at the Moon," she said, turning around, and then it was all gone—the face, the night, the Moon, the magic—and she was back in the grubby, stale little hole, facing an angry, stale little man. It was then that the eternal thud of the air-conditioning fans and the crackle of the electrostatic precipitators that sieved out the dust reached her consciousness again like the bite of a dentist's drill.

"Only wanted to look at the Moon!" he mimicked her in falsetto. "Only wanted to die like a little fool and make me that much more ashamed of you!" Then his voice went gruff and professional. "Here, count yourself."

She silently took the Geiger counter he held at arm's length, waited until it settled down to a steady ticking slower than a clock—due only to cosmic rays and indicating nothing dangerous—and then began to comb her body with the instrument. First her head and shoulders, then out along her arms and back along their under side. There was something oddly voluptuous about her movements, although her features were gray and sagging.

The ticking did not change its tempo until she came to her waist. Then it suddenly spurted, clicking faster and faster. Her husband gave an excited grunt, took a quick step forward, froze. She goggled for a moment in fear, then grinned foolishly, dug in the pocket of her grimy apron and guiltily pulled out a wristwatch.

He grabbed it as it dangled from her fingers, saw that it had a radium dial, cursed, heaved it up as if to smash it on the floor, but instead put it carefully on the table.

"You imbecile, you incredible imbecile," he softly chanted to himself through clenched teeth, with eyes half closed.

She shrugged faintly, put the Geiger counter on the table, and stood there slumped.

He waited until the chanting had soothed his anger, before speaking again. He said quietly, "I do suppose you still realize the sort of world you're living in?"

SHE NODDED slowly, staring at nothingness. Oh, she realized, all right, realized only too well. It was the world that hadn't realized. The world that had gone on stockpiling hydrogen bombs. The world that had put those bombs in cobalt shells, although it had promised it wouldn't, because the cobalt made them much more terrible and cost no more. The world that had started throwing those bombs, always telling itself that it hadn't thrown enough of them yet to make the air really dangerous with the deadly radioactive dust that came from the cobalt. Thrown them and kept on throwing until the danger point, where air and ground would become fatal to all human life, was approached.

Then, for about a month, the two great enemy groups had hesitated. And then each, unknown to the other, had decided it could risk one last gigantic and decisive attack without exceeding the danger point. It had been planned to strip off the cobalt cases, but someone forgot and then there wasn't time. Besides, the military scientists of each group were confident that the lands of the other had got the most dust. The two attacks came within an hour of each other.

After that, the Fury. The Fury of doomed men who think only of taking with them as many as possible of the enemy, and in this case—they hoped—all. The Fury of suicides who know they have botched up life for good. The Fury of cocksure men who realize they have been outsmarted by fate, the enemy, and themselves, and know that they will never be able to improvise a defense when arraigned before the high court of history—and whose unadmitted hope is that there will be no high court of history left to arraign them. More cobalt bombs were dropped during the Fury than in all the preceding years of the war.

After the Fury, the Terror. Men and women with death sifting into their bones through their nostrils and skin, fighting for bare survival under a dust-hazed sky that played fantastic tricks with the light of Sun and Moon, like the dust from Krakatoa that drifted around the world for years. Cities, countryside, and air were all poisoned, alive with deadly radiation.

The only realistic chance for continued existence was to retire, for the five or ten years the radiation would remain deadly, to some well-sealed and radiation-shielded place that must also be copiously supplied with food, water, power, and a means of air-conditioning.

Such places were prepared by the far-seeing, seized by the stronger, defended by them in turn against the desperate hordes of the dying... until there were no more of those.

After that, only the waiting, the enduring. A mole's existence, without beauty or tenderness, but with fear and guilt as constant companions. Never to see the Sun, to walk among the trees—or even know if there were still trees.

Oh, yes, she realized what the world was like.

"YOU UNDERSTAND, too, I suppose, that we were allowed to reclaim this ground-level apartment only because the Committee believed us to be responsible people, and because I've been making a damn good showing lately?"

"Yes, Hank."

"I thought you were eager for privacy. You want to go back to the basement tenements?"

God, no! Anything rather than that fetid huddling, that shameless communal sprawl. And yet, was this so much better? The nearness to the surface was meaningless; it only tantalized. And the privacy magnified Hank.

She shook her head dutifully and replied, "No, Hank."

"Then why aren't you careful? I've told you a million times, Effie, that glass is no protection against the dust that's outside that window. The lead shutter must never be touched! If you make one single slip like that and it gets around, the Committee will send us back to the lower levels without blinking an eye. And they'll think twice before trusting me with any important jobs."

"I'm sorry, Hank."

"Sorry? What's the good of being sorry? The only thing that counts is never to make a slip! Why the devil do you do such things, Effie? What drives you to it?"

She swallowed. "It's just that it's so dreadful being cooped up like this," she said hesitatingly, "shut away from the sky and the Sun. I'm just hungry for a little beauty."

"And do you suppose I'm not?" he demanded. "Don't you suppose I want to get outside, too, and be carefree and have a good time? But I'm not so damn selfish about it. I want my children to enjoy the Sun, and my children's children. Don't you see that that's the all-important thing and that we have to behave like mature adults and make sacrifices for it?"

"Yes, Hank."

He surveyed her slumped figure, her lined and listless face. "You're a fine one to talk about hunger for beauty," he told her. Then his voice grew softer, more deliberate. "You haven't forgotten, have you, Effie, that until last month the Committee was so concerned about your sterility? That they were about to enter my name on the list of those waiting to be allotted a free woman? Very high on the list, too!"

She could nod even at that one, but not while looking at him. She turned away. She knew very well that the Committee was justified in worrying about the birth rate. When the community finally moved back to the surface again, each additional healthy young person would be an asset, not only in the struggle for bare survival, but in the resumed war against Communism which some of the Committee members still counted on.

It was natural that they should view a sterile woman with disfavor, and not only because of the waste of her husband's germ-plasm, but because sterility might indicate that she had suffered more than the average from radiation. In that case, if she did bear children later on, they would be more apt to carry a defective heredity, producing an undue number of monsters and freaks in future generations, and so contaminating the race.

Of course she understood it. She could hardly remember the time when she didn't. Years ago? Centuries? There wasn't much difference in a place where time was endless.

HIS LECTURE finished, her husband smiled and grew almost cheerful.

"Now that you're going to have a child, that's all in the background again. Do you know, Effie, that when I first came in, I had some very good news for you? I'm to become a member of the Junior Committee and the announcement will be made at the banquet tonight." He cut short her mumbled congratulations. "So brighten yourself up and put on your best dress. I want the other Juniors to see what a handsome wife the new member has got." He paused. "Well, get a move on!"

She spoke with difficulty, still not looking at him. "I'm terribly sorry, Hank, but you'll have to go alone. I'm not well."

He straightened up with an indignant jerk. "There you go again! First that infantile, inexcusable business of the shutters, and now this! No feeling for my reputation at all. Don't be ridiculous, Effie. You're coming!"

"Terribly sorry," she repeated blindly, "but I really can't. I'd just be sick. I wouldn't make you proud of me at all."

"Of course you won't," he retorted sharply. "As it is, I have to spend half my energy running around making excuses for you—why you're so odd, why you always seem to be ailing, why you're always stupid and snobbish and say the wrong thing. But tonight's really important, Effie. It will cause a lot of bad comment if the new member's wife isn't present. You know how just a hint of sickness starts the old radiation-disease rumor going. You've *got* to come, Effie."

She shook her head helplessly.

"Oh, for heaven's sake, come on!" he shouted, advancing on her. "This is just a silly mood. As soon as you get going, you'll snap out of it. There's nothing really wrong with you at all."

He put his hand on her shoulder to turn her around, and at his touch her face suddenly grew so desperate and gray that for a moment he was alarmed in spite of himself.

"Really?" he asked, almost with a note of concern.

She nodded miserably.

"Hmm!" He stepped back and strode about irresolutely. "Well, of course, if that's the way it is..." He checked himself and a sad smile crossed his face. "So you don't care enough about your old husband's success to make one supreme effort in spite of feeling bad?"

Again the helpless headshake. "I just can't go out tonight, under any circumstances." And her gaze stole toward the lead shutters.

He was about to say something when he caught the direction of her gaze. His eyebrows jumped. For seconds he stared at her incredulously, as if some completely new and almost unbelievable possibility had popped into his mind. The look of incredulity slowly faded, to be replaced by a harder, more calculating expression. But when he spoke again, his voice was shockingly bright and kind.

"Well, it can't be helped naturally, and I certainly wouldn't want you to go if you weren't able to enjoy it. So you hop right into bed and get a good rest. I'll run over to the men's dorm to freshen up. No, really, I don't want you to have to make any effort at all. Incidentally, Jim Barnes isn't going to be able to come to the banquet either—touch of the old 'flu, he tells me, of all things."

He watched her closely as he mentioned the other man's name, but she didn't react noticeably. In fact, she hardly seemed to be hearing his chatter.

"I got a bit sharp with you, I'm afraid, Effie," he continued contritely. "I'm sorry about that. I was excited about my new job and I guess that was why things upset me. Made me feel let down when I found you weren't feeling as good as I was. Selfish of me. Now you get into bed right away and get well. Don't worry about me a bit. I know you'd come if you possibly could. And I know you'll be thinking about me. Well, I must be off now."

He started toward her, as if to embrace her, then seemed to think better of it. He turned back at the doorway and said, emphasizing the words, "You'll be completely alone for the next four hours." He waited for her nod, then bounced out.

S HE STOOD still until his footsteps died away. Then she straightened up, walked over to where he'd put down the wristwatch, picked it up and smashed it hard on the floor. The crystal shattered, the case flew apart, and something went *zing!*

She stood there breathing heavily. Slowly her sagged features lifted, formed themselves into the beginning of a smile. She stole another look at the shutters. The smile became more definite. She felt her hair, wet her fingers and ran them along her hairline and back over her ears. After wiping her hands on her apron, she took it off. She straightened her dress, lifted her head with a little flourish, and stepped smartly toward the window.

Then her face went miserable again and her steps slowed.

No, it couldn't be, and it won't be, she told herself. It had been just an illusion, a silly romantic dream that she had somehow projected out of her beauty-starved mind and given a moment's false reality. There couldn't be anything alive outside. There hadn't been for two whole years.

And if there conceivably were, it would be something altogether horrible. She remembered some of the pariahs—hairless, witless creatures, with radiation welts crawling over their bodies like worms, who had come begging for succor during the last months of the Terror—and been shot down. How they must have hated the people in refuges!

But even as she was thinking these things, her fingers were caressing the bolts, gingerly drawing them, and then she was opening the shutters gently, apprehensively.

No, there couldn't be anything outside, she assured herself wryly, peering out into the green night. Even her fears had been groundless.

But the face came floating up toward the window. She started back in terror, then checked herself.

For the face wasn't horrible at all, only very thin, with full lips and large eyes and a thin proud nose like the jutting beak of a bird. And no radiation welts or scars marred the skin, olive in the tempered moonlight. It looked, in fact, just as it had when she had seen it the first time.

For a long moment the face stared deep, deep into her brain. Then the full lips smiled and a half-clenched, thin-fingered hand materialized itself from the green darkness and rapped twice on the grimy pane.

Her heart pounding, she furiously worked the little crank that opened the window. It came unstuck from the frame with a tiny explosion of dust and a *zing* like that of the watch, only louder. A moment later it swung open wide and a puff of incredibly fresh air caressed her face and the inside of her nostrils, stinging her eyes with unanticipated tears.

The man outside balanced on the sill, crouching like a faun, head high, one elbow on knee. He was dressed in scarred, snug trousers and an old sweater.

"Is it tears I get for a welcome?" he mocked her gently in a musical voice. "Or are those only to greet God's own breath, the air?"

HE SWUNG down inside and now she could see that he was tall. Turning, he snapped his fingers and called, "Come, puss."

A black cat with a twisted stump of a tail and feet like small boxing gloves and ears almost as big as rabbits' hopped clumsily in view. He lifted it down, gave it a pat. Then, nodding familiarly to Effie, he unstrapped a little pack from his back and laid it on the table.

She couldn't move. She even found it hard to breathe.

"The window," she finally managed to get out.

He looked at her inquiringly, caught the direction of her stabbing finger. Moving without haste, he went over and closed it carelessly.

"The shutters, too," she told him, but he ignored that, looking around.

"It's a snug enough place you and your man have," he commented. "Or is it that this is a free-love town or a harem spot, or just a military post?" He checked her before she could answer. "But let's not be talking about such things now. Soon enough I'll be scared to death for both of us. Best enjoy the kick of meeting, which is always good for twenty minutes at the least." He smiled at her rather shyly. "Have you food? Good, then bring it."

She set cold meat and some precious canned bread before him and had water heating for coffee. Before he fell to, he shredded a chunk of meat and put it on the floor for the cat, which left off its sniffing inspection of the walls and ran up eagerly mewing. Then the man began to eat, chewing each mouthful slowly and appreciatively.

From across the table Effie watched him, drinking in his every deft movement, his every cryptic quirk of expression. She attended to making the coffee, but that took only a moment. Finally she could contain herself no longer.

"What's it like up there?" she asked breathlessly. "Outside, I mean."

He looked at her oddly for quite a space. Finally, he said flatly, "Oh, it's a wonderland for sure, more amazing than you tombed folk could ever imagine. A veritable fairyland." And he quickly went on eating.

"No, but really," she pressed.

Noting her eagerness, he smiled and his eyes filled with playful tenderness. "I mean it, on my oath," he assured her. "You think the bombs and the dust made only death and ugliness. That was true at first. But then, just as the doctors foretold, they changed the life in the seeds and loins that were brave enough to stay. Wonders bloomed and walked." He broke off suddenly and asked, "Do any of you ever venture outside?"

"A few of the men are allowed to," she told him, "for short trips in special protective suits, to hunt for canned food and fuels and batteries and things like that."

"Aye, and those blind-souled slugs would never see anything but what they're looking for," he said, nodding bitterly. "They'd never see the garden where a dozen buds blossom where one did before, and the flowers have petals a yard across, with stingless bees big as sparrows gently supping their nectar. Housecats grown spotted and huge as leopards (not little runts like Joe Louis here) stalk through those gardens. But they're gentle beasts, no more harmful than the rainbow-scaled snakes that glide around their paws, for the dust burned all the murder out of them, as it burned itself out.

"I've even made up a little poem about that. It starts, 'Fire can hurt me, or water, or the weight of Earth. But the dust is my friend.' Oh, yes, and then the robins like cockatoos and squirrels like a princess's ermine! All under a treasure chest of Sun and Moon and stars that the dust's magic powder changes from ruby to emerald and sapphire and amethyst and back again. Oh, and then the new children—"

"You're telling the truth?" she interrupted him, her eyes brimming with tears. "You're not making it up?"

"I am not," he assured her solemnly. "And if you could catch a glimpse of one of the new children, you'd never doubt me again. They have long limbs as brown as this coffee would be if it had lots of fresh cream in it, and smiling delicate faces and the whitish teeth and the finest hair. They're so nimble that I—a sprightly man and somewhat enlivened by the dust—

feel like a cripple beside them. And their thoughts dance like flames and make me feel a very imbecile.

"Of course, they have seven fingers on each hand and eight toes on each foot, but they're the more beautiful for that. They have large pointed ears that the Sun shines through. They play in the garden, all day long, slipping among the great leaves and blooms, but they're so swift that you can hardly see them, unless one chooses to stand still and look at you. For that matter, you have to look a bit hard for all these things I'm telling you."

"But it is true?" she pleaded.

"Every word of it," he said, looking straight into her eyes. He put down his knife and fork. "What's your name?" he asked softly. "Mine's Patrick."

"Effie," she told him.

He shook his head. "That can't be," he said. Then his face brightened. "Euphemia," he exclaimed. "That's what Effie is short for. Your name is Euphemia." As he said that, looking at her, she suddenly felt beautiful. He got up and came around the table and stretched out his hand toward her.

"Euphemia—" he began.

"Yes?" she answered huskily, shrinking from him a little, but looking up sideways, and very flushed.

"Don't either of you move," Hank said.

The voice was flat and nasal because Hank was wearing a nose respirator that was just long enough to suggest an elephant's trunk. In his right hand was a large blue-black automatic pistol.

THEY TURNED their faces to him. Patrick's was abruptly alert, shifty. But Effie's was still smiling tenderly, as if Hank could not break the spell of the magic garden and should be pitied for not knowing about it.

"You little—" Hank began with an almost gleeful fury, calling her several shameful names. He spoke in short phrases, closing tight his unmasked mouth between them while he sucked in breath through the respirator. His voice rose in a crescendo. "And not with a man of the community, but a pariah! *A pariah!*"

"I hardly know what you're thinking, man, but you're quite wrong," Patrick took the opportunity to put in hurriedly, conciliatingly. "I just happened to be coming by hungry tonight, a lonely tramp, and knocked at the window. Your wife was a bit foolish and let kindheartedness get the better of prudence—"

"Don't think you've pulled the wool over my eyes, Effie," Hank went on with a screechy laugh, disregarding the other man completely. "Don't think I don't know why you're suddenly going to have a child after four long years."

At that moment the cat came nosing up to his feet. Patrick watched him narrowly, shifting his weight forward a little, but Hank only kicked the animal aside without taking his eyes off them.

"Even that business of carrying the wristwatch in your pocket instead of on your arm," he went on with channeled hysteria. "A neat bit of camouflage, Effie. Very neat. And telling me it was my child, when all the while you've been seeing him for months!"

"Man, you're mad; I've not touched her!" Patrick denied hotly though still calculatingly, and risked a step forward, stopping when the gun instantly swung his way.

"Pretending you were going to give me a healthy child," Hank raved on, "when all the while you knew it would be—either in body or germ plasm—a thing like *that*!"

He waved his gun at the malformed cat, which had leaped to the top of the table and was eating the remains of Patrick's food, though its watchful green eyes were fixed on Hank.

"I should shoot him down!" Hank yelled, between sobbing, chest-racking inhalations through the mask. "I should kill him this instant for the contaminated pariah he is!"

All this while Effie had not ceased to smile compassionately. Now she stood up without haste and went to Patrick's side. Disregarding his warning, apprehensive glance, she put her arm lightly around him and faced her husband.

"Then you'd be killing the bringer of the best news we've ever had," she said, and her voice was like a flood of some warm sweet liquor in that musty, hate-charged room. "Oh, Hank, forget your silly, wrong jealousy and listen to me. Patrick here has something wonderful to tell us."

HANK STARED at her, and for once he screamed no reply. It was obvious that he was seeing for the first time how beautiful she had become, and that the realization jolted him terribly.

"What do you mean?" he finally asked unevenly, almost fearfully.

"I mean that we no longer need to fear the dust," she said, and now her smile was radiant. "It never really did hurt people the way the doctors said it would. Remember how it was with me, Hank, the exposure I had and recovered from, although the doctors said I wouldn't at first—and without even losing my hair? Hank, those who were brave enough to stay outside, and who weren't killed by terror and suggestion and panic—they adapted to the dust. They changed, but they changed for the better. Everything—"

"Effie, he told you lies!" Hank interrupted, but still in that same agitated, broken voice, cowed by her beauty.

"Everything that grew or moved was purified," she went on ringingly. "You men going outside have never seen it, because you've never had eyes for it. You've been blinded to beauty, to life itself. And now all the power in the dust has gone and faded, anyway, burned itself out. That's true, isn't it?"

She smiled at Patrick for confirmation. His face was strangely veiled, as if he were calculating obscure changes. He might have given a little nod; at any rate, Effie assumed that he did, for she turned back to her husband.

"You see, Hank? We can all go out now. We need never fear the dust again. Patrick is a living proof of that," she continued triumphantly, standing straighter, holding him a little tighter. "Look at him. Not a scar or a sign, and he's been out in the dust for years. How could he be this way, if the dust hurt the brave? Oh, believe me, Hank! Believe what you see. Test it if you want. Test Patrick here."

"Effie, you're all mixed up. You don't know—" Hank faltered, but without conviction of any sort.

"Just test him," Effie repeated with utter confidence, ignoring—not even noticing—Patrick's warning nudge.

"All right," Hank mumbled. He looked at the stranger dully. "Can you count?" he asked.

Patrick's face was a complete enigma. Then he suddenly spoke, and his voice was like a fencer's foil— light, bright, alert, constantly playing, yet utterly on guard.

"Can I count? Do you take me for a complete simpleton, man? Of course I can count!"

"Then count yourself," Hank said, barely indicating the table.

"Count myself, should I?" the other retorted with a quick facetious laugh. "Is this a kindergarten? But if you want me to, I'm willing." His voice was rapid. "I've two arms, and two legs, that's four. And ten fingers and ten toes—you'll take my word for them? —that's twenty-four. A head, twenty-five. And two eyes and a nose and a mouth—"

"With this, I mean," Hank said heavily, advanced to the table, picked up the Geiger counter, switched it on, and handed it across the table to the other man.

But while it was still an arm's length from Patrick, the clicks began to mount furiously, until they were like the rapid chatter of a pigmy machine gun.

Abruptly the clicks slowed, but that was only the counter shifting to a new scaling circuit, in which each click stood for 512 of the old ones.

WITH THOSE horrid, rattling little volleys, fear cascaded into the room and filled it, smashing like so much colored glass all the bright barriers of words Effie had raised against it. For no dreams can stand against the Geiger counter, the Twentieth Century's mouthpiece of ultimate truth. It was as if the dust and all the terrors of the dust had incarnated themselves in one dread invading shape that said in words stronger than audible speech, "Those were illusions, whistles in the dark. This is reality, the dreary, pitiless reality of the Burrowing Years."

Hank scuttled back to the wall. Through chattering teeth he babbled, "... enough radioactives... kill a thousand men... freak... a freak..." In his agitation he forgot for a moment to inhale through the respirator.

Even Effie—taken off guard, all the fears that had been drilled into her twanging like piano wires—shrank from the skeletal-seeming shape beside her, held herself to it only by desperation.

Patrick did it for her. He disengaged her arm and stepped briskly away. Then he whirled on them, smiling sardonically, and started to speak, but instead looked with distaste at the chattering Geiger counter he held between fingers and thumb.

"Have we listened to this racket long enough?" he asked.

Without waiting for an answer, he put down the instrument on the table. The cat hurried over to it curiously and the clicks began to mount in a minor crescendo. Effie lunged for it frantically, switched it off, darted back.

"That's right," Patrick said with another chilling smile. "You do well to cringe, for I'm death itself. Even in death I could kill you, like a snake." And with that his voice took on the tones of a circus barker. "Yes, I'm a freak, as the gentleman so wisely said. That's what one doctor who dared talk with me for a minute told me before he kicked me out. He couldn't tell me why, but somehow the dust doesn't kill me. Because I'm a freak, you see, just like the men who ate nails and walked on fire and ate arsenic and stuck themselves through with pins. Step right up, ladies and gentlemen—only not too close!—and examine the man the dust can't harm. Rappaccini's child, brought up to date; his embrace, death!

"And now," he said, breathing heavily, "I'll get out and leave you in your damned lead cave."

He started toward the window. Hank's gun followed him shakingly.

"Wait!" Effie called in an agonized voice. He obeyed. She continued falteringly, "When we were together earlier, you didn't act as if..."

"When we were together earlier, I wanted what I wanted," he snarled at her. "You don't suppose I'm a bloody saint, do you?"

"And all the beautiful things you told me?"

"That," he said cruelly, "is just a line I've found that women fall for. They're all so bored and so starved for beauty—as *they* generally put it."

"Even the garden?" Her question was barely audible through the sobs that threatened to suffocate her.

He looked at her and perhaps his expression softened just a trifle.

"What's outside," he said flatly, "is just a little worse than either of you can imagine." He tapped his temple. "The garden's all here."

"You've killed it," she wept. "You've killed it in me. You've both killed everything that's beautiful. But you're worse," she screamed at Patrick, "because he only killed beauty once, but you brought it to life just so you could kill it again. Oh, I can't stand it! I won't stand it!" And she began to scream.

P ATRICK started toward her, but she broke off and whirled away from him to the window, her eyes crazy.

"You've been lying to us," she cried. "The garden's there. I know it is. But you don't want to share it with anyone."

"No, no, Euphemia," Patrick protested anxiously. "It's hell out there, believe me. I wouldn't lie to you about it."

"Wouldn't lie to me!" she mocked. "Are you afraid, too?"

With a sudden pull, she jerked open the window and stood before the blank green-tinged oblong of darkness that seemed to press into the room like a menacing, heavy, wind-urged curtain.

At that Hank cried out a shocked, pleading, "Effie!"

She ignored him. "I can't be cooped up here any longer," she said. "And I won't, now that I know. I'm going to the garden."

Both men sprang at her, but they were too late. She leaped lightly to the sill, and by the time they had flung themselves against it, her footsteps were already hurrying off into the darkness.

"Effie, come back! Come back!" Hank shouted after her desperately, no longer thinking to cringe from the man beside him, or how the gun was pointed. "I love you, Effie. Come back!"

Patrick added. "Come back, Euphemia. You'll be safe if you come back right away. Come back to your home."

No answer to that at all.

They both strained their eyes through the greenish murk. They could barely make out a shadowy figure about half a block down the near-black canyon of the dismal, dust-blown street, into which the greenish moonlight hardly reached. It seemed to them that the figure was scooping something up from the pavement and letting it sift down along its arms and over its bosom.

"Go out and get her, man," Patrick urged the other. "For if I go out for her, I warn you I won't bring her back. She said something about having stood the dust better than most, and that's enough for me."

But Hank, chained by his painfully learned habits and by something else, could not move.

And then a ghostly voice came whispering down the street, chanting, "Fire can hurt me, or water, or the weight of Earth. But the dust is my friend."

Patrick spared the other man one more look. Then, without a word, he vaulted up and ran off.

Hank stood there. After perhaps a half minute he remembered to close his mouth when he inhaled. Finally he was sure the street was empty. As he started to close the window, there was a little *mew*.

He picked up the cat and gently put it outside. Then he did close the window, and the shutters, and bolted them, and took up the Geiger counter, and mechanically began to count himself.

OLD RAMBLING HOUSE
by FRANK HERBERT

*All the Grahams desired was a home they could call
their own... but what did the home want?*

O N HIS last night on Earth, Ted Graham
stepped out of a glass-walled telephone
booth, ducked to avoid a swooping moth
that battered itself in a frenzy against a
bare globe above the booth.

Ted Graham was a long-necked man with a
head of pronounced egg shape topped by prematurely
balding sandy hair. Something about his lanky, intense
appearance suggested his occupation: certified public
accountant.

He stopped behind his wife, who was studying
a newspaper classified page, and frowned. "They said

to wait here. They'll come get us. Said the place is hard to find at night."

Martha Graham looked up from the newspaper. She was a doll-faced woman, heavily pregnant, a kind of pink prettiness about her. The yellow glow from the light above the booth subdued the red-auburn cast of her ponytail hair.

"I just *have* to be in a house when the baby's born," she said. "What'd they sound like?"

"I dunno. There was a funny kind of interruption—like an argument in some foreign language."

"Did they sound foreign?"

"In a way." He motioned along the line of night-shrouded trailers toward one with two windows glowing amber. "Let's wait inside. These bugs out here are fierce."

"Did you tell them which trailer is ours?"

"Yes. They didn't sound at all anxious to look at it. That's odd—them wanting to trade their house for a trailer."

"There's nothing odd about it. They've probably just got itchy feet like we did."

He appeared not to hear her. "Funniest-sounding language you ever heard when that argument started—like a squirt of noise."

INSIDE the trailer, Ted Graham sat down on the green couch that opened into a double bed for company.

"They could use a good tax accountant around here," he said. "When I first saw the place, I got that definite feeling. The valley looks prosperous. It's a wonder nobody's opened an office here before."

His wife took a straight chair by the counter separating kitchen and living area, folded her hands across her heavy stomach.

"I'm just continental tired of wheels going around under me," she said. "I want to sit and stare at the same view for the rest of my life. I don't know how a trailer ever seemed glamorous when—"

"It was the inheritance gave us itchy feet," he said.

Tires gritted on gravel outside.

Martha Graham straightened. "Could that be them?"

"Awful quick, if it is." He went to the door, opened it, stared down at the man who was just raising a hand to knock.

"Are you Mr. Graham?" asked the man.

"Yes." He found himself staring at the caller.

"I'm Clint Rush. You called about the house?" The man moved farther into the light. At first, he'd appeared an old man, fine wrinkle lines in his face, a tired leather look to his skin. But as he moved his head in the light, the wrinkles seemed to dissolve— and with them, the years lifted from him.

"Yes, we called," said Ted Graham. He stood aside. "Do you want to look at the trailer now?"

Martha Graham crossed to stand beside her husband. "We've kept it in awfully good shape," she said. "We've never let anything get seriously wrong with it."

She sounds too anxious, thought Ted Graham. *I wish she'd let me do the talking for the two of us.*

"We can come back and look at your trailer tomorrow in daylight," said Rush. "My car's right out here, if you'd like to see our house."

Ted Graham hesitated. He felt a nagging worry tug at his mind, tried to fix his attention on what bothered him.

"Hadn't we better take our car?" he asked. "We could follow you."

"No need," said Rush. "We're coming back into town tonight anyway. We can drop you off then."

Ted Graham nodded. "Be right with you as soon as I lock up."

Inside the car, Rush mumbled introductions. His wife was a dark shadow in the front seat, her hair drawn back in a severe bun. Her features suggested gypsy blood. He called her Raimee.

Odd name, thought Ted Graham. And he noticed that she, too, gave that strange first impression of age that melted in a shift of light.

Mrs. Rush turned her gypsy features toward Martha Graham. "You are going to have a baby?"

It came out as an odd, veiled statement.

Abruptly, the car rolled forward.

Martha Graham said, "It's supposed to be born in about two months. We hope it's a boy."

Mrs. Rush looked at her husband. "I have changed my mind," she said.

Rush spoke without taking his attention from the road. "It is too..." He broke off, spoke in a tumble of strange sounds.

Ted Graham recognized it as the language he'd heard on the telephone.

Mrs. Rush answered in the same tongue, anger showing in the intensity of her voice. Her husband replied, his voice calmer.

Presently, Mrs. Rush fell moodily silent.

Rush tipped his head toward the rear of the car. "My wife has moments when she does not want to get rid of the old house. It has been with her for many years."

Ted Graham replied, "Oh." Then: "Are you Spanish?"

Rush hesitated. "No. We are Basque."

He turned the car down a well-lighted avenue that merged into a highway. They turned onto a side road. There followed more turns—left, right, right.

Ted Graham lost track.

They hit a jolting bump that made Martha gasp.

"I hope that wasn't too rough on you," said Rush. "We're almost there."

T HE CAR swung into a lane, its lights picking out the skeleton outlines of trees: peculiar trees—tall, gaunt, leafless. They added to Ted's feeling of uneasiness.

The lane dipped, ended at a low wall of a house—red brick with clerestory windows beneath overhanging eaves. The effect of the wall and a wide-beamed door seen to the left was ultramodern.

Ted Graham helped his wife out of the car, followed the Rushes to the door.

"I thought you told me it was an old house," he said.

"It was designed by one of the first modernists," said Rush. He fumbled with an odd curved key. The wide door swung open onto a hallway equally wide, carpeted by a deep pile rug. They could glimpse floor-to-ceiling view windows at the end of the hall, city lights beyond.

Martha Graham gasped, entered the hall as though in a trance. Ted Graham followed, heard the door close behind them.

"It's so—so—so *big*," exclaimed Martha Graham.

"You want to trade *this* for our trailer?" asked Ted Graham.

"It's too inconvenient for us," said Rush. "I work over the mountains on the coast." He shrugged. "We cannot sell it."

Ted Graham looked at him sharply. "Isn't there any money around here?" He had a sudden vision of a tax accountant with no customers.

"Plenty of money, but no customers for real estate."

They entered the living room. Sectional divans lined the walls. Subdued lighting glowed from the corners. Two paintings hung on the opposite walls—oblongs of odd lines and twists that made Ted Graham dizzy.

Warning bells clamored in his mind.

ARTHA Graham crossed to the windows, looked at the lights far away below. "I had no idea we'd climbed that far," she said. "It's like a fairy city."

Mrs. Rush emitted a short, nervous laugh.

Ted Graham glanced around the room, he thought: *If the rest of the house is like this, it's worth fifty or sixty thousand.* He thought of the trailer: *A good one, but not worth more than seven thousand.*

Uneasiness was like a neon sign flashing in his mind. "This seems so..." He shook his head.

"Would you like to see the rest of the house?" asked Rush.

Martha Graham turned from the window. "Oh, yes."

Ted Graham shrugged. *No harm in looking,* he thought.

When they returned to the living room, Ted Graham had doubled his previous estimate on the house's value. His brain reeled with the summing of it: a solarium with an entire ceiling covered by sun lamps, an automatic laundry where you dropped soiled clothing down a chute, took it washed and ironed from the other end...

"Perhaps you and your wife would like to discuss it in private," said Rush. "We will leave you for a moment."

And they were gone before Ted Graham could protest.

Martha Graham said, "Ted, I honestly never in my life dreamed—"

"Something's very wrong, honey."

"But, Ted—"

"This house is worth at least a hundred thousand dollars. Maybe more. And they want to trade *this*—" he looked around himself— "for a seven-thousand-dollar trailer?"

"Ted, they're foreigners. And if they're so foolish they don't know the value of this place, then why should—"

"I don't like it," he said. Again he looked around the room, recalled the fantastic equipment of the house. "But maybe you're right."

He stared out at the city lights. They had a lacelike quality: tall buildings linked by lines of flickering incandescence. Something like a Roman candle shot skyward in the distance.

"Okay!" he said. "If they want to trade, let's go push the deal..."

Abruptly, the house shuddered. The city lights blinked out. A humming sound filled the air.

Martha Graham clutched her husband's arm. "Ted! Wha— what was that?"

"I dunno." He turned. "Mr. Rush!"

No answer. Only the humming.

The door at the end of the room opened. A strange man came through it. He wore a short toga-like garment of gray, metallic cloth belted at the waist by something that glittered and shimmered through every color of the spectrum. An aura of coldness and power emanated from him—a sense of untouchable hauteur.

H E GLANCED around the room, spoke in the same tongue the Rushes had used.

Ted Graham said, "I don't understand you, mister."

The man put a hand to his flickering belt. Both Ted and Martha Graham felt themselves rooted to the floor, a tingling sensation vibrating along every nerve.

Again the strange language rolled from the man's tongue, but now the words were understood.

"Who are you?"

"My name's Graham. This is my wife. What's going—"

"How did you get here?"

"The Rushes—they wanted to trade this house for our trailer. They brought us. Now look, we—"

"What is your talent—your occupation?"

"Tax accountant. Say! Why all these—"

"That was to be expected," said the man. "Clever! Oh, excessively clever!" His hand moved again to the belt. "Now be very quiet. This may confuse you momentarily."

Colored lights filled both the Grahams' minds. They staggered.

"You are qualified," said the man. "You will serve."

"Where are we?" demanded Martha Graham.

"The coordinates would not be intelligible to you," he said. "I am of the Rojac. It is sufficient for you to know that you are under Rojac sovereignty."

TED GRAHAM said, "But—"

"You have, in a way, been kidnapped. And the Raimees have fled to your planet—an unregistered planet."

"I'm afraid," Martha Graham said shakily.

"You have nothing to fear," said the man. "You are no longer on the planet of your birth—nor even in the same galaxy." He glanced at Ted Graham's wrist. "That device on your wrist—it tells your local time?"

"Yes."

"That will help in the search. And your sun— can you describe its atomic cycle?"

Ted Graham groped in his mind for his memories of science lessons from school, from the Sunday supplements. "I can recall that our galaxy is a spiral like—"

"Most galaxies are spiral."

"Is this some kind of a practical joke?" asked Ted Graham.

The man smiled, a cold, superior smile. "It is no joke. Now I will make you a proposition."

Ted nodded warily. "All right, let's have the stinger."

"The people who brought you here were tax collectors we Rojac recruited from a subject planet. They were conditioned to make it impossible for them to leave their job untended. Unfortunately, they were clever enough to realize that if they brought someone else in who could do their job, they were released from their mental bonds. Very clever."

"But—"

"You may have their job," said the man. "Normally, you would be put to work in the lower echelons, but we believe in meting out justice wherever possible. The Raimees undoubtedly stumbled on your planet by accident and lured you into this position without—"

"How do you know I can do your job?"

"That moment of brilliance was an aptitude test. You passed. Well, do you accept?"

"What about our baby?" Martha Graham worriedly wanted to know.

"You will be allowed to keep it until it reaches the age of decision—about the time it will take the child to reach adult stature."

"Then what?" insisted Martha Graham.

"The child will take its position in society—according to its ability."

"Will we ever see our child after that?"

"Possibly."

Ted Graham said, "What's the joker in this?"

Again the cold, superior smile. "You will receive conditioning similar to that which we gave the Raimees. And we will want to examine your memories to aid us in our search for your planet. It would be good to find a new inhabitable place."

"Why did they trap us like this?" asked Martha Graham.

"It's lonely work," the man explained. "Your house is actually a type of space conveyance that travels along your collection route—and there is much travel to the job. And then—you will not have friends, nor time for much other than work. Our methods are necessarily severe at times."

"*Travel?*" Martha Graham repeated in dismay.

"Almost constantly."

Ted Graham felt his mind whirling. And behind him, he heard his wife sobbing.

THE RAIMEES sat in what had been the Grahams' trailer.

"For a few moments, I feared he would not succumb to the bait," she said. "I knew you could never overcome the mental compulsion enough to leave them there without their first agreeing."

Raimee chuckled. "Yes. And now I'm going to indulge in everything the Rojac never permitted. I'm going to write ballads and poems."

"And I'm going to paint," she said. "Oh, the delicious freedom!"

"Greed won this for us," he said. "The long study of the Grahams paid off. They couldn't refuse to trade."

"I knew they'd agree. The looks in their eyes when they saw the house! They both had..." She broke off, a look of horror coming into her eyes. "One of them did not agree!"

"They both did. You heard them."

"The baby?"

He stared at his wife. "But—but it is not at the age of decision!"

"In perhaps eighteen of this planet's years, it *will* be at the age of decision. What then?"

His shoulders sagged. He shuddered. "I will not be able to fight it off. I will have to build a transmitter, call the Rojac and confess!"

"And they will collect another inhabitable place," she said, her voice flat and toneless.

"I've spoiled it," he said. "I've spoiled it!"

PIPER IN THE WOODS

by PHILIP K. DICK

Earth maintained an important garrison on Asteroid Y-3. Now suddenly it was imperiled with a biological impossibility—men becoming plants!

ELL, CORPORAL Westerburg," Doctor Henry Harris said gently, "just why do you think you're a plant?"

As he spoke, Harris glanced down again at the card on his desk. It was from the Base Commander himself, made out in Cox's heavy scrawl: *Doc, this is the lad I told you about. Talk to him and try to find out how he got this delusion. He's from the new Garrison, the new check-station on Asteroid Y-3, and we don't want anything to go wrong there. Especially a silly damn thing like this!*

Harris pushed the card aside and stared back up at the youth across the desk from him. The young man seemed ill at ease and appeared to be avoiding answering the question Harris had put to him. Harris frowned. Westerburg was a good-looking chap, actually handsome in his Patrol uniform, a shock of blond hair over one eye. He was tall, almost six feet, a fine healthy lad, just two years out of Training, according to the card. Born in Detroit. Had measles when he was nine. Interested in jet engines, tennis, and girls. Twenty-six years old.

"Well, Corporal Westerburg," Doctor Harris said again. "Why do you think you're a plant?"

The Corporal looked up shyly. He cleared his throat. "Sir, I *am* a plant, I don't just think so. I've been a plant for several days, now."

"I see." The Doctor nodded. "You mean that you weren't always a plant?"

"No, sir. I just became a plant recently."

"And what were you before you became a plant?"

"Well, sir, I was just like the rest of you."

There was silence. Doctor Harris took up his pen and scratched a few lines, but nothing of importance came. A plant? And such a healthy-looking lad! Harris removed his steel-rimmed glasses and polished them with his handkerchief. He put them on again and leaned back in his chair. "Care for a cigarette, Corporal?"

"No, sir."

The Doctor lit one himself, resting his arm on the edge of the chair. "Corporal, you must realize that there are very few men who become plants, especially on such short notice. I have to admit you are the first person who has ever told me such a thing."

"Yes, sir, I realize it's quite rare."

"You can understand why I'm interested, then. When you say you're a plant, you mean you're not capable of mobility? Or do you mean you're a vegetable, as opposed to an animal? Or just what?"

The Corporal looked away. "I can't tell you any more," he murmured. "I'm sorry, sir."

"Well, would you mind telling me *how* you became a plant?"

Corporal Westerburg hesitated. He stared down at the floor, then out the window at the spaceport, then at a fly on the desk. At last he stood up, getting slowly to his feet. "I can't even tell you that, sir," he said.

"You can't? Why not?"

"Because—because I promised not to."

THE ROOM was silent. Doctor Harris rose, too, and they both stood facing each other. Harris frowned, rubbing his jaw. "Corporal, just *who* did you promise?"

"I can't even tell you that, sir. I'm sorry."

The Doctor considered this. At last he went to the door and opened it. "All right, Corporal. You may go now. And thanks for your time."

"I'm sorry I'm not more helpful." The Corporal went slowly out and Harris closed the door after him. Then he went across his office to the vidphone. He rang Commander Cox's letter. A moment later the beefy good-natured face of the Base Commander appeared.

"Cox, this is Harris. I talked to him, all right. All I could get is the statement that he's a plant. What else is there? What kind of behavior pattern?"

"Well," Cox said, "the first thing they noticed was that he wouldn't do any work. The Garrison Chief reported that this Westerburg would wander off outside the Garrison and just sit, all day long. Just sit."

"In the sun?"

"Yes. Just sit in the sun. Then at nightfall he would come back in. When they asked why he wasn't working in the jet repair building he told them he had to be out in the sun. Then he said—" Cox hesitated.

"Yes? Said what?"

"He said that work was unnatural. That it was a waste of time. That the only worthwhile thing was to sit and contemplate—outside."

"What then?"

"Then they asked him how he got that idea, and then he revealed to them that he had become a plant."

"I'm going to have to talk to him again, I can see," Harris said. "And he's applied for a permanent discharge from the Patrol? What reason did he give?"

"The same, that he's a plant now, and has no more interest in being a Patrolman. All he wants to do is sit in the sun. It's the damnedest thing I ever heard."

"All right. I think I'll visit him in his quarters." Harris looked at his watch. "I'll go over after dinner."

"Good luck," Cox said gloomily. "But who ever heard of a man turning into a plant? We told him it wasn't possible, but he just smiled at us."

"I'll let you know how I make out," Harris said.

H ARRIS walked slowly down the hall. It was after six; the evening meal was over. A dim concept was coming into his mind, but it was much too soon to be sure. He increased his pace, turning right at the end of the hall. Two nurses passed, hurrying by. Westerburg was quartered with a buddy, a man who had been injured in a jet blast and who was now almost recovered. Harris came to the dorm wing and stopped, checking the numbers on the doors.

"Can I help you, sir?" the robot attendant said, gliding up.

"I'm looking for Corporal Westerburg's room."

"Three doors to the right."

Harris went on. Asteroid Y-3 had only recently been garrisoned and staffed. It had become the primary check-point to halt and examine ships entering the system from outer space. The Garrison made sure that no dangerous bacteria, fungus, or what-not arrived to infect the system. A nice asteroid it was, warm, well-watered, with trees and lakes and lots of sunlight. And the most modern Garrison in the nine planets. He shook his head, coming to the third door. He stopped, raising his hand and knocking.

"Who's there?" sounded through the door.

"I want to see Corporal Westerburg."

The door opened. A bovine youth with horn-rimmed glasses looked out, a book in his hand. "Who are you?"

"Doctor Harris."

"I'm sorry, sir. Corporal Westerburg is asleep."

"Would he mind if I woke him up? I want very much to talk to him." Harris peered inside. He could see a neat room, with a desk, a rug and lamp, and two bunks. On one of the bunks was Westerburg, lying face up, his arms folded across his chest, his eyes tightly closed.

"Sir," the bovine youth said, "I'm afraid I can't wake him up for you, much as I'd like to."

"You can't? Why not?"

"Sir, Corporal Westerburg won't wake up, not after the sun sets. He just won't. He can't be wakened."

"Cataleptic? Really?"

"But in the morning, as soon as the sun comes up, he leaps out of bed and goes outside. Stays the whole day."

"I see," the Doctor said. "Well, thanks anyhow." He went back out into the hall and the door shut after him. "There's more to this than I realized," he murmured. He went on back the way he had come.

I T WAS a warm sunny day. The blue sky was almost free of clouds and a gentle wind moved through the cedars along the bank of the stream. There was a path leading from the hospital building down the slope to the stream. At the stream a small bridge led over to the other side, and a few patients were standing on the bridge, wrapped in their bathrobes, looking aimlessly down at the water.

It took Harris several long minutes to find Westerburg. The youth was not with the other patients, near or around the bridge. He had gone farther down, past the cedar trees and out onto a strip of bright meadow, where poppies and grass grew everywhere. He was sitting on the stream bank, on a flat grey stone, leaning back and staring up, his mouth open a little. He did not notice the Doctor until Harris was almost beside him.

"Hello," Harris said softly.

Westerburg opened his eyes, looking up. He smiled and got slowly to his feet, a graceful, flowing motion that was rather surprising for a man of his size. "Hello, Doctor. What brings you out here?"

"Nothing. Thought I'd get some sun."

"Here, you can share my rock." Westerburg moved over and Harris sat down gingerly, being careful not to catch his trousers on the sharp edges of the rock. He lit a cigarette and gazed silently down at the water. Beside him, Westerburg had resumed his strange position, leaning back, resting on his hands, staring up with his eyes shut tight.

"Nice day," the Doctor said.

"Yes."

"Do you come here every day?"

"Yes."

"You like it better out here than inside."

"I can't stay inside," Westerburg said.

"You can't? How do you mean, 'can't'?"

"You would die without *air*, wouldn't you?" the Corporal said.

"And you'd die without sunlight?"

Westerburg nodded.

"Corporal, may I ask you something? Do you plan to do this the rest of your life, sit out in the sun on a flat rock? Nothing else?"

Westerburg nodded.

"How about your job? You went to school for years to become a Patrolman. You wanted to enter the Patrol very badly. You were given a fine rating and a first-class position. How do you feel, giving all that up? You know, it won't be easy to get back in again. Do you realize that?"

"I realize it."

"And you're really going to give it all up?"

"That's right."

HARRIS was silent for a while. At last he put his cigarette out and turned toward the youth. "All right, let's say you give up your job and sit in the sun. Well, what happens, then? Someone else has to do the job instead of you. Isn't that true? The job has to be done, *your* job has to be done. And if you don't do it someone else has to."

"I suppose so."

"Westerburg, suppose everyone felt the way you do? Suppose everyone wanted to sit in the sun all day? What would happen? No one would check ships coming from outer space. Bacteria and toxic crystals would enter the system and cause mass death and suffering. Isn't that right?"

"If everyone felt the way I do they wouldn't be going into outer space."

"But they have to. They have to trade, they have to get minerals and products and new plants."

"Why?"

"To keep society going."

"Why?"

"Well—" Harris gestured. "People couldn't live without society."

Westerburg said nothing to that. Harris watched him, but the youth did not answer.

"Isn't that right?" Harris said.

"Perhaps. It's a peculiar business, Doctor. You know, I struggled for years to get through Training. I had to work and pay my own way. Washed dishes, worked in kitchens. Studied at night, learned, crammed, worked on and on. And you know what I think, now?"

"What?"

"I wish I'd become a plant earlier."

Doctor Harris stood up. "Westerburg, when you come inside, will you stop off at my office? I want to give you a few tests, if you don't mind."

"The shock box?" Westerburg smiled. "I knew that would be coming around. Sure, I don't mind."

Nettled, Harris left the rock, walking back up the bank a short distance. "About three, Corporal?"

The Corporal nodded.

Harris made his way up the hill, to the path, toward the hospital building. The whole thing was beginning to become more clear to him. A boy who had struggled all his life. Financial insecurity. Idealized goal, getting a Patrol assignment. Finally reached it, found the load too great. And on Asteroid Y-3 there was too much vegetation to look at all day. Primitive identification and projection on the flora of the asteroid. Concept of security involved in immobility and permanence. Unchanging forest.

He entered the building. A robot orderly stopped him almost at once. "Sir, Commander Cox wants you urgently, on the vidphone."

"Thanks." Harris strode to his office. He dialed Cox's letter and the Commander's face came presently into focus. "Cox? This is Harris. I've been out talking to the boy. I'm beginning to get this lined up, now. I can see the pattern, too much load too long. Finally gets what he wants and the idealization shatters under the—"

"Harris!" Cox barked. "Shut up and listen. I just got a report from Y-3. They're sending an express rocket here. It's on the way."

"An express rocket?"

"Five more cases like Westerburg. All say they're plants! The Garrison Chief is worried as hell. Says we *must* find out what it is or the Garrison will fall apart, right away. Do you get me, Harris? Find out what it is!"

"Yes, sir," Harris murmured. "Yes, sir."

B Y THE end of the week there were twenty cases, and all, of course, were from Asteroid Y-3.

Commander Cox and Harris stood together at the top of the hill, looking gloomily down at the stream below. Sixteen men and four women sat in the sun along the bank, none of them moving, none speaking. An hour had gone by since Cox and Harris appeared, and in all that time the twenty people below had not stirred.

"I don't get it," Cox said, shaking his head. "I just absolutely don't get it. Harris, is this the beginning of the end? Is everything going to start cracking around us? It gives me a hell of a strange feeling to see those people down there, basking away in the sun, just sitting and basking."

"Who's that man there with the red hair?"

"That's Ulrich Deutsch. He was Second in Command at the Garrison. Now look at him! Sits and dozes with his mouth open and his eyes shut. A week ago that man was climbing, going right up to the top. When the Garrison Chief retires he was supposed to take over. Maybe another year, at the most. All his life he's been climbing to get up there."

"And now he sits in the sun," Harris finished.

"That woman. The brunette, with the short hair. Career woman. Head of the entire office staff of the Garrison. And the man beside her. Janitor. And that cute little gal there, with the bosom. Secretary, just out of school. All kinds. And I got a note this morning, three more coming in sometime today."

Harris nodded. "The strange thing is—they really *want* to sit down there. They're completely rational; they could do something else, but they just don't care to."

"Well?" Cox said. "What are you going to do? Have you found anything? We're counting on you. Let's hear it."

"I couldn't get anything out of them directly," Harris said, "but I've had some interesting results with the shock box. Let's go inside and I'll show you."

"Fine," Cox turned and started toward the hospital. "Show me anything you've got. This is serious. Now I know how Tiberius felt when Christianity showed up in high places."

H ARRIS snapped off the light. The room was pitch black. "I'll run this first reel for you. The subject is one of the best biologists stationed at the Garrison. Robert Bradshaw. He came in yesterday. I got a good run from the shock box because Bradshaw's mind is so highly differentiated. There's a lot of repressed material of a non-rational nature, more than usual."

He pressed a switch. The projector whirred, and on the far wall a three-dimensional image appeared in color, so real that it might have been the man himself. Robert Bradshaw was a man of fifty, heavy-set, with iron grey hair and a square jaw. He sat in the chair calmly, his hands resting on the arms, oblivious to the electrodes attached to his neck and wrist. "There I go," Harris said. "Watch."

His film-image materialized, approaching Bradshaw. "Now, Mr. Bradshaw," his image said, "this won't hurt you at all, and it'll help us a lot." The image rotated the controls on the shock box. Bradshaw stiffened, and his jaw set, but otherwise he gave no sign. The image of Harris regarded him for a time and then stepped away from the controls.

"Can you hear me, Mr. Bradshaw?" the image asked.

"Yes."

"What is your name?"

"Robert C. Bradshaw."

"What is your position?"

"Chief Biologist at the check-station on Y-3."

"Are you there now?"

"No, I'm back on Terra. In a hospital."

"Why?"

"Because I admitted to the Garrison Chief that I had become a plant."

"Is that true? That you are a plant."

"Yes, in a non-biological sense. I retain the physiology of a human being, of course."

"What do you mean, then, that you're a plant?"

"The reference is to attitudinal response, to Weltanschauung."

"Go on."

"It is possible for a warm-blooded animal, an upper primate, to adopt the psychology of a plant, to some extent."

"Yes?"

"I refer to this."

"And the others? They refer to this also?"

"Yes."

"How did this occur, your adopting this attitude?"

Bradshaw's image hesitated, the lips twisting. "See?" Harris said to Cox. "Strong conflict. He wouldn't have gone on, if he had been fully conscious."

"I—"

"Yes?"

"I was taught to become a plant."

The image of Harris showed surprise and interest. "What do you mean, you were *taught* to become a plant?"

"They realized my problems and they taught me to become a plant. Now I'm free from them, the problems."

"Who? Who taught you?"

"The Pipers."

"Who? The Pipers? Who are the Pipers?"

There was no answer.

"Mr. Bradshaw, who are the Pipers?"

After a long, agonized pause, the heavy lips parted. "They live in the woods…"

Harris snapped off the projector, and the lights came on. He and Cox blinked. "That was all I could get," Harris said. "But I was lucky to get that. He wasn't supposed to tell, not at all. That was the thing they all promised not to do, tell who taught them to become plants. The Pipers who live in the woods, on Asteroid Y-3."

"You got this story from all twenty?"

"No." Harris grimaced. "Most of them put up too much fight. I couldn't even get *this* much from them."

Cox reflected. "The Pipers. Well? What do you propose to do? Just wait around until you can get the full story? Is that your program?"

"No," Harris said. "Not at all. I'm going to Y-3 and find out who the Pipers are, myself."

T HE SMALL patrol ship made its landing with care and precision, its jets choking into final silence. The hatch slid back and Doctor Henry Harris found himself staring out at a field, a brown, sun-baked landing field. At the end of the field was a tall signal tower. Around the field on all sides were long grey buildings, the Garrison check-station itself. Not far off a huge Venusian cruiser was parked, a vast green hulk, like an enormous lime. The technicians from the station were swarming all over it, checking and examining each inch of it for lethal life-forms and poisons that might have attached themselves to the hull.

"All out, sir," the pilot said.

Harris nodded. He took hold of his two suitcases and stepped carefully down. The ground was hot underfoot, and he blinked in the bright sunlight. Jupiter was in the sky, and the vast planet reflected considerable sunlight down onto the asteroid.

Harris started across the field, carrying his suitcases. A field attendant was already busy opening the storage compartment of the patrol ship, extracting his trunk. The attendant lowered the trunk into a waiting dolly and came after him, manipulating the little truck with bored skill.

As Harris came to the entrance of the signal tower the gate slid back and a man came forward, an older man, large and robust, with white hair and a steady walk.

"How are you, Doctor?" he said, holding his hand out. "I'm Lawrence Watts, the Garrison Chief."

They shook hands. Watts smiled down at Harris. He was a huge old man, still regal and straight in his dark blue uniform, with his gold epaulets sparkling on his shoulders.

"Have a good trip?" Watts asked. "Come on inside and I'll have a drink fixed for you. It gets hot around here, with the Big Mirror up there."

"Jupiter?" Harris followed him inside the building. The signal tower was cool and dark, a welcome relief. "Why is the gravity so near Terra's? I expected to go flying off like a kangaroo. Is it artificial?"

"No. There's a dense core of some kind to the asteroid, some kind of metallic deposit. That's why we picked this asteroid out of all the others. It made the construction problem much simpler, and it also explains why the asteroid has natural air and water. Did you see the hills?"

"The hills?"

"When we get up higher in the tower we'll be able to see over the buildings. There's quite a natural park here, a regular little forest, complete with everything you'd want. Come in here, Harris. This is my office." The old man strode at quite a clip, around the corner and into a large, well-furnished apartment. "Isn't this pleasant? I intend to make my last year here as amiable as possible." He frowned. "Of course, with Deutsch gone, I may be here forever. Oh, well." He shrugged. "Sit down, Harris."

"Thanks." Harris took a chair, stretching his legs out. He watched Watts as he closed the door to the hall. "By the way, any more cases come up?"

"Two more today," Watts was grim. "Makes almost thirty, in all. We have three hundred men in this station. At the rate it's going—"

"Chief, you spoke about a forest on the asteroid. Do you allow the crew to go into the forest at will? Or do you restrict them to the buildings and grounds?"

W ATTS rubbed his jaw. "Well, it's a difficult situation, Harris. I have to let the men leave the grounds sometimes. They can *see* the forest from the buildings, and as long as you can see a nice place to stretch out and relax that does it. Once every ten days they have a full period of rest. Then they go out and fool around."

"And then it happens?"

"Yes, I suppose so. But as long as they can see the forest they'll want to go. I can't help it."

"I know. I'm not censuring you. Well, what's your theory? What happens to them out there? What do they do?"

"What happens? Once they get out there and take it easy for a while they don't want to come back and work. It's boondoggling. Playing hookey. They don't want to work, so off they go."

"How about this business of their delusions?"

Watts laughed good-naturedly. "Listen, Harris. You know as well as I do that's a lot of poppycock. They're no more plants than you or I. They just don't want to work, that's all. When I was a cadet we had a few ways to make people work. I wish we could lay a few on their backs, like we used to."

"You think this is simple goldbricking, then?"

"Don't you think it is?"

"No," Harris said. "They really believe they're plants. I put them through the high-frequency shock treatment, the shock box. The whole nervous system is paralyzed, all inhibitions stopped cold. They tell the truth, then. And they said the same thing—and more."

Watts paced back and forth, his hands clasped behind his back. "Harris, you're a doctor, and I suppose you know what you're talking about. But look at the situation here. We have a garrison, a good modern garrison. We're probably the most modern outfit in the system. Every new device and gadget is here that science can produce. Harris, this garrison is one vast machine. The men are parts, and each has his job, the Maintenance Crew, the Biologists, the Office Crew, the Managerial Staff.

"Look what happens when one person steps away from his job. Everything else begins to creak. We can't service the bugs if no one services the machines. We can't order food to feed the crews if no one makes out reports, takes inventories. We can't direct any kind of activity if the Second in Command decides to go out and sit in the sun all day.

"Thirty people, one tenth of the Garrison. But we can't run without them. The Garrison is built that way. If you take the supports out the whole building falls. No one can leave. We're all tied here, and these people know it. They know they have no right to do that, run off on their own. No one has that right anymore. We're all too tightly interwoven to suddenly start doing what we want. It's unfair to the rest, the majority."

HARRIS nodded in agreement. "Chief, can I ask you something?"

"What is it?"

"Are there any inhabitants on the asteroid? Any natives?"

"Natives?" Watts considered. "Yes, there's some kind of aborigines living out there." He waved vaguely toward the window.

"What are they like? Have you seen them?"

"Yes, I've seen them. At least, I saw them when we first came here. They hung around for a while, watching us, then after a time they disappeared."

"Did they die off? Diseases of some kind?"

"No. They just—just disappeared. Into their forest. They're still there, someplace."

"What kind of people are they?"

"Well, the story is that they're originally from Mars. They don't look much like Martians, though. They're dark, a kind of coppery color. Thin. Very agile, in their own way. They hunt and fish. No written language. We don't pay much attention to them."

"I see." Harris paused. "Chief, have you ever heard of anything called—The Pipers?"

"The Pipers?" Watts frowned. "No. Why?"

"The patients mentioned something called The Pipers. According to Bradshaw, the Pipers taught him to become a plant. He learned it from them, a kind of teaching."

"The Pipers. What are they?"

"I don't know," Harris admitted. "I thought maybe you might know. My first assumption, of course, was that they're the natives. But now I'm not so sure, not after hearing your description of them."

"The natives are primitive savages. They don't have anything to teach anybody, especially a top-flight biologist."

Harris hesitated. "Chief, I'd like to go into the woods and look around. Is that possible?"

"Certainly. I can arrange it for you. I'll give you one of the men to show you around."

"I'd rather go alone. Is there any danger?"

"No, none that I know of. Except—"

"Except the Pipers," Harris finished. "I know. Well, there's only one way to find them, and that's it. I'll have to take my chances."

"I F YOU walk in a straight line," Chief Watts said, "you'll find yourself back at the Garrison in about six hours. It's a damn small asteroid. There's a couple of streams and lakes, so don't fall in."

"How about snakes or poisonous insects?"

"Nothing like that reported. We did a lot of tramping around at first, but it's grown back now, the way it was. We never encountered anything dangerous."

"Thanks, Chief," Harris said. They shook hands. "I'll see you before nightfall."

"Good luck." The Chief and his two armed escorts turned and went back across the rise, down the other side toward the Garrison. Harris watched them go until they disappeared inside the building. Then he turned and started into the grove of trees.

The woods were very silent around him as he walked. Trees towered up on all sides of him, huge dark-green trees like eucalyptus. The ground underfoot was soft with endless leaves that had fallen and rotted into soil. After a while the grove of high trees fell behind and he found himself crossing a dry meadow, the grass and weeds burned brown in the sun.

Insects buzzed around him, rising up from the dry weed-stalks. Something scuttled ahead, hurrying through the undergrowth. He caught sight of a grey ball with many legs, scampering furiously, its antennae weaving.

The meadow ended at the bottom of a hill. He was going up, now, going higher and higher. Ahead of him an endless expanse of green rose, acres of wild growth. He scrambled to the top finally, blowing and panting, catching his breath.

He went on. Now he was going down again, plunging into a deep gully. Tall ferns grew, as large as trees. He was entering a living Jurassic forest, ferns that stretched out endlessly ahead of him. Down he went, walking carefully. The air began to turn cold around him. The floor of the gully was damp and silent; underfoot the ground was almost wet.

He came out on a level table. It was dark, with the ferns growing up on all sides, dense growths of ferns, silent and unmoving. He came upon a natural path, an old stream bed, rough and rocky, but easy to follow. The air was thick and oppressive. Beyond the ferns he could see the side of the next hill, a green field rising up.

Something grey was ahead. Rocks, piled-up boulders, scattered and stacked here and there. The stream bed led directly to them. Apparently this had been a pool of some kind, a stream emptying from it. He climbed the first of the boulders awkwardly, feeling his way up. At the top he paused, resting again.

As yet he had had no luck. So far he had not met any of the natives. It would be through them that he would find the mysterious Pipers that were stealing the men away, if such really existed. If he could find the natives, talk to them, perhaps he could find out something. But as yet he had been unsuccessful. He looked around. The woods were very silent. A slight breeze moved through the ferns, rustling them, but that was all. Where were the natives? Probably they had a settlement of some sort, huts, a clearing. The asteroid was small; he should be able to find them by nightfall.

H E STARTED down the rocks. More rocks rose up ahead and he climbed them. Suddenly he stopped, listening. Far off, he could hear a sound, the sound of water. Was he approaching a pool of some kind? He went on again, trying to locate the sound. He scrambled down rocks and up rocks, and all around him there was silence, except for the splashing of distant water. Maybe a waterfall, water in motion. A stream. If he found the stream he might find the natives.

The rocks ended and the stream bed began again, but this time it was wet, the bottom muddy and overgrown with moss. He was on the right track; not too long ago this stream had flowed, probably during the rainy season. He went up on the side of the stream, pushing through the ferns and vines. A golden snake slid expertly out of his path. Something glinted ahead, something sparkling through the ferns. Water. A pool. He hurried, pushing the vines aside and stepping out, leaving them behind.

He was standing on the edge of a pool, a deep pool sunk in a hollow of grey rocks, surrounded by ferns and vines. The water was clear and bright, and in motion, flowing in a waterfall at the far end. It was beautiful, and he stood watching, marveling at it, the undisturbed quality of it. Untouched, it was. Just as it had always been, probably. As long as the asteroid existed. Was he the first to see it? Perhaps. It was so hidden, so concealed by the ferns. It gave him a strange feeling, a feeling almost of ownership. He stepped down a little toward the water.

And it was then he noticed her.

The girl was sitting on the far edge of the pool, staring down into the water, resting her head on one drawn-up knee. She had been bathing; he could see that at once. Her coppery body was still wet and glistening with moisture, sparkling in the sun. She had not seen him. He stopped, holding his breath, watching her.

She was lovely, very lovely, with long dark hair that wound around her shoulders and arms. Her body was slim, very slender, with a supple grace to it that made him stare, accustomed as he was to various forms of anatomy. How silent she was! Silent and unmoving, staring down at the water. Time passed, strange, unchanging time, as he watched the girl. Time might even have ceased, with the girl sitting on the rock staring into the water, and the rows of great ferns behind her, as rigid as if they had been painted there.

All at once the girl looked up. Harris shifted, suddenly conscious of himself as an intruder. He stepped back. "I'm sorry," he murmured. "I'm from the Garrison. I didn't mean to come poking around."

She nodded without speaking.

"You don't mind?" Harris asked presently.

"No."

So she spoke Terran! He moved a little toward her, around the side of the pool. "I hope you don't mind my bothering you. I won't be on the asteroid very long. This is my first day here. I just arrived from Terra."

She smiled faintly.

"I'm a doctor. Henry Harris." He looked down at her, at the slim coppery body, gleaming in the sunlight, a faint sheen of moisture on her arms and thighs. "You might be interested in why I'm here." He paused. "Maybe you can even help me."

She looked up a little. "Oh?"

"Would you like to help me?"

She smiled. "Yes. Of course."

"That's good. Mind if I sit down?" He looked around and found himself a flat rock. He sat down slowly, facing her. "Cigarette?"

"No."

"Well, I'll have one." He lit up, taking a deep breath. "You see, we have a problem at the Garrison. Something has been happening to some of the men, and it seems to be spreading. We have to find out what causes it or we won't be able to run the Garrison."

H E WAITED for a moment. She nodded slightly. How silent she was! Silent and unmoving. Like the ferns.

"Well, I've been able to find out a few things from them, and one very interesting fact stands out. They keep saying that something called—called The Pipers are responsible for their condition. They say the Pipers taught them—" He stopped. A strange look had flitted across her dark, small face. "Do you know the Pipers?"

She nodded.

Acute satisfaction flooded over Harris. "You do? I was sure the natives would know." He stood up again. "I was sure they would, if the Pipers really existed. Then they do exist, do they?"

"They exist."

Harris frowned. "And the Pipers are here, in the woods?"

"Yes."

"I see." He ground his cigarette out impatiently. "You don't suppose there's any chance you could take me to them, do you?"

"Take you?"

"Yes. I have this problem and I have to solve it. You see, the Base Commander on Terra has assigned this to me, this business about the Pipers. It has to be solved. And I'm the one assigned to the job. So it's important to me to find them. Do you see? Do you understand?"

She nodded.

"Well, will you take me to them?"

The girl was silent. For a long time she sat, staring down into the water, resting her head against her knee. Harris began to become impatient. He fidgeted back and forth, resting first on one leg and then on the other.

"Well, will you?" he said again. "It's important to the whole Garrison. What do you say?" He felt around in his pockets. "Maybe I could give you something. What do I have..." He brought out his lighter. "I could give you my lighter."

The girl stood up, rising slowly, gracefully, without motion or effort. Harris' mouth fell open. How supple she was, gliding to her feet in a single motion! He blinked. Without effort she had stood, seemingly without *change*. All at once she was standing instead of sitting, standing and looking calmly at him, her small face expressionless.

"Will you?" he said.

"Yes. Come along." She turned away, moving toward the row of ferns.

Harris followed quickly, stumbling across the rocks. "Fine," he said. "Thanks a lot. I'm really very interested to meet these Pipers. Where are you taking me, to your village? How much time do we have before nightfall?"

The girl did not answer. She had entered the ferns already, and Harris quickened his pace to keep from losing her. How silently she glided!

"Wait," he called. "Wait for me."

The girl paused, waiting for him, slim and lovely, looking silently back.

He entered the ferns, hurrying after her.

ELL, I'LL be damned!" said Commander Cox. "It sure didn't take you long." He leaped down the steps two at a time. "Let me give you a hand."

Harris grinned, lugging his heavy suitcases. He set them down and breathed a sigh of relief. "It isn't worth it," he said. "I'm going to give up taking so much."

"Come on inside. Soldier, give him a hand." A Patrolman hurried over and took one of the suitcases. The three men went inside and down the corridor to Harris' quarters. Harris unlocked the door and the Patrolman deposited his suitcase inside.

"Thanks," Harris said. He set the other down beside it. "It's good to be back, even for a little while."

"A little while?"

"I just came back to settle my affairs. I have to return to Y-3 tomorrow morning."

"Then you didn't solve the problem?"

"I solved it, but I haven't *cured* it. I'm going back and get to work right away. There's a lot to be done."

"But you found out what it is?"

"Yes. It was just what the men said. The Pipers."

"The Pipers do exist?"

"Yes." Harris nodded. "They do exist." He removed his coat and put it over the back of the chair. Then he went to the window and let it down. Warm spring air rushed into the room. He settled himself on the bed, leaning back.

"The Pipers exist, all right—in the minds of the Garrison crew! To the crew, the Pipers are real. The crew created them. It's a mass hypnosis, a group projection, and all the men there have it, to some degree."

"How did it start?"

"Those men on Y-3 were sent there because they were skilled, highly-trained men with exceptional ability. All their lives they've been schooled by complex modern society, fast tempo and high integration between people. Constant pressure toward some goal, some job to be done.

"Those men are put down suddenly on an asteroid where there are natives living the most primitive of existence, completely vegetable lives. No concept of goal, no concept of purpose, and hence no ability to plan. The natives live the way the animals live, from day to day, sleeping, picking food from the trees. A kind of Garden-of-Eden existence, without struggle or conflict."

"So? But—"

"Each of the Garrison crew sees the natives and *unconsciously* thinks of his own early life, when he was a child, when *he* had no worries, no responsibilities, before he joined modern society. A baby lying in the sun.

"But he can't admit this to himself! He can't admit that he might *want* to live like the natives, to lie and sleep all day. So he invents The Pipers, the idea of a mysterious group living in the woods who trap him, lead him into their kind of life. Then he can blame *them*, not himself. They 'teach' him to become a part of the woods."

"What are you going to do? Have the woods burned?"

"No." Harris shook his head. "That's not the answer; the woods are harmless. The answer is psychotherapy for the men. That's why I'm going right back, so I can begin work. They've got to be made to see that the Pipers are inside them, their own unconscious voices calling to them to give up their responsibilities. They've got to be made to realize that there are no Pipers, at least, not outside themselves. The woods are harmless and the natives have nothing to teach anyone. They're primitive savages, without even a written language. We're seeing a psychological projection by a whole Garrison of men who want to lay down their work and take it easy for a while."

The room was silent.

"I see," Cox said presently. "Well, it makes sense." He got to his feet. "I hope you can do something with the men when you get back."

"I hope so, too," Harris agreed. "And I think I can. After all, it's just a question of increasing their self-awareness. When they have that the Pipers will vanish."

Cox nodded. "Well, you go ahead with your unpacking, Doc. I'll see you at dinner. And maybe before you leave, tomorrow."

"Fine."

ARRIS opened the door and let the Commander out into the hall. Harris closed the door after him and then went back across the room. He looked out the window for a moment, his hands in his pockets.

It was becoming evening, the air was turning cool. The sun was just setting as he watched, disappearing behind the buildings of the city surrounding the hospital. He watched it go down.

Then he went over to his two suitcases. He was tired, very tired from his trip. A great weariness was beginning to descend over him. There were so many things to do, so terribly many. How could he hope to do them all? Back to the asteroid. And then what?

He yawned, his eyes closing. How sleepy he was! He looked over at the bed. Then he sat down on the edge of it and took his shoes off. So much to do, the next day.

He put his shoes in the corner of the room. Then he bent over, unsnapping one of the suitcases. He opened the suitcase. From it he took a bulging gunnysack. Carefully, he emptied the contents of the sack out on the floor. Dirt, rich soft dirt. Dirt he had collected during his last hours there, dirt he had carefully gathered up.

When the dirt was spread out on the floor he sat down in the middle of it. He stretched himself out, leaning back. When he was fully comfortable he folded his hands across his chest and closed his eyes. So much work to do—But later on, of course. Tomorrow. How warm the dirt was...

He was sound asleep in a moment.

SENTIMENT, INC.
by POUL ANDERSON

The way we feel about another person, or about objects,
is often bound up in associations that have no direct
connection with the person or object at all. Often, what
we call a "change of heart" comes about sheerly from a
change in the many associations which make up our
present viewpoint. Now, suppose that these associations
could be altered artificially, at the option of the person
who was in charge of the process...

S HE WAS twenty-two years old, fresh out of college, full of life and hope, and all set to conquer the world. Colin Fraser happened to be on vacation on Cape Cod, where she was playing summer stock, and went to more shows than he had planned. It wasn't hard to get an introduction, and before long he and Judy Sanders were seeing a lot of each other.

"Of course," she told him one afternoon on the beach, "my real name is Harkness."

He raised his arm, letting the sand run through his fingers. The beach was big and dazzling white around them, the sea galloped in with a steady roar, and a gull rode the breeze overhead. "What was wrong with it?" he asked. "For a professional monicker, I mean."

She laughed and shook the long hair back over her shoulders. "I wanted to live under the name of Sanders," she explained.

"Oh—oh, yes, of course. Winnie the Pooh." He grinned. "Soulmates, that's what we are." It was about then that he decided he'd been a bachelor long enough.

In the fall she went to New York to begin the upward grind—understudy, walk-on parts, shoestring-theaters, and roles in outright turkeys. Fraser returned to Boston for awhile, but his work suffered—he had to keep dashing off to see her.

By spring she was beginning to get places; she had talent and everybody enjoys looking at a brown-eyed blonde. His weekly proposals were also beginning to show some real progress, and he thought that a month or two of steady siege might finish the campaign. So he took leave from his job and went down to New York himself. He'd saved up enough money, and was good enough in his work, to afford it; anyway, he was his own boss—consulting engineer, specializing in mathematical analysis.

He got a furnished room in Brooklyn, and filled in his leisure time—as he thought of it—with some special math courses at Columbia. And he had a lot of friends in town, in a curious variety of professions. Next to Judy, he saw most of the physicist Sworsky, who was an entertaining companion though most of his work was too top-secret even to be mentioned. It was a happy period.

There is always a jarring note, to be sure. In this case, it was the fact that Fraser had plenty of competition. He wasn't good-looking himself—a tall gaunt man of twenty-eight, with a dark hatchet face and perpetually-rumpled clothes. But still, Judy saw more of him than of anyone else, and admitted she was seriously considering his proposal and no other.

He called her up once for a date. "Sorry," she answered. "I'd love to, Colin, but I've already promised tonight. Just so you won't worry, it's Matthew Snyder."

"Hm—the industrialist?"

"Uh-huh. He asked me in such a way it was hard to refuse. But I don't think you have to be jealous, honey. 'Bye now."

Fraser lit his pipe with a certain smugness. Snyder was several times a millionaire, but he was close to sixty, a widower of notably dull conversation. Judy wasn't—Well, no worries, as she'd said. He dropped over to Sworsky's apartment for an evening of chess and bull-shooting.

I T WAS early in May, when the world was turning green again, that Judy called Fraser up. "Hi," she said breathlessly. "Busy tonight?"

"Well, I was hoping I'd be, if you get what I mean," he said.

SENTIMENT, INC.

"Look, I want to take you out for a change. Just got some unexpected money and dammit, I want to feel rich for one evening."

"Hmm—" He scowled into the phone. "I dunno—"

"Oh, get off it, Galahad. I'll meet you in the Dixie lobby at seven. Okay?" She blew him a kiss over the wires, and hung up before he could argue further. He sighed and shrugged. Why not, if she wanted to?

They were in a little Hungarian restaurant, with a couple of Tzigani strolling about playing for them alone, it seemed, when he asked for details. "Did you get a bonus, or what?"

"No." She laughed at him over her drink. "I've turned guinea pig."

"I hope you quit *that* job well before we're married!"

"It's a funny deal," she said thoughtfully. "It'd interest you. I've been out a couple of times with this Snyder, you know, and if anything was needed to drive me into your arms, Colin, it's his political lectures."

"Well, bless the Republican Party!" He laid his hand over hers; she didn't withdraw it, but she frowned just a little.

"Colin, you know I want to get somewhere before I marry—see a bit of the world, the theatrical world, before turning hausfrau. Don't be so—Oh, never mind. I like you anyway."

Sipping her drink and setting it down again: "Well, to carry on with the story. I finally gave Comrade Snyder the complete brush-off, and I must say he took it very nicely. But today, this morning, he called asking me to have lunch with him, and I did after he explained. It seems he's got a psychiatrist

friend doing research, measuring brain storms or
something, and—Do I mean storms? Waves, I guess.
Anyway, he wants to measure as many different kinds
of people as possible, and Snyder had suggested me. I
was supposed to come in for three afternoons running
—about two hours each time—and I'd get a hundred
dollars per session."

"Hm," said Fraser. "I didn't know psych
research was that well-heeled. Who is this mad
scientist?"

"His name is Kennedy. Oh, by the way, I'm not
supposed to tell anybody; they want to spring it on
the world as a surprise or something. But you're different, Colin. I'm excited; I want to talk to somebody
about it."

"Sure," he said. "You had a session already?"

"Yes, my first was today. It's a funny place to
do research—Kennedy's got a big suite on Fifth
Avenue, right up in the classy district. Beautiful office.
The name of his outfit is Sentiment, Inc."

"Hm. Why should a research-team take such a
name? Well, go on."

"Oh, there isn't much else to tell. Kennedy was
very nice. He took me into a laboratory full of all sorts
of dials and meters and blinking lights and os—what
do you call them? Those things that make wiggly
pictures."

"Oscilloscopes. You'll never make a scientist,
my dear."

She grinned. "But I know one scientist who'd
like to—Never mind! Anyway, he sat me down in a
chair and put bands around my wrists and ankles—
just like the hot squat—and a big thing like a beauty-
parlor hair-drier over my head. Then he fiddled with

his dials for awhile, making notes. Then he started saying words at me, and showing me pictures. Some of them were very pretty; some ugly; some funny; some downright horrible... Anyway, that's all there was to it. After a couple of hours he gave me a check for a hundred dollars and told me to come back tomorrow."

"Hm." Fraser rubbed his chin. "Apparently he was measuring the electric rhythms corresponding to pleasure and dislike. I'd no idea anybody'd made an encephalograph that accurate."

"Well," said Judy, "I've told you why we're celebrating. Now come on, the regular orchestra's tuning up. Let's dance."

They had a rather wonderful evening. Afterward Fraser lay awake for a long time, not wanting to lose a state of happiness in sleep. He considered sleep a hideous waste of time: if he lived to be ninety, he'd have spent almost thirty years unconscious.

J UDY WAS engaged for the next couple of evenings, and Fraser himself was invited to dinner at Sworsky's the night after that. So it wasn't till the end of the week that he called her again.

"Hullo, sweetheart," he said exuberantly. "How's things? I refer to Charles Addams Things, of course."

"Oh—Colin." Her voice was very small, and it trembled.

"Look, I've got two tickets to see *H. M. S. Pinafore*. So put on your own pinafore and meet me."

"Colin—I'm sorry, Colin. I can't."

"Huh?" He noticed how odd she sounded, and a leadenness grew within him. "You aren't sick, are you?"

"Colin, I—I'm going to be married."

"*What?*"

"Yes. I'm in love now; really in love. I'll be getting married in a couple of months."

"But—but—"

"I didn't want to hurt you." He heard her begin to cry.

"But who—how—"

"It's Matthew," she gulped. "Matthew Snyder."

He sat quiet for a long while, until she asked if he was still on the line. "Yeah," he said tonelessly. "Yeah, I'm still here, after a fashion." Shaking himself: "Look, I've got to see you. I want to talk to you."

"I can't."

"You sure as hell can," he said harshly.

They met at a quiet little bar which had often been their rendezvous. She watched him with frightened eyes while he ordered martinis.

"All right," he said at last. "What's the story?"

"I—" He could barely hear her. "There isn't any story. I suddenly realized I loved Matt. That's all."

"*Snyder!*" He made it a curse. "Remember what you told me about him before?"

"I felt different then," she whispered. "He's a wonderful man when you get to know him."

And rich. He suppressed the words and the thought. "What's so wonderful specifically?" he asked.

"He—" Briefly, her face was rapt. Fraser had seen her looking at him that way, now and then.

"Go on," he said grimly. "Enumerate Mr. Snyder's good qualities. Make a list. He's courteous, cultured, intelligent, young, handsome, amusing—To hell! *Why*, Judy?"

"I don't know," she said in a high, almost fearful tone. "I just love him, that's all." She reached over the table and stroked his cheek. "I like you a lot, Colin. Find yourself a nice girl and be happy."

His mouth drew into a narrow line. "There's something funny here," he said. "Is it blackmail?"

"No!" She stood up, spilling her drink, and the flare of temper showed him how overwrought she was. "He just happens to be the man I love. That's enough out of you, good-bye, Mr. Fraser."

He sat watching her go. Presently he took up his drink, gulped it barbarously, and called for another.

II

JUAN MARTINEZ had come from Puerto Rico as a boy and made his own way ever since. Fraser had gotten to know him in the army, and they had seen each other from time to time since then. Martinez had gone into the private-eye business and made a good thing of it; Fraser had to get past a very neat-looking receptionist to see him.

"Hi, Colin," said Martinez, shaking hands. He was a small, dark man, with a large nose and beady black eyes that made him resemble a sympathetic mouse. "You look like the very devil."

"I feel that way, too," said Fraser, collapsing into a chair. "You can't go on a three-day drunk without showing it."

"Well, what seems to be the trouble? Cigarette?" Martinez held out a pack. "Girlfriend give you the air?"

"As a matter of fact, yes; that's what I want to see you about."

"This isn't a lonely-hearts club," said Martinez. "And I've told you time and again a private dick isn't a wisecracking superman. Our work is ninety-nine percent routine; and for the other one percent, we call in the police."

"Let me give you the story," said Fraser. He rubbed his eyes wearily as he told it. At the end, he sat staring at the floor.

"Well," said Martinez, "it's too bad and all that. But what the hell, there are other dames. New York has more beautiful women per square inch than any other city except Paris. Latch on to somebody else. If you want, I can give you a phone number—"

"You don't understand," said Fraser "I want you to investigate this; I want to know why she did it."

Martinez squinted through a haze of smoke. "Snyder's a rich and powerful man," he said. "Isn't that enough?"

"No," said Fraser, too tired to be angry at the hint. "Judy isn't that kind of a girl. Neither is she the kind to go overboard in a few days, especially when I was there. Sure, that sounds conceited, but dammit, I *know* she cared for me."

"Okay. You suspect pressure was brought to bear?"

"Yeah. It's hard to imagine what. I called up Judy's family in Maine, and they said they were all right, no worries. Nor do I think anything in her own life would give a blackmailer or an extortionist any-thing to go on. Still—I want to know."

Martinez drummed the desk-top with nervous fingers. "I'll look into it if you insist," he said, "though it'll cost you a pretty penny. Rich men's lives aren't easy to pry into if they've got something they want to hide. But I don't think we'd find out much; your case seems to be only one of a rash of similar ones in the past year."

"Huh?" Fraser looked sharply up.

"Yeah. I follow all the news; and remember the odd facts. There've been a good dozen cases recently, where beautiful young women suddenly married rich men or became their mistresses. It doesn't all get into the papers, but I've got my contacts. I know. In every instance, there was no obvious reason; in fact, the dames seemed very much in love with daddy."

"And the era of the gold-digger is pretty well gone—" Fraser sat staring out the window. It didn't seem right that the sky should be so full of sunshine.

"Well," said Martinez, "you don't need me. You need a psychologist."

Psychologist!

"By God, Juan, I'm going to give you a job anyway!" Fraser leaped to his feet. "You're going to check into an outfit called Sentiment, Inc."

A WEEK later, Martinez said, "Yeah, we found it easily enough. It's not in the phone-book, but they've got a big suite right in the high-rent district on Fifth. The ad-dress is here, in my written report. Nobody else in the building knows much about 'em, except that they're a quiet, well-behaved bunch and call themselves re-search psychologists. They have a staff of four: a secretary-receptionist; a full-time secretary; and a couple of husky boys who may be bodyguards for the boss. That's this Kennedy, Robert Kennedy. My man couldn't get into his office; the girl said he was too busy and never saw anybody except some regular clients. Nor could he date either of the girls, but he did investigate them.

"The receptionist is just a working girl for routine stuff, married, hardly knows or cares what's going on. The steno is unmarried, has a degree in psych, lives alone, and seems to have no friends except her boss. Who's not her lover, by the way."

"Well, how about Kennedy himself?" asked Fraser.

"I've found out a good bit, but it's all legitimate," said Martinez. "He's about fifty years old, a widower, very steady private life. He's a licensed psychiatrist who used to practice in Chicago, where he also did research in collaboration with a physicist named Gavotti, who's since then died. Shortly after that happened—

"No, there isn't any suspicion of foul play; the physicist was an old man and died of a heart attack. Anyway, Kennedy moved to New York. He still practices, officially, but he doesn't take just anybody; claims that his research only leaves him time for a few." Martinez narrowed his eyes. "The only thing you could hold against him is that he occasionally sees a guy named Bryce, who's in a firm that has some dealings with Amtorg."

"The Russian trading corporation? Hm."

"Oh, that's pretty remote guilt by association, Colin. Amtorg does have legitimate business, you know. We buy manganese from them, among other things. And the rest of Kennedy's connections are all strictly blue ribbon. *Crème de la crème*—business, finance, politics, and one big union-leader who's known to be a conservative. In fact, Kennedy's friends are so powerful you'd have real trouble doing anything against him."

Fraser slumped in his chair. "I suppose my notion was pretty wild," he admitted.

"Well, there is one queer angle. You know these rich guys who've suddenly made out with such highly desirable dames? As far as I could find out, every one of them is a client of Kennedy's."

"Eh?" Fraser jerked erect.

"'S a fact. Also, my man showed the building staff, elevator pilots and so on, pictures of these women, and a couple of 'em were remembered as having come to see Kennedy."

"Shortly before they—fell in love?"

"Well, that I can't be sure of. You know how people are with remembering dates. But it's possible."

Fraser shook his dark head. "It's unbelievable," he said. "I thought Svengali was outworn melodrama."

"I know something about hypnotism, Colin. It won't do anything like what you think happened to those girls."

Fraser got out his pipe and fumbled tobacco into it. "I think," he said, "I'm going to call on Dr. Robert Kennedy myself."

"Take it easy, boy," said Martinez. "You been reading too many weird stories; you'll just get tossed out on your can."

Fraser tried to smile. It was hard—Judy wouldn't answer his calls and letters any more. "Well," he said, "it'll be in a worthy cause."

T HE ELEVATOR let him out on the nineteenth floor. It held four big suites, with the corridor running between them. He studied the frosted-glass doors. On one side was the Eagle Publishing Company and Frank & Dayles, Brokers. On the other was the Messenger Advertising Service, and Sentiment, Inc. He entered their door and stood in a quiet, oak-paneled reception room. Behind the railing were a couple of desks, a young woman working at each, and two burly men who sat boredly reading magazines.

The pretty girl, obviously the receptionist, looked up as Fraser approached and gave him a professional smile. "Yes, sir?" she asked.

"I'd like to see Dr. Kennedy, please," he said, trying hard to be casual.

"Do you have an appointment, sir?"

"No, but it's urgent."

"I'm sorry, sir; Dr. Kennedy is very busy. He can't see anybody except his regular patients and research subjects."

"Look, just take this note in to him, will you? Thanks."

Fraser sat uneasily for some minutes, wondering if he'd worded the note correctly. *I must see you about Miss Judy Harkness. Important.* Well, what the devil else could you say?

The receptionist came out again. "Dr. Kennedy can spare you a few minutes, sir," she said. "Go right on in."

"Thanks." Fraser slouched toward the inner door. The two men lowered their magazines to follow him with watchful eyes.

There was a big, handsomely-furnished office inside, with a door beyond that must lead to the laboratory. Kennedy looked up from some papers and rose, holding out his hand. He was a medium-sized man, rather plump, graying hair brushed thickly back from a broad, heavy face behind rimless glasses. "Yes?" His voice was low and pleasant. "What can I do for you?"

"My name's Fraser." The visitor sat down and accepted a cigarette. Best to act urbanely. "I know Miss Harkness well. I understand you made some encephalographic studies of her."

"Indeed?" Kennedy looked annoyed, and Fraser recalled that Judy had been asked not to tell anyone. "I'm not sure; I would have to consult my records first." He wasn't admitting anything, thought Fraser.

"Look," said the engineer, "there's been a marked change in Miss Harkness recently. I know enough psychology to be certain that such changes don't happen overnight without cause. I wanted to consult you."

"I'm not her psychiatrist," said Kennedy coldly. "Now if you will excuse me, I have a lot to do—"

"All right," said Fraser. There was no menace in his voice tone, only a weariness. "If you insist, I'll play it dirty. Such abrupt changes indicate mental instability. But I know she was perfectly sane before. It begins to look as if your experiments may have—injured her mind. If that is the case, I should have to report you for malpractice."

Kennedy flushed. "I am a licensed psychiatrist," he said, "and any other doctor will confirm that Miss Harkness is still in mental health. If you tried to get an investigation started, you would only be wasting your own time and that of the authorities. She herself will testify that no harm was done to her; no compulsion applied; and that you are an infernal busybody with some delusions of your own. Good afternoon."

"Ah," said Fraser, "so she *was* here."

Kennedy pushed a button. His men entered. "Show this gentleman the way out, please," he said.

Fraser debated whether to put up a fight, decided it was futile, and went out between the two others. When he got to the street, he found he was shaking, and badly in need of a drink.

FRASER asked, "Jim, did you ever read *Trilby?*"

Sworsky's round, freckled face lifted to regard him. "Years ago," he answered. "What of it?"

"Tell me something. Is it possible—even theoretically possible—to do what Svengali did? Change emotional attitudes, just like that." Fraser snapped his fingers.

"I don't know," said Sworsky. "Nuclear cross-sections are more in my line. But offhand, I should imagine it might be done... sometime in the far future. Thought-habits, associational-patterns, the labeling of this as good and that as bad, seem to be matters of established neural paths. If you could selectively alter the polarization of individual neurons—But it's a pretty remote prospect; we hardly know a thing about the brain today."

He studied his friend sympathetically. "I know it's tough to get jilted," he said, "but don't go off your trolley about it."

"I could stand it if someone else had gotten her in the usual kind of way," said Fraser thinly. "But this—Look, let me tell you all I've found out."

Sworsky shook his head at the end of the story. "That's a mighty wild speculation," he murmured. "I'd forget it if I were you."

"Did you know Kennedy's old partner? Gavotti, at Chicago."

"Sure, I met him a few times. Nice old guy, very unworldly, completely wrapped up in his work. He got interested in neurology from the physics angle toward the end of his life, and contributed a lot to cybernetics. What of it?"

"I don't know," said Fraser; "I just don't know. But do me a favor, will you, Jim? Judy won't see me at all, but she knows you and likes you. Ask her to dinner or something. Insist that she come. Then you and your wife find out—whatever you can. Just exactly how she feels about the whole business. What her attitudes are toward everything."

"The name is Sworsky, not Holmes. But sure, I'll do what I can, if you'll promise to try and get rid of this fixation. You ought to see a head-shrinker your-self, you know."

In vino veritas—sometimes too damn much *veritas*.

T OWARD the end of the evening, Judy was talking freely, if not quite coherently. "I cared a lot for Colin," she said. "It was pretty wonderful having him around. He's a grand guy. Only Matt—I don't know. Matt hasn't got half of what Colin has; Matt's a single-track mind. I'm afraid I'm just going to be an ornamental convenience to him. Only if you've ever been so you got all dizzy when someone was around, and thought about him all the time he was away—well, that's how he is. Nothing else matters."

"Colin's gotten a funny obsession," said Sworsky cautiously. "He thinks Kennedy hypnotized you for Snyder. I keep telling him it's impossible, but he can't get over the idea."

"Oh, no, no, no," she said with too much fervor. "It's nothing like that. I'll tell you just what happened. We had those two measuring sessions; it was kind of dull but nothing else. And then the third time Kennedy did put me under hypnosis—he called it that, at least. I went to sleep and woke up about an hour later and he sent me home. I felt all good inside, happy, and shlo—slowly I began to see what Matt meant to me.

"I called him up that same evening. He said Kennedy's machine *did* speed up people's minds for a short while, sometimes, so they decided quick-like what they'd've worked out anyway. Kennedy is—I don't know. It's funny how ordinary he seemed at first. But when you get to know him, he's like—God, almost. He's strong and wise and good. He—" Her voice trailed off and she sat looking foolishly at her glass.

"You know," said Sworsky, "perhaps Colin is right after all."

"Don't say that!" She jumped up and slapped his face. "Kennedy's *good*, I tell you! All you little lice sitting here making sly remarks behind his back, and he's so, much bigger than all of you and—" She broke into tears and stormed out of the apartment.

Sworsky reported the affair to Fraser. "I wonder," he said. "It doesn't seem natural, I'll agree. But what can anybody do? The police?"

"I've tried," said Fraser dully. "They laughed. When I insisted, I damn near got myself jugged. That's no use. The trouble is, none of the people who've been under the machine will testify against Kennedy. He fixes it so they worship him."

"I still think you're crazy. There *must* be a simpler hypothesis; I refuse to believe your screwy notions without some real evidence. But what are you going to do now?"

"Well," said Fraser with a tautness in his voice, "I've got several thousand dollars saved up, and Juan Martinez will help. Ever hear the fable about the lion? He licked hell out of the bear and the tiger and the rhinoceros, but a little gnat finally drove him nuts. Maybe I can be the gnat." He shook his head. "But I'll have to hurry. The wedding's only six weeks off."

III

I T CAN be annoying to be constantly shadowed; to have nasty gossip about you spreading through the places where you work and live; to find your tires slashed; to be accosted by truculent drunks when you stop in for a quick one; to have loud horns blow under your window every night. And it doesn't do much good to call the police; your petty tormentors always fade out of sight.

Fraser was sitting in his room some two weeks later, trying unsuccessfully to concentrate on matrix algebra, when the phone rang. He never picked it up without a fluttering small hope that it might be Judy, and it never was. This time it was a man's voice: "Mr. Fraser?"

"Yeah," he grunted. "Wha'dya want?"

"This is Robert Kennedy. I'd like to talk to you."

Fraser's heart sprang in his ribs, but he held his voice stiff. "Go on, then. Talk."

"I want you to come up to my place. We may be having a long conversation."

"Mmm—well—" It was more than he had allowed himself to hope for, but he remained curt: "Okay. But a full report of this business, and what I think you're doing, is in the hands of several people. If anything should happen to me—"

"You've been reading too many hard-boileds," said Kennedy. "Nothing will happen. Anyway, I have a pretty good idea who those people are; I can hire detectives of my own, you know."

"I'll come over, then." Fraser hung up and realized, suddenly, that he was sweating.

The night air was cool as he walked down the street. He paused for a moment, feeling the city like a huge impersonal machine around him, grinding and grinding. Human civilization had grown too big, he thought. It was beyond anyone's control; it had taken on a will of its own and was carrying a race which could no longer guide it. Sometimes—reading the papers, or listening to the radio, or just watching the traffic go by like a river of steel—a man could feel horribly helpless.

He took the subway to Kennedy's address, a swank apartment in the lower Fifties. He was admitted by the psychiatrist in person; no one else was around.

"I assume," said Kennedy, "that you don't have some wild idea of pulling a gun on me. That would accomplish nothing except to get you in trouble."

"No," said Fraser, "I'll be good." His eyes wandered about the living room. One wall was covered with books which looked used; there were some quality reproductions, a Capehart, and fine, massive furniture. It was a tasteful layout. He looked a little more closely at three pictures on the mantel: a middle-aged woman and two young men in uniform.

"My wife," said Kennedy, "and my boys. They're all dead. Would you like a drink?"

"No. I came to talk."

"I'm not Satan, you know," said Kennedy. "I like books and music, good wine, good conversation. I'm as human as you are, only I have a purpose."

Fraser sat down and began charging his pipe. "Go ahead," he said. "I'm listening."

Kennedy pulled a chair over to face him. The big smooth countenance behind the rimless glasses held little expression. "Why have you been annoying me?" he asked.

"I?" Fraser lifted his brows.

Kennedy made an impatient gesture. "Let's not chop words. There are no witnesses tonight. I intend to talk freely, and want you to do the same. I know that you've got Martinez sufficiently convinced to help you with this childish persecution-campaign. What do you hope to get out of it?"

"I want my girl back," said Fraser tonelessly. "I was hoping my nuisance-value—"

KENNEDY winced a bit. "You know, I'm damned sorry about that. It's the one aspect of my work which I hate. I'd like you to believe that I'm not just a scientific procurer. Actually, I have to satisfy the minor desires of my clients, so they'll stay happy and agree to my major wishes. It's the plain truth that those women have been only the minutest fraction of my job."

"Nevertheless, you're a free-wheeling son, doing something like that—"

"Really, now, what's so horrible about it? Those girls are in love—the normal, genuine article. It's not any kind of zombie state, or whatever your overheated imagination has thought up. They're entirely sane, unharmed, and happy. In fact, happiness of that kind is so rare in this world that if I wanted to, I could pose as their benefactor."

"You've got a machine," said Fraser; "it changes the mind. As far as I'm concerned, that's as gross a violation of liberty as throwing somebody into a concentration camp."

"How free do you think anyone is? You're born with a fixed heredity. Environment molds you like clay. Your society teaches you what and how to think. A million tiny factors, all depending on blind, uncontrollable chance, determine the course of your life—including your love-life... Well, we needn't waste any time on philosophy. Go on, ask some questions. I admit I've hurt you—unwittingly, to be sure—but I do want to make amends."

"Your machine, then," said Fraser. "How did you get it? How does it work."

"I was practicing in Chicago," said Kennedy, "and collaborating on the side with Gavotti. How much do you know of cybernetics? I don't mean computers and automata, which are only one aspect of the field; I mean control and communication, in the animal as well as in the machine."

"Well, I've read Wiener's books, and studied Shannon's work, too." Despite himself, Fraser was thawing, just a trifle. "It's exciting stuff. Communications theory seems to be basic, in biology and psychology as well as in electronics."

"Quite. The future may remember Wiener as the Galileo of neurology. If Gavotti's work ever gets published, he'll be considered the Newton. So far, frankly, I've suppressed it. He died suddenly, just when his machine was completed and he was getting ready to publish his results. Nobody but I knew anything more than rumors; he was inclined to be secretive till he had a *fait accompli* on hand. I realized what an opportunity had been given me, and took it; I brought the machine here without saying much to anyone."

Kennedy leaned back in his chair. "I imagine it was mostly luck which took Gavotti and me so far," he went on. "We made a long series of improbably good guesses, and thus telescoped a century of work into a decade. If I were religious, I'd be down on my knees, thanking the Lord for putting this thing of the future into my hands."

"Or the devil," said Fraser.

Briefly, anger flitted across Kennedy's face. "I grant you, the machine is a terrible power, but it's harmless to a man if it's used properly—as I have used it. I'm not going to tell you just how it works; to be perfectly honest, I only understand a fraction of its theory and its circuits myself. But look, you know something of encephalography. The various basic rhythms of the brain have been measured. The standard method is already so sensitive that it can detect abnormalities like a developing tumor or a strong emotional disturbance, that will give trouble unless corrected. Half of Gavotti's machine is a still more delicate encephalograph. It can measure and analyze the minute variations in electrical pulses corresponding to the basic emotional states. It won't read thoughts, no; but once calibrated for a given individual, it will tell you if he's happy, sorrowful, angry, disgusted, afraid— any fundamental neuro-glandular condition, or any combination of them."

He paused. "All right," said Fraser. "What else does it do?"

"It does *not* make monsters," said Kennedy. "Look, the specific emotional reaction to a given stimulus is, in the normal individual, largely a matter of conditioned reflex, instilled by social environment or the accidental associations of his life.

"Anyone in decent health will experience fear in the presence of danger; desire in the presence of a sexual object, and so on. That's basic biology, and the machine can't change that. But most of our evaluations are learned. For instance, to an American the word 'mother' has powerful emotional connotations, while to a Samoan it means nothing very exciting. You had to develop a taste for liquor, tobacco, coffee—in fact most of what you consume. If you're in love with a particular woman, it's a focusing of the general sexual libido on her, brought about by the symbolizing part of your mind: she *means* something to you. There are cultures without romantic love, you know. And so on. All these specific, conditioned reactions can be changed."

"How?"

KENNEDY thought for a moment "The encephalographic part of the machine measures the exact pulsations in the individual corresponding to the various emotional reactions. It takes me about four hours to determine those with the necessary precision; then I have to make statistical analyses of the data, to winnow out random variations. Thereafter I put the subject in a state of light hypnosis—that's only to increase suggestibility, and make the process faster. As I pronounce the words and names I'm interested in, the machine feeds back the impulses corresponding to the emotions I want: a sharply-focused beam on the brain center concerned.

"For instance, suppose you were an alcoholic and I wanted to cure you. I'd put you in hypnosis and stand there whispering 'wine, whisky, beer, gin,' and so on; meanwhile, the machine would be feeding the impulses corresponding to your reactions of hate, fear, and disgust into your brain. You'd come out unchanged, except that your appetite for alcohol would be gone; you could, in fact, come out hating the stuff so much that you'd join the Prohibition Party—though, in actual practice, it would probably be enough just to give you a mild aversion."

"Mmm—I see. Maybe." Fraser scowled. "And the—subject—doesn't remember what you've done?"

"Oh, no. It all takes place on the lower subconscious levels. A new set of conditioned neural pathways is opened, you see, and old ones are closed off. The brain does that by itself, through its normal symbolizing mechanism. All that happens is that the given symbol—such as liquor—becomes reflectively associated with the given emotional state, such as dislike."

Kennedy leaned forward with an air of urgency. "The end result is in no way different from ordinary means of persuasion. Propaganda does the same thing by sheer repetition. If you're courting a girl, you try to identify yourself in her mind with the things she desires, by appropriate behavior... I'm sorry; I shouldn't have used that example... The machine is only a direct, fast way of doing this, producing a more stable result."

"It's still—tampering," said Fraser. "How do you know you're not creating side-effects, doing irreparable long-range damage?"

"Oh, for Lord's sake!" exploded Kennedy. "Take your mind off that shelf, will you? I've told you how delicate the whole thing is. A few microwatts of power more or less, a frequency-shift of less than one percent, and it doesn't work at all. There's no effect whatsoever." He cooled off fast, adding reflectively: "On the given subject, that is. It might work on some-one else. These pulsations are a highly individual mat-ter; I have to calibrate every case separately."

There was a long period of silence. Then Fraser strained forward and said in an ugly voice:

"All right You've told me how you do it. Now tell me *why*. What possible reason or excuse, other than your own desire to play God? This thing could be the greatest psychiatric tool in history, and you're using it to—pimp!"

"I told you that was not important," said Kennedy quietly. "I'm doing much more. I set up in practice here in New York a couple of years ago. Once I had a few chance people under control—no, I tell you again, I didn't make robots of them. I merely asso-ciated myself, in their own minds, with the father-image. That's something I do to everyone who comes under the machine, just as a precaution if nothing else, Kennedy is all-wise, all-powerful; Kennedy can do no wrong. It isn't a conscious realization; to the waking mind, I am only a shrewd adviser and a damn swell fellow. But the subconscious mind knows other-wise. It wouldn't *let* my subjects act against me; it wouldn't even let them want to.

"Well, you see how it goes. I got those first few people to recommend me to certain selected friends, and these in turn recommended me to others. Not necessarily as a psychiatrist; I have variously been a doctor, a counsellor, or merely a research-man looking for data. But I'm building up a group of the people I want. People who'll back me up, who'll follow my advice—not with any knowledge of being dominated, but because the workings of their own subconscious minds will lead them inevitably to think that my advice is the only sound policy to follow and my requests are things any decent man must grant."

"Yeah," said Fraser. "I get it. Big businessmen. Labor-leaders. Politicians. Military men. And Soviet spies!"

KENNEDY nodded. "I have connections with the Soviets; their agents think I'm on their side. But it isn't treason, though I may help them out from time to time.

"That's why I have to do these services for my important clients, such as getting them the women they want—or, what I actually do more often, influencing their competitors and associates. You see, the subconscious mind knows I am all-powerful, but the conscious mind doesn't. It has to be satisfied by occasional proofs that I *am* invaluable; otherwise conflicts would set in, my men would become unstable and eventually psychotic, and be of no further use to me.

"Of course," he added, almost pedantically, "my men don't know how I persuade these other people—they only know that I do, somehow, and their regard for their own egos, as well as for me, sets up a bloc which prevents them from reasoning out the fact that they themselves are dominated. They're quite content to accept the results of my help, without inquiring further into the means than the easy rationalization that I have a 'persuasive personality.'

"I don't like what I'm doing, Fraser. But it's got to be done."

"You still haven't said *what's* got to be done," answered the engineer coldly.

"I've been given something unbelievable," said Kennedy. His voice was very soft now. "If I'd made it public, can you imagine what would have happened? Psychiatrists would use it, yes; but so would criminals, dictators, power-hungry men of all kinds. Even in this country, I don't think libertarian principles could long survive. It would be too simple—

"And yet it would have been cowardly to break the machine and burn Gavotti's notes. Chance has given me the power to be more than a chip in the river —a river that's rapidly approaching a waterfall, war, destruction, tyranny, no matter who the Pyrrhic victor may be. I'm in a position to do something for the causes in which I believe."

"And what are they?" asked Fraser.

Kennedy gestured at the pictures on the mantel. "Both my sons were killed in the last war. My wife died of cancer—a disease which would be licked now if a fraction of the money spent on armaments had been diverted to research. That brought it home to me; but there are hundreds of millions of people in worse cases. And war isn't the only evil—there is poverty, oppression, inequality, want and suffering. It could be changed.

"I'm building up my own lobby, you might say. In a few more years, I hope to be the indispensable adviser of all the men who, between them, really run this country. And yes, I have been in touch with

Soviet agents—have even acted as a transmitter of stolen information. The basic problem of spying, you know, is not to get the information in the first place as much as to get it to the homeland. Treason? No. I think not. I'm getting my toehold in world communism. I already have some of its agents; sooner or later, I'll get to the men who really matter. Then communism will no longer be a menace."

He sighed. "It's a hard row to hoe. It'll take my lifetime, at least; but what else have I got to give my life to?"

Fraser sat quiet. His pipe was cold, he knocked it out and began filling it afresh. The scratching of his match seemed unnaturally loud. "It's too much," he said. "It's too big a job for one man to tackle. The world will stumble along somehow, but you'll just get things into a worse mess."

"I've got to try," said Kennedy.

"And I still want my girl back."

"I can't do that; I need Snyder too much. But I'll make it up to you somehow." Kennedy sighed. "Lord, if you knew how much I've wanted to tell all this!"

With sudden wariness: "Not that it's to be repeated. In fact, you're to lay off me; call off your dogs. Don't try to tell anyone else what I've told you. You'd never be believed and I already have enough power to suppress the story, if you should get it out somehow. And if you give me any more trouble at all, I'll see to it that you—stop."

"Murder?"

"Or commitment to an asylum. I can arrange that too."

Fraser sighed. He felt oddly unexcited, empty, as if the interview had drained him of his last will to resist. He held the pipe loosely in his fingers, letting it go out.

"Ask me a favor," urged Kennedy. "I'll do it, if it won't harm my own program. I tell you, I want to square things."

"Well—"

"Think about it. Let me know."

"All right." Fraser got up. "I may do that." He went out the door without saying goodnight.

IV

H E SAT with his feet on the table, chair tilted back and teetering dangerously, hands clasped behind his head, pipe filling the room with blue fog. It was his usual posture for attacking a problem.

And damn it, he thought wearily, this was a question such as he made his living on. An industrial engineer comes into the office. We want this and that —a machine for a very special purpose, let's say. What should we do, Mr. Fraser? Fraser prowls around the plant, reads up on the industry, and then sits down and thinks. The elements of the problem are such-and-such; how can they be combined to yield a solution?

Normally, he uses the mathematical approach, especially in machine design. Most practicing engineers have a pathetic math background—they use ten pages of elaborate algebra and rusty calculus to figure out something that three vector equations would solve. But you have to get the logical basics straight first, before you can set up your equations.

All right, what is the problem? To get Judy back. That means forcing Kennedy to restore her normal emotional reactions—no, he didn't want her thrust into love of him; he just wanted her as she had been.

What are the elements of the problem? Kennedy acts outside the law, but he has blocked all official channels. He even has connections extending through the Iron Curtain.

Hmm—he could appeal to the FBI? Kennedy couldn't have control over them—*yet*. However, if Fraser tried to tip off the FBI, they'd act cautiously, if they investigated at all. They'd have to go slow. And Kennedy would find out in time to do something about it.

Martinez could help no further. Sworsky had closer contact with Washington. He'd been so thoroughly cleared that they'd be inclined to trust whatever he said. But Sworsky doubted the whole story; like many men who'd suffered through irresponsible Congressional charges, he was almost fanatic about having proof before accusing anyone of anything. Moreover, Kennedy knew that Sworsky was Fraser's friend; he'd probably be keeping close tabs on the physicist and ready to block any attempts he might make to help. With the backing of a man like Snyder, Kennedy could hire as many detectives as he wanted.

In fact, whatever the counter-attack, it was necessary to go warily.

Kennedy's threat to get rid of Fraser if the engineer kept working against him was not idle mouthing. He could do it—and, being a fanatic, would.

But Kennedy, like the demon of legend, would grant one wish—just to salve his own conscience. Only what should the wish be? Another woman? Or merely to be reconciled, artificially, to an otherwise-intolerable situation?

Judy, Judy, Judy!

Fraser swore at himself. Damn it to hell, this was a problem in logic. No room for emotion. Of course, it might be a problem without a solution. There are plenty of those.

He squinted, trying to visualize the office. He thought of burglary, stealing evidence—silly thought. But let's see, now. What was the layout, exactly? Four suites on one floor of the skyscraper, three of them unimportant offices of unimportant men. And—

Oh, Lord!

Fraser sat for a long while, hardly moving. Then he uncoiled himself and ran, downstairs and into the street and to the nearest pay phone. His own line might be tapped—

"Hello, hello, Juan?... Yes, I know I got you out of bed, and I'm not sorry. This is too bloody important... Okay, okay... Look, I want a complete report on the Messenger Advertising Service... When? Immediately, if not sooner. And I mean *complete*... That's right, Messenger... Okay, fine. I'll buy you a drink sometime."

"Hello, Jim? Were you asleep too?... Sorry... But look, would you make a list of all the important men you know fairly well? I need it bad... No, don't come over. I think I'd better not see you for a while. Just mail it to me... All right, so I am paranoid..."

J EROME K. FERRIS was a large man, with a
sense of his own importance that was even larger. He sat hunched in the chair, his head
dwarfed by the aluminum helmet, his breathing
shallow. Around him danced and flickered a
hundred meters, indicator lights, tubes. There was a
low humming in the room, otherwise it was altogether silent, blocked and shielded against the outside
world. The fluorescent lights were a muted glow.

Fraser sat watching the greenish trace on the
huge oscilloscope screen. It was an intricate set of
convolutions, looking more like a plate of spaghetti
than anything else. He wondered how many fre-
quencies were involved. Several thousand, at the very
least.

"Fraser," repeated Kennedy softly into the ear
of the hypnotized man. "Colin Fraser. Colin Fraser."
He touched a dial with infinite care. "Colin Fraser.
Colin Fraser."

The oscilloscope flickered as he readjusted, a
new trace appeared. Kennedy waited for a while, then:
"Robert Kennedy. Sentiment, Inc. Robert Kennedy.
Sentiment, Inc. Robert Kennedy. Sentiment—"

He turned off the machine, its murmur and
glow died away. Facing Fraser with a tight little smile,
he said: "All right. Your job is done. Are we even
now?"

"As even, as we'll ever get, I suppose," replied
Fraser.

"I wish you'd trust me," said Kennedy with a
hint of wistfulness. "I'd have done the job honestly;
you didn't have to watch."

"Well, I was interested," said Fraser.

"Frankly, I still don't see what you stand to gain by the doglike devotion of this Ferris. He's rich, but he's too weak and short-sighted to be a leader. I'd never planned on conditioning him for my purposes."

"I've explained that," said Fraser patiently. "Ferris is a large stockholder in a number of corporations. His influence can swing a lot of business my way."

"Yes, I know. I didn't grant your wish blindly, you realize. I had Ferris studied; he's unable to harm me." Kennedy regarded Fraser with hard eyes. "And just in case you still have foolish notions, please remember that I gave him the father-conditioning with respect to myself. He'll do a lot for you, but not if it's going to hurt me in any way."

"I know when I'm licked," said Fraser bleakly; "I'm getting out of town as soon as I finish those courses I'm signed up for."

Kennedy snapped his fingers. "All right, Ferris, wake up now."

Ferris blinked. "What's been happening?" he asked.

"Nothing much," said Kennedy, unbuckling the electrodes. "I've taken my readings. Thank you very much for the help, sir. I'll see that you get due credit when my research is published."

"Ah—yes. Yes." Ferris puffed himself out. Then he put an arm around Fraser's shoulder. "If you aren't busy," he said, "maybe we could go have lunch."

"Thanks," said Fraser. "I'd like to talk to you about a few things."

He lingered for a moment after Ferris had left the room. "I imagine this is goodbye for us," he said.

"Well, so long, at least. We'll probably hear from each other again." Kennedy shook Fraser's hand. "No hard feelings? I did go to a lot of trouble for you —wangling your introduction to Ferris when you'd named him, and having one of my men persuade him to come here. And right when I'm so infernally busy, too."

"Sure," said Fraser. "It's all right. I can't pretend to love you for what you've done, but you aren't a bad sort."

"No worse than you," said Kennedy with a short laugh. "You've used the machine for your own ends, now."

"Yeah," said Fraser. "I guess I have."

S WORSKY asked, "Why do you insist on calling me from drugstores? And why at my office? I've got a home phone, you know."

"I'm not sure but that our own lines are tapped," said Fraser. "Kennedy's a smart cookie, and don't you forget it. I think he's about ready to dismiss me as a danger, but you're certainly being watched; you're on his list."

"You're getting a persecution-complex. Honest, Colin, I'm worried."

"Well, bear with me for a while. Now, have you had any information on Kennedy since I called last?"

"Hm, no. I did mention to Thomson, as you asked me to, that I'd heard rumors of some revolutionary encephalographic techniques and would be interested in seeing the work. Why did you want me to do that?"

"Thomson," said Fraser, "is one of Kennedy's men. Now look, Jim, before long you're going to be invited to visit Kennedy. He'll give you a spiel about his research and ask to measure your brain waves. I want you to say yes. Then I want to know the exact times of the three appointments he'll give you—the first two, at least."

"Hmm—if Kennedy is in fact doing what you claim—"

"Jim, it's a necessary risk, but *I'm* the one who's taking it. You'll be okay, I promise you; though perhaps later you'll read of me being found in the river. You see, I got Kennedy to influence a big stockowner for me. One of the lesser companies in which he has a loud voice is Messenger. I don't suppose Kennedy knows that. I hope not!"

S WORSKY looked as if he'd been sandbagged. He was white, and the hand that poured a drink shook.

"Lord," he muttered. "Lord, Colin, you were right."

Fraser's teeth drew back from his lips. "You went through with it, eh?"

"Yes. I let the son hypnotize me, and afterward I walked off with a dreamy expression, as you told me to. Just three hours ago, he dropped around here in person. He gave me a long rigmarole about the stupidity of military secrecy, and how the Soviet Union stands for peace and justice. I hope I acted impressed; I'm not much of an actor."

"You don't have to be. Just so you didn't overdo it. To one of Kennedy's victims, obeying his advice comes so naturally that it doesn't call for any awe-struck wonderment."

"And he wanted data from me! Bombardment cross-sections. Critical values. Resonance levels. My Lord, if the Russians found that out through spies it'd save them three years of research. This is an FBI case, all right."

"No, not yet." Fraser laid an urgent hand on Sworsky's arm. "You've stuck by me so far, Jim. Go along a little further."

"What do you want me to do?"

"Why—" Fraser's laugh jarred out. "Give him what he wants, of course."

KENNEDY looked up from his desk, scowling. "All right, Fraser," he said. "You've been a damned nuisance, and it's pretty patient of me to see you again. But this is the last time. Wha'd'you want?"

"It's the last time I'll need to see you, perhaps." Fraser didn't sit down. He stood facing Kennedy. "You've had it, friend; straight up."

"What do you mean?" Kennedy's hand moved toward his buzzer.

"Listen before you do anything," said Fraser harshly. "I know you tried to bring Jim Sworsky under the influence. You asked him for top-secret data. A few hours ago, you handed the file he brought you on to Bryce, who's no doubt at the Amtorg offices this minute. That's high treason, Kennedy; they execute people for doing that."

The psychologist slumped back.

"Don't try to have your bully boys get rid of me," said Fraser. "Sworsky is sitting by the phone, waiting to call the FBI. I'm the only guy who can stop him."

"But—" Kennedy's tongue ran around his lips. "But he committed treason himself. He gave me the papers!"

Fraser grinned. "You don't think those were authentic, do you? I doubt if you'll be very popular in the Soviet Union either, once they've tried to build machines using your data."

Kennedy looked down at the floor. "How did you do it?" he whispered.

"Remember Ferris? The guy you fixed up for me? He owns a share of your next-door neighbor, the Messenger Advertising Service. I fed him a song and dance about needing an office to do some important work, only my very whereabouts had to be secret. The Messenger people were moved out without anybody's knowing. I installed myself there one night, also a simple little electric oscillator.

"Encephalography is damn delicate work; it involves amplifications up to several million. The apparatus misbehaves if you give it a hard look. Naturally, your lab and the machine were heavily shielded, but even so, a radio emitter next door would be bound to throw you off. My main trouble was in lousing you up just a little bit, not enough to make you suspect anything.

"I only worked at that during your calibrating sessions with Sworsky. I didn't have to be there when you turned the beam on him, because it would be calculated from false data and be so far from his pattern as to have no effect. You told me yourself how precise an adjustment was needed. Sworsky played along, then. Now we've got proof—not that you meddled with human lives, but that you are a spy."

Kennedy sat without moving. His voice was a broken mumble. "I was going to change the world. I had hopes for all humankind. And you, for the sake of one woman—"

"I never trusted anybody with a messiah complex. The world is too big to change single-handed; you'd just have bungled it up worse than it already is. A lot of dictators started out as reformers and ended up as mass-executioners; you'd have done the same."

Fraser leaned over his desk. "I'm willing to make a deal, though," he went on. "Your teeth are pulled; there's no point in turning you in. Sworsky and Martinez and I are willing just to report on Bryce, and let you go, if you'll change back all your subjects. We're going to read your files, and watch and see that you do it. Every one."

Kennedy bit his lip. "And the machine—?"

"I don't know. We'll settle that later. Okay, God, here's the phone number of Judy Harkness. Ask her to come over for a special treatment. At once."

A MONTH later, the papers had a story about a plausible maniac who had talked his way into the Columbia University laboratories, where Gavotti's puzzling machine was being studied, and pulled out a hammer and smashed it into ruin before he could be stopped. Taken to jail, he committed suicide in his cell. The maniac's name was Kennedy.

Fraser felt vague regret, but it didn't take him long to forget it; he was too busy making plans for his wedding.

THE TUNNEL UNDER THE WORLD

By FREDERIK POHL

Pinching yourself is no way to see if you are dreaming.
Surgical instruments?
Well, yes—but a mechanic's kit is best of all!

O N THE morning of June 15th, Guy Burckhardt woke up screaming out of a dream.

It was more real than any dream he had ever had in his life. He could still hear and feel the sharp, ripping-metal explosion, the violent heave that had tossed him furiously out of bed, the searing wave of heat.

THE TUNNEL UNDER THE WORLD

He sat up convulsively and stared, not believing what he saw, at the quiet room and the bright sunlight coming in the window.

He croaked, "Mary?"

His wife was not in the bed next to him. The covers were tumbled and awry, as though she had just left it, and the memory of the dream was so strong that instinctively he found himself searching the floor to see if the dream explosion had thrown her down.

BUT SHE wasn't there. Of course she wasn't, he told himself, looking at the familiar vanity and slipper chair, the uncracked window, the unbuckled wall. It had only been a dream.

"Guy?" His wife was calling him querulously from the foot of the stairs. "Guy, dear, are you all right?"

He called weakly, "Sure."

There was a pause. Then Mary said doubtfully, "Breakfast is ready. Are you sure you're all right? I thought I heard you yelling—"

Burckhardt said more confidently, "I had a bad dream, honey. Be right down."

IN THE shower, punching the lukewarm-and-cologne he favored, he told himself that it had been a beaut of a dream. Still, bad dreams weren't unusual, especially bad dreams about explosions. In the past thirty years of H-bomb jitters, who had not dreamed of explosions?

Even Mary had dreamed of them, it turned out, for he started to tell her about the dream, but she cut him off. "You *did*?" Her voice was astonished. "Why, dear, I dreamed the same thing! Well, almost the same thing. I didn't actually *hear* anything. I dreamed that something woke me up, and then there was a sort of quick bang, and then something hit me on the head. And that was all. Was yours like that?"

Burckhardt coughed. "Well, no," he said. Mary was not one of these strong-as-a-man, brave-as-a-tiger women. It was not necessary, he thought, to tell her all the little details of the dream that made it seem so real. No need to mention the splintered ribs, and the salt bubble in his throat, and the agonized knowledge that this was death. He said, "Maybe there really was some kind of explosion downtown. Maybe we heard it and it started us dreaming."

Mary reached over and patted his hand absently. "Maybe," she agreed. "It's almost half-past eight, dear. Shouldn't you hurry? You don't want to be late to the office."

He gulped his food, kissed her and rushed out —not so much to be on time as to see if his guess had been right.

But downtown Tylerton looked as it always had. Coming in on the bus, Burckhardt watched critically out the window, seeking evidence of an explosion. There wasn't any. If anything, Tylerton looked better than it ever had before: It was a beautiful crisp day, the sky was cloudless, the buildings were clean and inviting. They had, he observed, steam-blasted the Power & Light Building, the town's only skyscraper—

that was the penalty of having Contro Chemical's main plant on the outskirts of town; the fumes from the cascade stills left their mark on stone buildings.

None of the usual crowd were on the bus, so there wasn't anyone Burckhardt could ask about the explosion. And by the time he got out at the corner of Fifth and Lehigh and the bus rolled away with a muted diesel moan, he had pretty well convinced himself that it was all imagination.

He stopped at the cigar stand in the lobby of his office building, but Ralph wasn't behind the counter. The man who sold him his pack of cigarettes was a stranger.

"Where's Mr. Stebbins?" Burckhardt asked.

The man said politely, "Sick, sir. He'll be in tomorrow. A pack of Marlins today?"

"Chesterfields," Burckhardt corrected.

"Certainly, sir," the man said. But what he took from the rack and slid across the counter was an unfamiliar green-and-yellow pack.

"Do try these, sir," he suggested. "They contain an anti-cough factor. Ever notice how ordinary cigarettes make you choke every once in a while?"

Burckhardt said suspiciously, "I never heard of this brand."

"Of course not. They're something new." Burckhardt hesitated, and the man said persuasively, "Look, try them out at my risk. If you don't like them, bring back the empty pack and I'll refund your money. Fair enough?"

Burckhardt shrugged. "How can I lose? But give me a pack of Chesterfields, too, will you?"

H E OPENED the pack and lit one while he waited for the elevator. They weren't bad, he decided, though he was suspicious of cigarettes that had the tobacco chemically treated in any way. But he didn't think much of Ralph's stand-in; it would raise hell with the trade at the cigar stand if the man tried to give every customer the same high-pressure sales talk.

The elevator door opened with a low-pitched sound of music. Burckhardt and two or three others got in and he nodded to them as the door closed. The thread of music switched off and the speaker in the ceiling of the cab began its usual commercials.

No, not the *usual* commercials, Burckhardt realized. He had been exposed to the captive-audience commercials so long that they hardly registered on the outer ear any more, but what was coming from the recorded program in the basement of the building caught his attention. It wasn't merely that the brands were mostly unfamiliar; it was a difference in pattern.

There were jingles with an insistent, bouncy rhythm, about soft drinks he had never tasted. There was a rapid patter dialogue between what sounded like two ten-year-old boys about a candy bar, followed by an authoritative bass rumble: "Go right out and get a DELICIOUS Choco-Bite and eat your TANGY Choco-Bite *all up*. That's *Choco-Bite!*" There was a sobbing female whine: "I *wish* I had a Feckle Freezer! I'd do *anything* for a Feckle Freezer!" Burckhardt reached his floor and left the elevator in the middle of the last one. It left him a little uneasy. The commercials were not for familiar brands; there was no feeling of use and custom to them.

But the office was happily normal—except that Mr. Barth wasn't in. Miss Mitkin, yawning at the reception desk, didn't know exactly why. "His home phoned, that's all. He'll be in tomorrow."

"Maybe he went to the plant. It's right near his house."

She looked indifferent. "Yeah."

A thought struck Burckhardt. "But today is June 15th! It's quarterly tax return day—he has to sign the return!"

Miss Mitkin shrugged to indicate that that was Burckhardt's problem, not hers. She returned to her nails.

Thoroughly exasperated, Burckhardt went to his desk. It wasn't that he couldn't sign the tax returns as well as Barth, he thought resentfully. It simply wasn't his job, that was all; it was a responsibility that Barth, as office manager for Contro Chemicals' downtown office, should have taken.

HE THOUGHT briefly of calling Barth at his home or trying to reach him at the factory, but he gave up the idea quickly enough. He didn't really care much for the people at the factory and the less contact he had with them, the better. He had been to the factory once, with Barth; it had been a confusing and, in a way, a frightening experience. Barring a handful of executives and engineers, there wasn't a soul in the factory—that is, Burckhardt corrected himself, remembering what Barth had told him, not a *living* soul—just the machines.

According to Barth, each machine was controlled by a sort of computer which reproduced, in its electronic snarl, the actual memory and mind of a human being. It was an unpleasant thought. Barth, laughing, had assured him that there was no Frankenstein business of robbing graveyards and implanting brains in machines. It was only a matter, he said, of transferring a man's habit patterns from brain cells to vacuum-tube cells. It didn't hurt the man and it didn't make the machine into a monster.

But they made Burckhardt uncomfortable all the same.

He put Barth and the factory and all his other little irritations out of his mind and tackled the tax returns. It took him until noon to verify the figures—which Barth could have done out of his memory and his private ledger in ten minutes, Burckhardt resentfully reminded himself.

He sealed them in an envelope and walked out to Miss Mitkin. "Since Mr. Barth isn't here, we'd better go to lunch in shifts," he said. "You can go first."

"Thanks." Miss Mitkin languidly took her bag out of the desk drawer and began to apply makeup.

Burckhardt offered her the envelope. "Drop this in the mail for me, will you? Uh—wait a minute. I wonder if I ought to phone Mr. Barth to make sure. Did his wife say whether he was able to take phone calls?"

"Didn't say." Miss Mitkin blotted her lips carefully with a Kleenex. "Wasn't his wife, anyway. It was his daughter who called and left the message."

"The kid?" Burckhardt frowned. "I thought she was away at school."

"She called, that's all I know."

Burckhardt went back to his own office and stared distastefully at the unopened mail on his desk. He didn't like nightmares; they spoiled his whole day. He should have stayed in bed, like Barth.

A FUNNY thing happened on his way home. There was a disturbance at the corner where he usually caught his bus—someone was screaming something about a new kind of deep-freeze—so he walked an extra block. He saw the bus coming and started to trot. But behind him, someone was calling his name. He looked over his shoulder; a small harried-looking man was hurrying toward him.

Burckhardt hesitated, and then recognized him. It was a casual acquaintance named Swanson. Burckhardt sourly observed that he had already missed the bus.

He said, "Hello."

Swanson's face was desperately eager as he approached. "Burckhardt?" he asked inquiringly, with an odd intensity. And then he just stood there silently, watching Burckhardt's face, with a burning eagerness that dwindled to a faint hope and died to a regret. He was searching for something, waiting for something, Burckhardt thought. But whatever it was he wanted, Burckhardt didn't know how to supply it.

Burckhardt coughed and said again, "Hello, Swanson."

Swanson didn't even acknowledge the greeting. He merely sighed a very deep sigh.

"Nothing doing," he mumbled, apparently to himself. He nodded abstractedly to Burckhardt and turned away.

Burckhardt watched the slumped shoulders disappear in the crowd. It was an *odd* sort of day, he thought, and one he didn't much like. Things weren't going right.

Riding home on the next bus, he brooded about it. It wasn't anything terrible or disastrous; it was something out of his experience entirely. You live your life, like any man, and you form a network of impressions and reactions. You *expect* things. When you open your medicine chest, your razor is expected to be on the second shelf; when you lock your front door, you expect to have to give it a slight extra tug to make it latch.

It isn't the things that are right and perfect in your life that make it familiar. It is the things that are just a little bit wrong—the sticking latch, the light switch at the head of the stairs that needs an extra push because the spring is old and weak, the rug that unfailingly skids underfoot.

It wasn't just that things were wrong with the pattern of Burckhardt's life; it was that the *wrong* things were wrong. For instance, Barth hadn't come into the office, yet Barth *always* came in.

Burckhardt brooded about it through dinner. He brooded about it, despite his wife's attempt to interest him in a game of bridge with the neighbors, all through the evening. The neighbors were people he liked—Anne and Farley Dennerman. He had known them all their lives. But they were odd and brooding, too, this night and he barely listened to Dennerman's complaints about not being able to get good phone service or his wife's comments on the disgusting variety of television commercials they had these days.

Burckhardt was well on the way to setting an all-time record for continuous abstraction when, around midnight, with a suddenness that surprised him—he was strangely *aware* of it happening—he turned over in his bed and, quickly and completely, fell asleep.

II

ON THE morning of June 15th, Burckhardt woke up screaming.

I T WAS more real than any dream he had ever had in his life. He could still hear the explosion, feel the blast that crushed him against a wall. It did not seem right that he should be sitting bolt upright in bed in an undisturbed room.

His wife came pattering up the stairs. "Darling!" she cried. "What's the matter?"

He mumbled, "Nothing. Bad dream."

She relaxed, hand on heart. In an angry tone, she started to say: "You gave me such a shock—"

But a noise from outside interrupted her. There was a wail of sirens and a clang of bells; it was loud and shocking.

The Burckhardts stared at each other for a heartbeat, then hurried fearfully to the window.

There were no rumbling fire engines in the street, only a small panel truck, cruising slowly along. Flaring loudspeaker horns crowned its top. From them issued the screaming sound of sirens, growing in intensity, mixed with the rumble of heavy-duty engines and the sound of bells. It was a perfect record of fire engines arriving at a four-alarm blaze.

Burckhardt said in amazement, "Mary, that's against the law! Do you know what they're doing? They're playing records of a fire. What are they up to?"

"Maybe it's a practical joke," his wife offered.

"Joke? Waking up the whole neighborhood at six o'clock in the morning?" He shook his head. "The police will be here in ten minutes," he predicted. "Wait and see."

But the police weren't—not in ten minutes, or at all. Whoever the pranksters in the car were, they apparently had a police permit for their games.

The car took a position in the middle of the block and stood silent for a few minutes. Then there was a crackle from the speaker, and a giant voice chanted:

"Feckle Freezers!
Feckle Freezers!
Gotta have a
Feckle Freezer!
Feckle, Feckle, Feckle,
Feckle, Feckle, Feckle—"

It went on and on. Every house on the block had faces staring out of windows by then. The voice was not merely loud; it was nearly deafening.

Burckhardt shouted to his wife, over the uproar, "What the hell is a Feckle Freezer?"

"Some kind of a freezer, I guess, dear," she shrieked back unhelpfully.

ABRUPTLY the noise stopped and the truck stood silent. It was still misty morning; the Sun's rays came horizontally across the rooftops. It was impossible to believe that, a moment ago, the silent block had been bellowing the name of a freezer.

"A crazy advertising trick," Burckhardt said bitterly. He yawned and turned away from the window. "Might as well get dressed. I guess that's the end of—"

The bellow caught him from behind; it was almost like a hard slap on the ears. A harsh, sneering voice, louder than the arch-angel's trumpet, howled:

"Have you got a freezer? *It stinks!* If it isn't a Feckle Freezer, *it stinks*! If it's a last year's Feckle Freezer, *it stinks*! Only this year's Feckle Freezer is any good at all! You know who owns an Ajax Freezer? Fairies own Ajax Freezers! You know who owns a Triplecold Freezer? Commies own Triplecold Freezers! Every freezer but a brand-new Feckle Freezer *stinks*!"

The voice screamed inarticulately with rage. "I'm warning you! Get out and buy a Feckle Freezer right away! Hurry up! Hurry for Feckle! Hurry for Feckle! Hurry, hurry, hurry, Feckle, Feckle, Feckle, Feckle, Feckle, Feckle..."

It stopped eventually. Burckhardt licked his lips. He started to say to his wife, "Maybe we ought to call the police about—" when the speakers erupted again. It caught him off guard; it was intended to catch him off guard. It screamed:

"Feckle, Feckle, Feckle, Feckle, Feckle, Feckle, Feckle, Feckle. Cheap freezers ruin your food. You'll get sick and throw up. You'll get sick and die. Buy a

Feckle, Feckle, Feckle, Feckle! Ever take a piece of meat out of the freezer you've got and see how rotten and moldy it is? Buy a Feckle, Feckle, Feckle, Feckle, Feckle. Do you want to eat rotten, stinking food? Or do you want to wise up and buy a Feckle, Feckle, Feckle—"

That did it. With fingers that kept stabbing the wrong holes, Burckhardt finally managed to dial the local police station. He got a busy signal—it was apparent that he was not the only one with the same idea—and while he was shakingly dialing again, the noise outside stopped.

He looked out the window. The truck was gone.

BURCKHARDT loosened his tie and ordered another Frosty-Flip from the waiter. If only they wouldn't keep the Crystal Cafe so *hot*! The new paint job—searing reds and blinding yellows—was bad enough, but someone seemed to have the delusion that this was January instead of June; the place was a good ten degrees warmer than outside.

He swallowed the Frosty-Flip in two gulps. It had a kind of peculiar flavor, he thought, but not bad. It certainly cooled you off, just as the waiter had promised. He reminded himself to pick up a carton of them on the way home; Mary might like them. She was always interested in something new.

He stood up awkwardly as the girl came across the restaurant toward him. She was the most beautiful thing he had ever seen in Tylerton. Chin-height, honey-blonde hair and a figure that—well, it was all hers. There was no doubt in the world that the dress that clung to her was the only thing she wore. He felt as if he were blushing as she greeted him.

"Mr. Burckhardt." The voice was like distant tomtoms. "It's wonderful of you to let me see you, after this morning."

He cleared his throat. "Not at all. Won't you sit down, Miss—"

"April Horn," she murmured, sitting down—beside him, not where he had pointed on the other side of the table. "Call me April, won't you?"

She was wearing some kind of perfume, Burckhardt noted with what little of his mind was functioning at all. It didn't seem fair that she should be using perfume as well as everything else. He came to with a start and realized that the waiter was leaving with an order for *filets mignon* for two.

"Hey!" he objected.

"Please, Mr. Burckhardt." Her shoulder was against his, her face was turned to him, her breath was warm, her expression was tender and solicitous. "This is all on the Feckle Corporation. Please let them—it's the *least* they can do."

He felt her hand burrowing into his pocket.

"I put the price of the meal into your pocket," she whispered conspiratorially. "Please do that for me, won't you? I mean I'd appreciate it if you'd pay the waiter—I'm old-fashioned about things like that."

She smiled meltingly, then became mock-businesslike. "But you must take the money," she insisted. "Why, you're letting Feckle off lightly if you do! You could sue them for every nickel they've got, disturbing your sleep like that."

ITH A dizzy feeling, as though he had just seen someone make a rabbit disappear into a top hat, he said, "Why, it really wasn't so bad, uh, April. A little noisy, maybe, but—"

"Oh, Mr. Burckhardt!" The blue eyes were wide and admiring. "I knew you'd understand. It's just that —well, it's such a *wonderful* freezer that some of the outside men get carried away, so to speak. As soon as the main office found out about what happened, they sent representatives around to every house on the block to apologize. Your wife told us where we could phone you—and I'm so very pleased that you were willing to let me have lunch with you, so that I could apologize, too. Because truly, Mr. Burckhardt, it is a *fine* freezer.

"I shouldn't tell you this, but—" the blue eyes were shyly lowered, "I'd do almost anything for Feckle Freezers. It's more than a job to me." She looked up. She was enchanting. "I bet you think I'm silly, don't you?"

Burckhardt coughed. "Well, I—"

"Oh, you don't want to be unkind!" She shook her head. "No, don't pretend. You think it's silly. But really, Mr. Burckhardt, you wouldn't think so if you knew more about the Feckle. Let me show you this little booklet—"

Burckhardt got back from lunch a full hour late. It wasn't only the girl who delayed him. There had been a curious interview with a little man named Swanson, whom he barely knew, who had stopped him with desperate urgency on the street—and then left him cold.

But it didn't matter much. Mr. Barth, for the first time since Burckhardt had worked there, was out for the day—leaving Burckhardt stuck with the quarterly tax returns.

What did matter, though, was that somehow he had signed a purchase order for a twelve-cubic-foot Feckle Freezer, upright model, self-defrosting, list price $625, with a ten per cent "courtesy" discount— "Because of that *horrid* affair this morning, Mr. Burckhardt," she had said.

And he wasn't sure how he could explain it to his wife.

H E NEEDN'T have worried. As he walked in the front door, his wife said almost immediately, "I wonder if we can't afford a new freezer, dear. There was a man here to apologize about that noise and—well, we got to talking and—"

She had signed a purchase order, too.

It had been the damnedest day, Burckhardt thought later, on his way up to bed. But the day wasn't done with him yet. At the head of the stairs, the weakened spring in the electric light switch refused to click at all. He snapped it back and forth angrily and, of course, succeeded in jarring the tumbler out of its pins. The wires shorted and every light in the house went out.

"Damn!" said Guy Burckhardt.

"Fuse?" His wife shrugged sleepily. "Let it go till the morning, dear."

Burckhardt shook his head. "You go back to bed. I'll be right along."

It wasn't so much that he cared about fixing the fuse, but he was too restless for sleep. He disconnected the bad switch with a screwdriver, stumbled down into the black kitchen, found the flashlight and climbed gingerly down the cellar stairs. He located a spare fuse, pushed an empty trunk over to the fuse box to stand on and twisted out the old fuse.

When the new one was in, he heard the starting click and steady drone of the refrigerator in the kitchen overhead.

He headed back to the steps, and stopped.

Where the old trunk had been, the cellar floor gleamed oddly bright. He inspected it in the flashlight beam. It was metal!

"Son of a gun," said Guy Burckhardt. He shook his head unbelievingly. He peered closer, rubbed the edges of the metallic patch with his thumb and acquired an annoying cut—the edges were *sharp*.

The stained cement floor of the cellar was a thin shell. He found a hammer and cracked it off in a dozen spots—everywhere was metal.

The whole cellar was a copper box. Even the cement-brick walls were false fronts over a metal sheath!

BAFFLED, he attacked one of the foundation beams. That, at least, was real wood. The glass in the cellar windows was real glass.

He sucked his bleeding thumb and tried the base of the cellar stairs. Real wood. He chipped at the bricks under the oil burner. Real bricks. The retaining walls, the floor—they were faked.

It was as though someone had shored up the house with a frame of metal and then laboriously concealed the evidence.

The biggest surprise was the upside-down boat hull that blocked the rear half of the cellar, relic of a brief home workshop period that Burckhardt had gone through a couple of years before. From above, it looked perfectly normal. Inside, though, where there should have been thwarts and seats and lockers, there was a mere tangle of braces, rough and unfinished.

"But I *built* that!" Burckhardt exclaimed, forgetting his thumb. He leaned against the hull dizzily, trying to think this thing through. For reasons beyond his comprehension, someone had taken his boat and his cellar away, maybe his whole house, and replaced them with a clever mock-up of the real thing.

"That's crazy," he said to the empty cellar. He stared around in the light of the flash. He whispered, "What in the name of Heaven would anybody do that for?"

Reason refused an answer; there wasn't any reasonable answer. For long minutes, Burckhardt contemplated the uncertain picture of his own sanity.

He peered under the boat again, hoping to reassure himself that it was a mistake, just his imagination. But the sloppy, unfinished bracing was unchanged. He crawled under for a better look, feeling the rough wood incredulously. Utterly impossible!

He switched off the flashlight and started to wriggle out. But he didn't make it. In the moment between the command to his legs to move and the crawling out, he felt a sudden draining weariness flooding through him.

Consciousness went—not easily, but as though it were being taken away, and Guy Burckhardt was asleep.

III

ON THE morning of June 16th, Guy Burckhardt woke up in a cramped position huddled under the hull of the boat in his basement—and raced upstairs to find it was June 15th.

The first thing he had done was to make a frantic, hasty inspection of the boat hull, the faked cellar floor, the imitation stone. They were all as he had remembered them—all completely unbelievable.

The kitchen was its placid, unexciting self. The electric clock was purring soberly around the dial. Almost six o'clock, it said. His wife would be waking at any moment.

Burckhardt flung open the front door and stared out into the quiet street. The morning paper was tossed carelessly against the steps—and as he retrieved it, he noticed that this was the 15th day of June.

But that was impossible. *Yesterday* was the 15th of June. It was not a date one would forget—it was quarterly tax-return day.

He went back into the hall and picked up the telephone; he dialed for Weather Information, and got a well-modulated chant: "—and cooler, some showers.

Barometric pressure thirty point zero four, rising...
United States Weather Bureau forecast for June 15th.
Warm and sunny, with high around—"

He hung the phone up. June 15th.

"Holy heaven!" Burckhardt said prayerfully.
Things were very odd indeed. He heard the ring of his
wife's alarm and bounded up the stairs.

Mary Burckhardt was sitting upright in bed
with the terrified, uncomprehending stare of someone
just waking out of a nightmare.

"Oh!" she gasped, as her husband came in the
room. "Darling, I just had the most *terrible* dream! It
was like an explosion and—"

"Again?" Burckhardt asked, not very sympathetically. "Mary, something's funny! I *knew* there was
something wrong all day yesterday and—"

He went on to tell her about the copper box
that was the cellar, and the odd mock-up someone
had made of his boat. Mary looked astonished, then
alarmed, then placatory and uneasy.

She said, "Dear, are you *sure*? Because I was
cleaning that old trunk out just last week and I didn't
notice anything."

"Positive!" said Guy Burckhardt. "I dragged it
over to the wall to step on it to put a new fuse in after
we blew the lights out and—"

"After we what?" Mary was looking more than
merely alarmed.

"After we blew the lights out. You know, when
the switch at the head of the stairs stuck. I went down
to the cellar and—"

Mary sat up in bed. "Guy, the switch didn't
stick. I turned out the lights myself last night."

Burckhardt glared at his wife. "Now I *know* you didn't! Come here and take a look!"

He stalked out to the landing and dramatically pointed to the bad switch, the one that he had unscrewed and left hanging the night before...

Only it wasn't. It was as it had always been. Unbelieving, Burckhardt pressed it and the lights sprang up in both halls.

MARY, LOOKING pale and worried, left him to go down to the kitchen and start breakfast. Burckhardt stood staring at the switch for a long time. His mental processes were gone beyond the point of disbelief and shock; they simply were not functioning.

He shaved and dressed and ate his breakfast in a state of numb introspection. Mary didn't disturb him; she was apprehensive and soothing. She kissed him good-by as he hurried out to the bus without another word.

Miss Mitkin, at the reception desk, greeted him with a yawn. "Morning," she said drowsily. "Mr. Barth won't be in today."

Burckhardt started to say something, but checked himself. She would not know that Barth hadn't been in yesterday, either, because she was tearing a June 14th pad off her calendar to make way for the "new" June 15th sheet.

He staggered to his own desk and stared unseeingly at the morning's mail. It had not even been opened yet, but he knew that the Factory Distributors envelope contained an order for twenty thousand feet

of the new acoustic tile, and the one from Finebeck &
Sons was a complaint.

After a long while, he forced himself to open
them. They were.

By lunchtime, driven by a desperate sense of
urgency, Burckhardt made Miss Mitkin take her
lunch hour first—the June-fifteenth-that-was-yester-
day, *he* had gone first. She went, looking vaguely worried about his strained insistence, but it made no difference to Burckhardt's mood.

The phone rang and Burckhardt picked it up
abstractedly. He answered, "Contro Chemicals Downtown, Burckhardt speaking."

The voice said, "This is Swanson," and stopped.

Burckhardt waited expectantly, but that was
all. He said, "Hello?"

Again the pause. Then Swanson asked in sad
resignation, "Still nothing, eh?"

"Nothing what? Swanson, is there something
you want? You came up to me yesterday and went
through this routine. You—"

The voice crackled: "Burckhardt! Oh, my good
heavens, *you remember*! Stay right there—I'll be down
in half an hour!"

"What's this all about?"

"Never mind," the little man said exultantly.
"Tell you about it when I see you. Don't say any more
over the phone—somebody may be listening. Just wait
there. Say, hold on a minute. Will you be alone in the
office?"

"Well, no. Miss Mitkin will probably—"

"Hell. Look, Burckhardt, where do you eat
lunch? Is it good and noisy?"

"Why, I suppose so. The Crystal Cafe. It's just about a block—"

"I know where it is. Meet you in half an hour!" And the receiver clicked.

THE CRYSTAL Café was no longer painted red, but the temperature was still up. And they had added piped-in music interspersed with commercials. The advertisements were for Frosty-Flip, Marlin Cigarettes— "They're sanitized," the announcer purred—and something called Choco-Bite candy bars that Burckhardt couldn't remember ever having heard of before. But he heard more about them quickly enough.

While he was waiting for Swanson to show up, a girl in the cellophane skirt of a nightclub cigarette vendor came through the restaurant with a tray of tiny scarlet-wrapped candies.

"Choco-Bites are *tangy*," she was murmuring as she came close to his table. "Choco-Bites are *tangier* than tangy!"

Burckhardt, intent on watching for the strange little man who had phoned him, paid little attention. But as she scattered a handful of the confections over the table next to his, smiling at the occupants, he caught a glimpse of her and turned to stare.

"Why, Miss Horn!" he said.

The girl dropped her tray of candies.

Burckhardt rose, concerned over the girl. "Is something wrong?"

But she fled.

The manager of the restaurant was staring suspiciously at Burckhardt, who sank back in his seat and tried to look inconspicuous. He hadn't insulted the girl! Maybe she was just a very strictly reared young lady, he thought—in spite of the long bare legs under the cellophane skirt—and when he addressed her, she thought he was a masher.

Ridiculous idea. Burckhardt scowled uneasily and picked up his menu.

"Burckhardt!" It was a shrill whisper.

Burckhardt looked up over the top of his menu, startled. In the seat across from him, the little man named Swanson was sitting, tensely poised.

"Burckhardt!" the little man whispered again. "Let's get out of here! They're on to you now. If you want to stay alive, come on!"

There was no arguing with the man. Burckhardt gave the hovering manager a sick, apologetic smile and followed Swanson out. The little man seemed to know where he was going. In the street, he clutched Burckhardt by the elbow and hurried him off down the block.

"Did you see her?" he demanded. "That Horn woman, in the phone booth? She'll have them here in five minutes, believe me, so hurry it up!"

ALTHOUGH the street was full of people and cars, nobody was paying any attention to Burckhardt and Swanson. The air had a nip in it—more like October than June, Burckhardt thought, in spite of the weather bureau. And he felt like a fool, following this mad little man down the street, running away from some "them" to-ward—toward what? The little man might be crazy, but he was afraid. And the fear was infectious.

"In here!" panted the little man.

It was another restaurant—more of a bar, really, and a sort of second-rate place that Burckhardt had never patronized.

"Right straight through," Swanson whispered; and Burckhardt, like a biddable boy, side-stepped through the mass of tables to the far end of the restaurant.

It was "L"-shaped, with a front on two streets at right angles to each other. They came out on the side street, Swanson staring coldly back at the question-looking cashier, and crossed to the opposite sidewalk.

They were under the marquee of a movie thea-ter. Swanson's expression began to relax.

"Lost them!" he crowed softly. "We're almost there."

He stepped up to the window and bought two tickets. Burckhardt trailed him in to the theater. It was a weekday matinee and the place was almost empty. From the screen came sounds of gunfire and horse's hoofs. A solitary usher, leaning against a bright brass rail, looked briefly at them and went back to staring boredly at the picture as Swanson led Burckhardt down a flight of carpeted marble steps.

They were in the lounge and it was empty. There was a door for men and one for ladies; and there was a third door, marked "MANAGER" in gold letters. Swanson listened at the door, and gently opened it and peered inside.

"Okay," he said, gesturing.

Burckhardt followed him through an empty office, to another door—a closet, probably, because it was unmarked.

But it was no closet. Swanson opened it warily, looked inside, then motioned Burckhardt to follow.

It was a tunnel, metal-walled, brightly lit. Empty, it stretched vacantly away in both directions from them.

Burckhardt looked wondering around. One thing he knew and knew full well:

No such tunnel belonged under Tylerton.

THERE was a room off the tunnel with chairs and a desk and what looked like television screens. Swanson slumped in a chair, panting.

"We're all right for a while here," he wheezed. "They don't come here much any more. If they do, we'll hear them and we can hide."

"Who?" demanded Burckhardt.

The little man said, "Martians!" His voice cracked on the word and the life seemed to go out of him. In morose tones, he went on: "Well, I think they're Martians. Although you could be right, you know; I've had plenty of time to think it over these last few weeks, after they got you, and it's possible they're Russians after all. Still—"

"Start from the beginning. Who got me when?"

Swanson sighed. "So we have to go through the whole thing again. All right. It was about two months ago that you banged on my door, late at night.

You were all beat up—scared silly. You begged me to help you—"

"*I* did?"

"Naturally you don't remember any of this. Listen and you'll understand. You were talking a blue streak about being captured and threatened, and your wife being dead and coming back to life, and all kinds of mixed-up nonsense. I thought you were crazy. But —well, I've always had a lot of respect for you. And you begged me to hide you and I have this darkroom, you know. It locks from the inside only. I put the lock on myself. So we went in there—just to humor you— and along about midnight, which was only fifteen or twenty minutes after, we passed out."

"Passed out?"

Swanson nodded. "Both of us. It was like being hit with a sandbag. Look, didn't that happen to you again last night?"

"I guess it did," Burckhardt shook his head uncertainly.

"Sure. And then all of a sudden we were awake again, and you said you were going to show me something funny, and we went out and bought a paper. And the date on it was June 15th."

"June 15th? But that's today! I mean—"

"You got it, friend. It's *always* today!"

It took time to penetrate.

Burckhardt said wonderingly, "You've hidden out in that darkroom for how many weeks?"

"How can I tell? Four or five, maybe. I lost count. And every day the same—always the 15th of June, always my landlady, Mrs. Keefer, is sweeping the front steps, always the same headline in the papers at the corner. It gets monotonous, friend."

IV

IT WAS Burckhardt's idea and Swanson despised it, but he went along. He was the type who always went along.

"It's dangerous," he grumbled worriedly. "Suppose somebody comes by? They'll spot us and—"

"What have we got to lose?"

Swanson shrugged. "It's dangerous," he said again. But he went along.

Burckhardt's idea was very simple. He was sure of only one thing—the tunnel went somewhere. Martians or Russians, fantastic plot or crazy hallucination, whatever was wrong with Tylerton had an explanation, and the place to look for it was at the end of the tunnel.

They jogged along. It was more than a mile before they began to see an end. They were in luck—at least no one came through the tunnel to spot them. But Swanson had said that it was only at certain hours that the tunnel seemed to be in use.

Always the 15th of June. Why? Burckhardt asked himself. Never mind the how. *Why?*

And falling asleep, completely involuntarily—everyone at the same time, it seemed. And not remembering, never remembering anything—Swanson had said how eagerly he saw Burckhardt again, the morning after Burckhardt had incautiously waited five minutes too many before retreating into the darkroom. When Swanson had come to, Burckhardt was gone. Swanson had seen him in the street that afternoon, but Burckhardt had remembered nothing.

And Swanson had lived his mouse's existence for weeks, hiding in the woodwork at night, stealing out by day to search for Burckhardt in pitiful hope, scurrying around the fringe of life, trying to keep from the deadly eyes of *them*.

Them. One of "them" was the girl named April Horn. It was by seeing her walk carelessly into a telephone booth and never come out that Swanson had found the tunnel. Another was the man at the cigar stand in Burckhardt's office building. There were more, at least a dozen that Swanson knew of or suspected.

They were easy enough to spot, once you knew where to look—for they, alone in Tylerton, changed their roles from day to day. Burckhardt was on that 8:51 bus, every morning of every day-that-was-June-15th, never different by a hair or a moment. But April Horn was sometimes gaudy in the cellophane skirt, giving away candy or cigarettes; sometimes plainly dressed; sometimes not seen by Swanson at all.

Russians? Martians? Whatever they were, what could they be hoping to gain from this mad masquerade?

Burckhardt didn't know the answer—but perhaps it lay beyond the door at the end of the tunnel. They listened carefully and heard distant sounds that could not quite be made out, but nothing that seemed dangerous. They slipped through.

And, through a wide chamber and up a flight of steps, they found they were in what Burckhardt recognized as the Contro Chemicals plant.

NOBODY was in sight. By itself, that was not so very odd—the automatized factory had never had very many persons in it. But Burckhardt remembered, from his single visit, the endless, ceaseless busyness of the plant, the valves that opened and closed, the vats that emptied themselves and filled themselves and stirred and cooked and chemically tasted the bubbling liquids they held inside themselves. The plant was never populated, but it was never still.

Only—now it *was* still. Except for the distant sounds, there was no breath of life in it. The captive electronic minds were sending out no commands; the coils and relays were at rest.

Burckhardt said, "Come on." Swanson reluctantly followed him through the tangled aisles of stainless steel columns and tanks.

They walked as though they were in the presence of the dead. In a way, they were, for what were the automatons that once had run the factory, if not corpses? The machines were controlled by computers that were really not computers at all, but the electronic analogues of living brains. And if they were turned off, were they not dead? For each had once been a human mind.

Take a master petroleum chemist, infinitely skilled in the separation of crude oil into its fractions. Strap him down, probe into his brain with searching electronic needles. The machine scans the patterns of the mind, translates what it sees into charts and sine waves. Impress these same waves on a robot computer and you have your chemist. Or a thousand copies of your chemist, if you wish, with all of his knowledge and skill, and no human limitations at all.

Put a dozen copies of him into a plant and they will run it all, twenty-four hours a day, seven days of every week, never tiring, never overlooking anything, never forgetting...

Swanson stepped up closer to Burckhardt. "I'm scared," he said.

They were across the room now and the sounds were louder. They were not machine sounds, but voices; Burckhardt moved cautiously up to a door and dared to peer around it.

It was a smaller room, lined with television screens, each one—a dozen or more, at least—with a man or woman sitting before it, staring into the screen and dictating notes into a recorder. The viewers dialed from scene to scene; no two screens ever showed the same picture.

The pictures seemed to have little in common. One was a store, where a girl dressed like April Horn was demonstrating home freezers. One was a series of shots of kitchens. Burckhardt caught a glimpse of what looked like the cigar stand in his office building.

It was baffling and Burckhardt would have loved to stand there and puzzle it out, but it was too busy a place. There was the chance that someone would look their way or walk out and find them.

THEY FOUND another room. This one was empty. It was an office, large and sumptuous. It had a desk, littered with papers. Burckhardt stared at them, briefly at first—then, as the words on one of them caught his attention, with incredulous fascination.

He snatched up the topmost sheet, scanned it, and another, while Swanson was frenziedly searching through the drawers.

Burckhardt swore unbelievingly and dropped the papers to the desk.

Swanson, hardly noticing, yelped with delight: "Look!" He dragged a gun from the desk. "And it's loaded, too!"

Burckhardt stared at him blankly, trying to assimilate what he had read. Then, as he realized what Swanson had said, Burckhardt's eyes sparked. "Good man!" he cried. "We'll take it. We're getting out of here with that gun, Swanson. And we're going to the police! Not the cops in Tylerton, but the F.B.I., maybe. Take a look at this!"

The sheaf he handed Swanson was headed: "Test Area Progress Report. Subject: Marlin Cigarettes Campaign." It was mostly tabulated figures that made little sense to Burckhardt and Swanson, but at the end was a summary that said:

Although Test 47-K3 pulled nearly double the number of new users of any of the other tests conducted, it probably cannot be used in the field because of local sound-truck control ordinances.

The tests in the 47-K12 group were second best and our recommendation is that retests be conducted in this appeal, testing each of the three best campaigns with and without the addition of sampling techniques.

An alternative suggestion might be to proceed directly with the top appeal in the K12 series, if the client is unwilling to go to the expense of additional tests.

All of these forecast expectations have an 80% probability of being within one-half of one per cent of results forecast, and more than 99% probability of coming within 5%.

Swanson looked up from the paper into Burckhardt's eyes. "I don't get it," he complained.

Burckhardt said, "I don't blame you. It's crazy, but it fits the facts, Swanson, *it fits the facts*. They aren't Russians and they aren't Martians. These people are advertising men! Somehow—heaven knows how they did it—they've taken Tylerton over. They've got us, all of us, you and me and twenty or thirty thousand other people, right under their thumbs.

"Maybe they hypnotize us and maybe it's something else; but however they do it, what happens is that they let us live a day at a time. They pour advertising into us the whole damned day long. And at the end of the day, they see what happened—and then they wash the day out of our minds and start again the next day with different advertising."

S WANSON'S jaw was hanging. He managed to close it and swallow. "Nuts!" he said flatly. Burckhardt shook his head. "Sure, it sounds crazy—but this whole thing is crazy. How else would you explain it? You can't deny that most of Tylerton lives the same day over and over again. You've *seen* it! And that's the crazy part and we have to admit that that's true—unless we are the crazy ones. And once you admit that somebody, somehow, knows how to accomplish that, the rest of it makes all kinds of sense.

"Think of it, Swanson! They test every last detail before they spend a nickel on advertising! Do you
have any idea what that means? Lord knows how
much money is involved, but I know for a fact that
some companies spend twenty or thirty million dollars a year on advertising. Multiply it, say, by a hundred companies. Say that every one of them learns
how to cut its advertising cost by only ten per cent.
And that's peanuts, believe me!

"If they know in advance what's going to
work, they can cut their costs in half—maybe to less
than half, I don't know. But that's saving two or three
hundred million dollars a year—and if they pay only
ten or twenty per cent of that for the use of Tylerton,
it's still dirt cheap for them and a fortune for whoever
took over Tylerton."

Swanson licked his lips. "You mean," he offered hesitantly, "that we're a—well, a kind of captive
audience?"

Burckhardt frowned. "Not exactly." He paused
and thought for a minute. "You know how a doctor
tests something like penicillin? He sets up a series of
little colonies of germs on gelatine disks and he tries
the stuff on one after another, changing it a little each
time. Well, that's us—we're the germs, Swanson. Only
it's even more efficient than that. They don't have to
test more than one colony, because they can use it over
and over again."

It was too hard for Swanson to take in. He
only said: "What do we do about it?"

"We go to the police. They can't use human
beings for guinea pigs!"

"How do we get to the police?"

Burckhardt hesitated. "I think—" he began slowly. "Sure. This place is the office of somebody important. We've got a gun. We'll stay right here until he comes along. And he'll get us out of here."

Simple and direct. Swanson subsided and found a place to sit, against the wall, out of sight of the door. Burckhardt took up a position behind the door itself—

And waited.

THE WAIT was not as long as it might have been. Thirty minutes, perhaps. Then Burckhardt heard approaching voices and had time for a swift whisper to Swanson before he flattened himself against the wall.

It was a man's voice, and a girl's. The man was saying, "—reason why you couldn't report on the phone? You're ruining your whole day's test! What the devil's the matter with you, Janet?"

"I'm sorry, Mr. Dorchin," she said in a sweet, clear tone. "I thought it was important."

The man grumbled, "Important! One lousy unit out of twenty-one thousand."

"But it's the Burckhardt one, Mr. Dorchin. Again. And the way he got out of sight, he must have had some help."

"All right, all right. It doesn't matter, Janet; the Choco-Bite program is ahead of schedule anyhow. As long as you're this far, come on in the office and make out your worksheet. And don't worry about the Burckhardt business. He's probably just wandering around. We'll pick him up tonight and—"

They were inside the door. Burckhardt kicked it shut and pointed the gun.

"That's what you think," he said triumphantly.

It was worth the terrified hours, the bewildered sense of insanity, the confusion and fear. It was the most satisfying sensation Burckhardt had ever had in his life. The expression on the man's face was one he had read about but never actually seen: Dorchin's mouth fell open and his eyes went wide, and though he managed to make a sound that might have been a question, it was not in words.

The girl was almost as surprised. And Burckhardt, looking at her, knew why her voice had been so familiar. The girl was the one who had introduced herself to him as April Horn.

Dorchin recovered himself quickly. "Is this the one?" he asked sharply.

The girl said, "Yes."

Dorchin nodded. "I take it back. You were right. Uh, you—Burckhardt. What do you want?"

SWANSON piped up, "Watch him! He might have another gun."

"Search him then," Burckhardt said. "I'll tell you what we want, Dorchin. We want you to come along with us to the FBI and explain to them how you can get away with kidnapping twenty thousand people."

"Kidnapping?" Dorchin snorted. "That's ridiculous, man! Put that gun away—you can't get away with this!"

Burckhardt hefted the gun grimly. "I think I can."

Dorchin looked furious and sick—but, oddly, not afraid. "Damn it—" he started to bellow, then closed his mouth and swallowed. "Listen," he said persuasively, "you're making a big mistake. I haven't kidnapped anybody, believe me!"

"I don't believe you," said Burckhardt bluntly. "Why should I?"

"But it's true! Take my word for it!"

Burckhardt shook his head. "The FBI can take your word if they like. We'll find out. Now how do we get out of here?"

Dorchin opened his mouth to argue.

Burckhardt blazed: "Don't get in my way! I'm willing to kill you if I have to. Don't you understand that? I've gone through two days of hell and every second of it I blame on you. Kill you? It would be a pleasure and I don't have a thing in the world to lose! Get us out of here!"

Dorchin's face went suddenly opaque. He seemed about to move; but the blonde girl he had called Janet slipped between him and the gun.

"Please!" she begged Burckhardt. "You don't understand. You mustn't shoot!"

"*Get out of my way!*"

"But, Mr. Burckhardt—"

She never finished. Dorchin, his face unreadable, headed for the door. Burckhardt had been pushed one degree too far. He swung the gun, bellowing. The girl called out sharply. He pulled the trigger. Closing on him with pity and pleading in her eyes, she came again between the gun and the man.

Burckhardt aimed low instinctively, to cripple, not to kill. But his aim was not good.

The pistol bullet caught her in the pit of the stomach.

DORCHIN was out and away, the door slamming behind him, his footsteps racing into the distance.

Burckhardt hurled the gun across the room and jumped to the girl.

Swanson was moaning. "That finishes us, Burckhardt. Oh, why did you do it? We could have got away. We could have gone to the police. We were practically out of here! We—"

Burckhardt wasn't listening. He was kneeling beside the girl. She lay flat on her back, arms helter-skelter. There was no blood, hardly any sign of the wound; but the position in which she lay was one that no living human being could have held.

Yet she wasn't dead.

She wasn't dead—and Burckhardt, frozen beside her, thought: *She isn't alive, either.*

There was no pulse, but there was a rhythmic ticking of the outstretched fingers of one hand.

There was no sound of breathing, but there was a hissing, sizzling noise.

The eyes were open and they were looking at Burckhardt. There was neither fear nor pain in them, only a pity deeper than the Pit.

She said, through lips that writhed erratically, "Don't—worry, Mr. Burckhardt. I'm—all right."

Burckhardt rocked back on his haunches, staring. Where there should have been blood, there was a clean break of a substance that was not flesh; and a curl of thin golden-copper wire.

Burckhardt moistened his lips.

"You're a robot," he said.

The girl tried to nod. The twitching lips said, "I am. And so are you."

V

SWANSON, after a single inarticulate sound, walked over to the desk and sat staring at the wall. Burckhardt rocked back and forth beside the shattered puppet on the floor. He had no words.

The girl managed to say, "I'm—sorry all this happened." The lovely lips twisted into a rictus sneer, frightening on that smooth young face, until she got them under control. "Sorry," she said again. "The—nerve center was right about where the bullet hit. Makes it difficult to—control this body."

Burckhardt nodded automatically, accepting the apology. Robots. It was obvious, now that he knew it. In hindsight, it was inevitable. He thought of his mystic notions of hypnosis or Martians or something stranger still—idiotic, for the simple fact of created robots fitted the facts better and more economically.

All the evidence had been before him. The automatized factory, with its transplanted minds—why not transplant a mind into a humanoid robot, give it its original owner's features and form?

Could it know that it was a robot?

"All of us," Burckhardt said, hardly aware that he spoke out loud. "My wife and my secretary and you and the neighbors. All of us the same."

"No." The voice was stronger. "Not exactly the same, all of us. I chose it, you see. I—" this time the convulsed lips were not a random contortion of the nerves—"I was an ugly woman, Mr. Burckhardt, and nearly sixty years old. Life had passed me. And when Mr. Dorchin offered me the chance to live again as a beautiful girl, I jumped at the opportunity. Believe me, I *jumped*, in spite of its disadvantages. My flesh body is still alive—it is sleeping, while I am here. I could go back to it. But I never do."

"And the rest of us?"

"Different, Mr. Burckhardt. I work here. I'm carrying out Mr. Dorchin's orders, mapping the results of the advertising tests, watching you and the others live as he makes you live. I do it by choice, but you have no choice. Because, you see, you are dead."

"Dead?" cried Burckhardt; it was almost a scream.

The blue eyes looked at him unwinkingly and he knew that it was no lie. He swallowed, marveling at the intricate mechanisms that let him swallow, and sweat, and eat.

He said: "Oh. The explosion in my dream."

"It was no dream. You are right—the explosion. That was real and this plant was the cause of it. The storage tanks let go and what the blast didn't get, the fumes killed a little later. But almost everyone died in the blast, twenty-one thousand persons. You died with them and that was Dorchin's chance."

"The damned ghoul!" said Burckhardt.

THE TWISTED shoulders shrugged with an odd grace. "Why? You were gone. And you and all the others were what Dorchin wanted—a whole town, a perfect slice of America. It's as easy to transfer a pattern from a dead brain as a living one. Easier—the dead can't say no. Oh, it took work and money—the town was a wreck —but it was possible to rebuild it entirely, especially because it wasn't necessary to have all the details exact.

"There were the homes where even the brains had been utterly destroyed, and those are empty inside, and the cellars that needn't be too perfect, and the streets that hardly matter. And anyway, it only has to last for one day. The same day—June 15th—over and over again; and if someone finds something a little wrong, somehow, the discovery won't have time to snowball, wreck the validity of the tests, because all errors are canceled out at midnight."

The face tried to smile. "That's the dream, Mr. Burckhardt, that day of June 15th, because you never really lived it. It's a present from Mr. Dorchin, a dream that he gives you and then takes back at the end of the day, when he has all his figures on how many of you responded to what variation of which appeal, and the maintenance crews go down the tunnel to go through the whole city, washing out the new dream with their little electronic drains, and then the dream starts all over again. On June 15th.

"Always June 15th, because June 14th is the last day any of you can remember alive. Sometimes the crews miss someone—as they missed you, because you were under your boat. But it doesn't matter. The ones who are missed give themselves away if they show it—and if they don't, it doesn't affect the test. But they don't drain us, the ones of us who work for Dorchin. We sleep when the power is turned off, just as you do. When we wake up, though, we remember." The face contorted wildly. "If I could only forget!"

Burckhardt said unbelievingly, "All this to sell merchandise! It must have cost millions!"

The robot called April Horn said, "It did. But it has made millions for Dorchin, too. And that's not the end of it. Once he finds the master words that make people act, do you suppose he will stop with that? Do you suppose—"

The door opened, interrupting her. Burckhardt whirled. Belatedly remembering Dorchin's flight, he raised the gun.

"Don't shoot," ordered the voice calmly. It was not Dorchin; it was another robot, this one not disguised with the clever plastics and cosmetics, but shining and plain. It said metallically: "Forget it, Burckhardt. You're not accomplishing anything. Give me that gun before you do any more damage. Give it to me *now*."

BURCKHARDT bellowed angrily. The gleam on this robot torso was steel; Burckhardt was not at all sure that his bullets would pierce it, or do much harm if they did. He would have put it to the test—

But from behind him came a whimpering, scurrying whirlwind; its name was Swanson, hysterical with fear. He catapulted into Burckhardt and sent him sprawling, the gun flying free.

"Please!" begged Swanson incoherently, prostrate before the steel robot. "He would have shot you —please don't hurt me! Let me work for you, like that girl. I'll do anything, anything you tell me—"

The robot voice said. "We don't need your help." It took two precise steps and stood over the gun —and spurned it, left it lying on the floor.

The wrecked blonde robot said, without emotion, "I doubt that I can hold out much longer, Mr. Dorchin."

"Disconnect if you have to," replied the steel robot.

Burckhardt blinked. "But you're not Dorchin!"

The steel robot turned deep eyes on him. "I am," it said. "Not in the flesh—but this is the body I am using at the moment. I doubt that you can damage this one with the gun. The other robot body was more vulnerable. Now will you stop this nonsense? I don't want to have to damage you; you're too expensive for that. Will you just sit down and let the maintenance crews adjust you?"

Swanson groveled. "You—you won't punish us?"

The steel robot had no expression, but its voice was almost surprised. "Punish you?" it repeated on a rising note. "How?"

Swanson quivered as though the word had been a whip; but Burckhardt flared: "Adjust *him*, if he'll let you—but not me! You're going to have to do me a lot of damage, Dorchin. I don't care what I cost or how much trouble it's going to be to put me back together again. But I'm going out of that door! If you want to stop me, you'll have to kill me. You won't stop me any other way!"

The steel robot took a half-step toward him, and Burckhardt involuntarily checked his stride. He stood poised and shaking, ready for death, ready for attack, ready for anything that might happen.

Ready for anything except what did happen. For Dorchin's steel body merely stepped aside, between Burckhardt and the gun, but leaving the door free.

"Go ahead," invited the steel robot. "Nobody's stopping you."

OUTSIDE the door, Burckhardt brought up sharp. It was insane of Dorchin to let him go! Robot or flesh, victim or beneficiary, there was nothing to stop him from going to the FBI or whatever law he could find away from Dorchin's synthetic empire, and telling his story. Surely the corporations who paid Dorchin for test results had no notion of the ghoul's technique he used; Dorchin would have to keep it from them, for the breath of publicity would put a stop to it. Walking out meant death, perhaps—but at that moment in his pseudo-life, death was no terror for Burckhardt.

There was no one in the corridor. He found a window and stared out of it. There was Tylerton—an ersatz city, but looking so real and familiar that Burckhardt almost imagined the whole episode a dream. It was no dream, though. He was certain of that in his heart and equally certain that nothing in Tylerton could help him now.

It had to be the other direction.

It took him a quarter of an hour to find a way, but he found it—skulking through the corridors, dodging the suspicion of footsteps, knowing for certain that his hiding was in vain, for Dorchin was undoubtedly aware of every move he made. But no one stopped him, and he found another door.

It was a simple enough door from the inside. But when he opened it and stepped out, it was like nothing he had ever seen.

First there was light—brilliant, incredible, blinding light. Burckhardt blinked upward, unbelieving and afraid.

He was standing on a ledge of smooth, finished metal. Not a dozen yards from his feet, the ledge dropped sharply away; he hardly dared approach the brink, but even from where he stood he could see no bottom to the chasm before him. And the gulf extended out of sight into the glare on either side of him.

NO WONDER Dorchin could so easily give him his freedom! From the factory, there was nowhere to go—but how incredible this fantastic gulf, how impossible the hundred white and blinding suns that hung above!

A voice by his side inquired, "Burckhardt?" And thunder rolled the name, mutteringly soft, back and forth in the abyss before him.

Burckhardt wet his lips. "Y-yes?" he croaked.

"This is Dorchin. Not a robot this time, but Dorchin in the flesh, talking to you on a hand mike.

Now you have seen, Burckhardt. Now will you be reasonable and let the maintenance crews take over?"

Burckhardt stood paralyzed. One of the moving mountains in the blinding glare came toward him.

It towered hundreds of feet over his head; he stared up at its top, squinting helplessly into the light.

It looked like—

Impossible!

The voice in the loudspeaker at the door said, "Burckhardt?" But he was unable to answer.

A heavy rumbling sigh. "I see," said the voice. "You finally understand. There's no place to go. You know it now. I could have told you, but you might not have believed me, so it was better for you to see it yourself. And after all, Burckhardt, why would I reconstruct a city just the way it was before? I'm a businessman; I count costs. If a thing has to be full-scale, I build it that way. But there wasn't any need to in this case."

From the mountain before him, Burckhardt helplessly saw a lesser cliff descend carefully toward him. It was long and dark, and at the end of it was whiteness, five-fingered whiteness...

"Poor little Burckhardt," crooned the loudspeaker, while the echoes rumbled through the enormous chasm that was only a workshop. "It must have been quite a shock for you to find out you were living in a town built on a table top."

VI

I T WAS the morning of June 15th, and Guy Burckhardt woke up screaming out of a dream.

It had been a monstrous and incomprehensible dream, of explosions and shadowy figures that were not men and terror beyond words.

He shuddered and opened his eyes.

Outside his bedroom window, a hugely amplified voice was howling.

Burckhardt stumbled over to the window and stared outside. There was an out-of-season chill to the air, more like October than June; but the scent was normal enough—except for the sound-truck that squatted at curbside halfway down the block. Its speaker horns blared:

"Are you a coward? Are you a fool? Are you going to let crooked politicians steal the country from you? NO! Are you going to put up with four more years of graft and crime? NO! Are you going to vote straight Federal Party all up and down the ballot? YES! *You just bet you are!*"

Sometimes he screams, sometimes he wheedles, threatens, begs, cajoles... but his voice goes on and on through one June 15th after another.

YEAR OF THE BIG THAW
by MARION ZIMMER BRADLEY

Mr. Emmett did his duty by the visitor from another world—never doubting the right of it.

YOU SAY that Matthew is your own son, Mr. Emmett?

Yes, Rev'rend Doane, and a better boy never stepped, if I say it as shouldn't. I've trusted him to drive team for me since he was eleven, and you can't say more than that for a farm boy. Way back when he was a little shaver so high, when the war came on, he was bounden he was going to sail with this Admiral Farragut. You know boys that age—like runaway colts. I couldn't see no good in his being cabin boy on some tarnation Navy ship and I told him so. If he'd wanted to sail out on a whaling ship, I 'low I'd have let him go. But Marthy—that's the boy's Ma—took on so that Matt stayed home. Yes, he's a good boy and a good son.

We'll miss him a powerful lot if he gets this scholarship thing. But I 'low it'll be good for the boy to get some learnin' besides what he gets in the school here. It's right kind of you, Rev'rend, to look over this application thing for me.

WELL, IF *he is your own son, Mr. Emmett, why did you write 'birthplace unknown' on the line here?*

Rev'rend Doane, I'm glad you asked me that question. I've been turnin' it over in my mind and I've jest about come to the conclusion it wouldn't be no-how fair to hold it back. I didn't lie when I said Matt was my son, because he's been a good son to me and Marthy. But I'm not his Pa and Marthy ain't his Ma, so could be I stretched the truth jest a mite. Rev'rend Doane, it's a tarnal funny yarn but I'll walk into the meetin' house and swear to it on a stack o'Bibles as thick as a cord of wood.

You know I've been farming the old Corning place these past seven year? It's good flat Connecticut bottom-land, but it isn't like our land up in Hampshire where I was born and raised. My Pa called it the Hampshire Grants and all that was King's land when *his* Pa came in there and started farming at the foot of Scuttock Mountain. That's Injun for fires, folks say, because the Injuns used to build fires up there in the spring for some of their heathen doodads. Anyhow, up there in the mountains we see a tarnal power of quare things.

Y OU CALL to mind the year we had the big thaw, about twelve years before the war? You mind the blizzard that year? I heard tell it spread down most to York. And at Fort Orange, the place they call Albany now, the Hudson froze right over, so they say. But those York folks do a sight of exaggerating, I'm told.

Anyhow, when the ice went out there was an almighty good thaw all over, and when the snow run off Scuttock mountain there was a good-sized hunk of farmland in our valley went under water. The crick on my farm flowed over the bank and there was a foot of water in the cowshed, and down in the swimmin' hole in the back pasture wasn't nothing but a big gully fifty foot and more across, rushing through the pasture, deep as a lake and brown as the old cow. You know freshet-floods? Full up with sticks and stones and old dead trees and somebody's old shed floatin' down the middle. And I swear to goodness, Parson, that stream was running along so fast I saw four-inch cobble-stones floating and bumping along.

I tied the cow and the calf and Kate—she was our white mare; you mind she went lame last year and I had to shoot her, but she was just a young mare then and skittish as all get-out—but she was a good little mare.

Anyhow, I tied the whole kit and caboodle of them in the woodshed up behind the house, where they'd be dry, then I started to get the milk-pail. Right then I heard the gosh-awfullest screech I ever heard in my life. Sounded like thunder and a freshet and a forest-fire all at once. I dropped the milk-pail as I heard Marthy scream inside the house, and I run outside. Marthy was already there in the yard and she points up in the sky and yelled, "Look up yander!"

We stood looking up at the sky over Scuttuck mountain where there was a great big—shoot now, I d'no as I can call its name but it was like a trail of fire in the sky, and it was makin' the dangdest racket you ever heard, Rev'rend. Looked kind of like one of them Fourth-of-July skyrockets, but it was big as a house. Marthy was screaming and she grabbed me and hollered, "Hez! Hez, what in tunket is it?" And when Marthy cusses like that, Rev'rend, she don't know what she's saying, she's so scared.

I was plumb scared myself. I heard Liza— that's our young-un, Liza Grace, that got married to the Taylor boy. I heard her crying on the stoop, and she came flying out with her pinny all black and hollered to Marthy that the pea soup was burning. Marthy let out another screech and ran for the house. That's a woman for you. So I quietened Liza down some and I went in and told Marthy it weren't no more than one of them shooting stars. Then I went and did the milking.

But you know, while we were sitting down to supper there came the most awful grinding, screeching, pounding crash I ever heard. Sounded if it were in the back pasture but the house shook as if somethin' had hit it.

Marthy jumped a mile and I never saw such a look on her face.

"Hez, what was that?" she asked.

"Shoot, now, nothing but the freshet," I told her.

But she kept right on about it. "You reckon that shooting star fell in our back pasture, Hez?"

"Well, now, I don't 'low it did nothing like that," I told her. But she was jittery as an old hen and it weren't like her nohow. She said it sounded like trouble and I finally quieted her down by saying I'd saddle Kate up and go have a look. I kind of thought, though I didn't tell Marthy, that somebody's house had floated away in the freshet and run aground in our back pasture.

S O I SADDLED up Kate and told Marthy to get some hot rum ready in case there was some poor soul run aground back there. And I rode Kate back to the back pasture.

It was mostly uphill because the top of the pasture is on high ground, and it sloped down to the crick on the other side of the rise.

Well, I reached the top of the hill and looked down. The crick were a regular river now, rushing along like Niagary. On the other side of it was a stand of timber, then the slope of Scuttuck mountain. And I saw right away the long streak where all the timber had been cut out in a big scoop with roots standing up in the air and a big slide of rocks down to the water.

It was still raining a mite and the ground was sloshy and squanchy under foot. Kate scrunched her hooves and got real balky, not likin' it a bit. When we got to the top of the pasture she started to whine and whicker and stamp, and no matter how loud I whoa'ed she kept on a-stamping and I was plumb scared she'd pitch me off in the mud. Then I started to smell a funny smell, like somethin' burning. Now, don't ask me

how anything could burn in all that water, because I
don't know.

WHEN WE came up on the rise I saw
the contraption.
Rev'rend, it was the most
tarnal crazy contraption I ever saw in
my life. It was bigger nor my cowshed and it was long
and thin and as shiny as Marthy's old pewter pitcher
her Ma brought from England. It had a pair of red
rods sticking out behind and a crazy globe fitted up
where the top ought to be. It was stuck in the mud,
turned halfway over on the little slide of roots and
rocks, and I could see what had happened, all right.

The thing must have been—now, Rev'rend,
you can say what you like but that thing must have
flew across Scuttuck and landed on the slope in the
trees, then turned over and slid down the hill. That
must have been the crash we heard. The rods weren't
just red, they were *red-hot*. I could hear them sizzle as
the rain hit 'em.

In the middle of the infernal contraption there
was a door, and it hung all to-other as if every hinge
on it had been wrenched halfway off. As I pushed old
Kate alongside it I heared somebody hollering alongside the contraption. I didn't nohow get the words but
it must have been for help, because I looked down and
there was a man a-flopping along in the water.

He was a big fellow and he wasn't swimming,
just thrashin' and hollering. So I pulled off my coat
and boots and hove in after him. The stream was running fast but he was near the edge and I managed to

catch on to an old tree-root and hang on, keeping his head out of the water till I got my feet aground. Then I hauled him onto the bank. Up above me Kate was still whinnying and raising Ned and I shouted at her as I bent over the man.

Wal, Rev'rend, he sure did give me a surprise —weren't no proper man I'd ever seed before. He was wearing some kind of red clothes, real shiny and sort of stretchy and not wet from the water, like you'd expect, but dry and it felt like that silk and India-rubber stuff mixed together. And it was such a bright red that at first I didn't see the blood on it. When I did I knew he were a goner. His chest were all stove in, smashed to pieces. One of the old tree-roots must have jabbed him as the current flung him down. I thought he were dead already, but then he opened up his eyes.

A funny color they were, greeny yellow. And I swear, Rev'rend, when he opened them eyes I *felt* he was readin' my mind. I thought maybe he might be one of them circus fellers in their flying contraptions that hang at the bottom of a balloon.

He spoke to me in English, kind of choky and stiff, not like Joe the Portygee sailor or like those tarnal dumb Frenchies up Canady way, but—well, funny. He said, "My baby—in ship. Get—baby..." He tried to say more but his eyes went shut and he moaned hard.

I YELPED, "Godamighty!" 'Scuse me, Rev'rend, but I was so blame upset that's just what I did say, "Godamighty, man, you mean there's a baby in that there dingfol contraption?" The man just moaned so after spreadin' my coat around the man a little bit I just plunged in that there river again.

Rev'rend, I heard tell once about some tom-fool idiot going over Niagary in a barrel, and I tell you it was like that when I tried crossin' that freshet to reach the contraption.

I went under and down, and was whacked by floating sticks and whirled around in the freshet. But somehow, I d'no how except by the pure grace of God, I got across that raging torrent and clumb up to where the crazy dingfol machine was sitting.

Ship, he'd called it. But that were no ship, Rev'rend, it was some flying dragon kind of thing. It was a real scarey lookin' thing but I clumb up to the little door and hauled myself inside it. And, sure enough, there was other people in the cabin, only they was all dead.

There was a lady and a man and some kind of an animal looked like a bobcat only smaller, with a funny-shaped rooster-comb thing on its head. They all —even the cat-thing—was wearing those shiny, stretchy clo'es. And they all was so battered and smashed I didn't even bother to hunt for their heart-beats. I could see by a look they was dead as a doornail.

THEN I heard a funny little whimper, like a kitten, and in a funny, rubber-cushioned thing there's a little boy baby, looked about six months old. He was howling lusty enough, and when I lifted him out of the cradle kind of thing, I saw why. That boy baby, he was wet, and his little arm was twisted under him. That there flying contraption must have smashed down awful hard, but that rubber hammock was so soft and cushiony all it did to him was jolt him good.

I looked around but I couldn't find anything to wrap him in. And the baby didn't have a stitch on him except a sort of spongy paper diaper, wet as sin. So I finally lifted up the lady, who had a long cape thing around her, and I took the cape off her real gentle. I knew she was dead and she wouldn't be needin' it, and that boy baby would catch his death if I took him out bare-naked like that. She was probably the baby's Ma; a right pretty woman she was but smashed up something shameful.

So anyhow, to make a long story short, I got that baby boy back across that Niagary falls somehow, and laid him down by his Pa. The man opened his eyes kind, and said in a choky voice, "Take care—baby."

I told him I would, and said I'd try to get him up to the house where Marthy could doctor him. The man told me not to bother. "I dying," he says. "We come from planet—star up there—crash here—" His voice trailed off into a language I couldn't understand, and he looked like he was praying.

I bent over him and held his head on my knees real easy, and I said, "Don't worry, mister, I'll take care of your little fellow until your folks come after him. Before God I will."

So the man closed his eyes and I said, *Our Father which art in Heaven*, and when I got through he was dead.

I got him up on Kate, but he was cruel heavy for all he was such a tall and skinny fellow. Then I wrapped that there baby up in the cape thing and took him home and give him to Marthy. And the next day I buried the fellow in the south medder and next meetin' day we had the baby baptized Matthew Daniel Emmett, and brung him up just like our own kids. That's all.

ALL? MR. *Emmett, didn't you ever find out where that ship really came from?*

Why, Rev'rend, he said it come from a star. Dying men don't lie, you know that. I asked the Teacher about them planets he mentioned and she says that on one of the planets—can't rightly remember the name, March or Mark or something like that—she says some big scientist feller with a telescope saw canals on that planet, and they'd hev to be pretty near as big as this-here Erie canal to see them so far off. And if they could build canals on that planet I d'no why they couldn't build a flying machine.

I went back the next day when the water was down a little, to see if I couldn't get the rest of them folks and bury them, but the flying machine had broke up and washed down the crick.

Marthy's still got the cape thing. She's a powerful saving woman. We never did tell Matt, though. Might make him feel funny to think he didn't really b'long to us.

B UT—BUT—*Mr. Emmett, didn't anybody ask questions about the baby—where you got it?*

Well, now, I'll 'low they was curious, because Marthy hadn't been in the family way and they knew it. But up here folks minds their own business pretty well, and I jest let them wonder. I told Liza Grace I'd found her new little brother in the back pasture, and o'course it was the truth. When Liza Grace growed up she thought it was jest one of those yarns old folks tell the little shavers.

A ND HAS *Matthew ever shown any differences from the other children that you could see?*

Well, Rev'rend, not so's you could notice it. He's powerful smart, but his real Pa and Ma must have been right smart too to build a flying contraption that could come so far.

O'course, when he were about twelve years old he started reading folks' minds, which didn't seem exactly right. He'd tell Marthy what I was thinkin' and things like that. He was just at the pesky age. Liza Grace and Minnie were both a-courtin' then, and he'd drive their boy friends crazy telling them what Liza Grace and Minnie were a-thinking and tease the gals by telling them what the boys were thinking about.

There weren't no harm in the boy, though, it was all teasing. But it just weren't decent, somehow. So I tuk him out behind the woodshed and give his britches a good dusting just to remind him that that kind of thing weren't polite nohow. And Rev'rend Doane, he ain't never done it sence.

YOUTH

by ISAAC ASIMOV

*Red and Slim found the two strange little animals
the morning after they heard the thunder sounds.
They knew that they could never show
their new pets to their parents.*

THERE was a spatter of pebbles against the window and the youngster stirred in his sleep. Another, and he was awake.

He sat up stiffly in bed. Seconds passed while he interpreted his strange surroundings. He wasn't in his own home, of course. This was out in the country. It was colder than it should be and there was green at the window.

"Slim!"

The call was a hoarse, urgent whisper, and the youngster bounded to the open window.

Slim wasn't his real name, but the new friend he had met the day before had needed only one look at his slight figure to say, "You're Slim." He added, "I'm Red."

Red wasn't his real name, either, but its appropriateness was obvious. They were friends instantly with the quick unquestioning friendship of young ones not yet quite in adolescence, before even the first stains of adulthood began to make their appearance.

Slim cried, "Hi, Red!" and waved cheerfully, still blinking the sleep out of himself.

Red kept to his croaking whisper, "Quiet! You want to wake somebody?"

Slim noticed all at once that the sun scarcely topped the low hills in the east, that the shadows were long and soft, and that the grass was wet.

Slim said, more softly, "What's the matter?"

Red only waved for him to come out.

Slim dressed quickly, gladly confining his morning wash to the momentary sprinkle of a little lukewarm water. He let the air dry the exposed portions of his body as he ran out, while bare skin grew wet against the dewy grass.

Red said, "You've got to be quiet. If Mom wakes up or Dad or your Dad or even any of the hands then it'll be 'Come on in or you'll catch your death of cold.'"

He mimicked voice and tone faithfully, so that Slim laughed and thought that there had never been so funny a fellow as Red.

Slim said, eagerly, "Do you come out here every day like this, Red? Real early? It's like the whole world is just yours, isn't it, Red? No one else around and all like that." He felt proud at being allowed entrance into this private world.

Red stared at him sidelong. He said carelessly, "I've been up for hours. Didn't you hear it last night?"

"Hear what?"

"Thunder."

"Was there a thunderstorm?" Slim never slept through a thunderstorm.

"I guess not. But there was thunder. I heard it, and then I went to the window and it wasn't raining. It was all stars and the sky was just getting sort of almost gray. You know what I mean?"

Slim had never seen it so, but he nodded.

"So I just thought I'd go out," said Red.

T HEY WALKED along the grassy side of the concrete road that split the panorama right down the middle all the way down to where it vanished among the hills. It was so old that Red's father couldn't tell Red when it had been built. It didn't have a crack or a rough spot in it.

Red said, "Can you keep a secret?"

"Sure, Red. What kind of a secret?"

"Just a secret. Maybe I'll tell you and maybe I won't. I don't know yet." Red broke a long, supple stem from a fern they passed, methodically stripped it of its leaflets and swung what was left whip-fashion. For a moment, he was on a wild charger, which reared and champed under his iron control. Then he got tired, tossed the whip aside and stowed the charger away in a corner of his imagination for future use.

He said, "There'll be a circus around."

Slim said, "That's no secret. I knew that. My Dad told me even before we came here—"

"That's not the secret. Fine secret! Ever see a circus?"

"Oh, sure. You bet."

"Like it?"

"Say, there isn't anything I like better."

Red was watching out of the corner of his eyes again. "Ever think you would like to be with a circus? I mean, for good?"

Slim considered, "I guess not. I think I'll be an astronomer like my Dad. I think he wants me to be."

"Huh! Astronomer!" said Red.

Slim felt the doors of the new, private world closing on him and astronomy became a thing of dead stars and black, empty space.

He said, placatingly, "A circus *would* be more fun."

"You're just saying that."

"No, I'm not. I mean it."

Red grew argumentative. "Suppose you had a chance to join the circus right now. What would you do?"

"I—I—"

"See!" Red affected scornful laughter.

Slim was stung. "I'd join up."

"Go on."

"Try me."

Red whirled at him, strange and intense. "You meant that? You want to go in with me?"

"HAT DO you mean?" Slim stepped back a bit, surprised by the unexpected challenge.

"I got something that can get us into the circus. Maybe someday we can even have a circus of our own. We could be the biggest circus-fellows in the world. That's if you want to go in with me. Otherwise—Well, I guess I can do it on my own. I just thought: Let's give good old Slim a chance."

The world was strange and glamorous, and Slim said, "Sure thing, Red. I'm in! What is it, huh, Red? Tell me what it is."

"Figure it out. What's the most important thing in circuses?"

Slim thought desperately. He wanted to give the right answer. Finally, he said, "Acrobats?"

"Holy Smokes! I wouldn't go five steps to look at acrobats."

"I don't know then."

"Animals, that's what! What's the best side-show? Where are the biggest crowds? Even in the main rings the best acts are animal acts." There was no doubt in Red's voice.

"Do you think so?"

"Everyone thinks so. You ask anyone. Anyway, I found animals this morning. Two of them."

"And you've got them?"

"Sure. That's the secret. Are you telling?"

"Of course not."

"Okay. I've got them in the barn. Do you want to see them?"

They were almost at the barn; its huge open door black. Too black. They had been heading there all the time. Slim stopped in his tracks.

He tried to make his words casual. "Are they big?"

"Would I fool with them if they were big? They can't hurt you. They're only about so long. I've got them in a cage."

They were in the barn now and Slim saw the large cage suspended from a hook in the roof. It was covered with stiff canvas.

Red said, "We used to have some bird there or something. Anyway, they can't get away from there. Come on, let's go up to the loft."

They clambered up the wooden stairs and Red hooked the cage toward them.

Slim pointed and said, "There's sort of a hole in the canvas."

Red frowned. "How'd that get there?" He lifted the canvas, looked in, and said, with relief, "They're still there."

"The canvas appeared to be burned," worried Slim.

"You want to look, or don't you?"

Slim nodded slowly. He wasn't sure he wanted to, after all. They might be—

But the canvas had been jerked off and there they were. Two of them, the way Red said. They were small, and sort of disgusting-looking. The animals moved quickly as the canvas lifted and were on the side toward the youngsters. Red poked a cautious finger at them.

"Watch out," said Slim, in agony.

"They don't hurt you," said Red. "Ever see any-thing like them?"

"No."

"Can't you see how a circus would jump at a chance to have these?"

"Maybe they're too small for a circus."

Red looked annoyed. He let go the cage which swung back and forth pendulum-fashion. "You're just trying to back out, aren't you?"

"No, I'm not. It's just—"

"They're not too small, don't worry. Right now, I've only got one worry."

"What's that?"

"Well, I've got to keep them till the circus comes, don't I? I've got to figure out what to feed them meanwhile."

The cage swung and the little trapped crea-tures clung to its bars, gesturing at the youngsters with queer, quick motions—almost as though they were intelligent.

II

T HE ASTRONOMER entered the dining room with decorum. He felt very much the guest.

He said, "Where are the young-sters? My son isn't in his room."

The Industrialist smiled. "They've been out for hours. However, breakfast was forced into them among the women some time ago, so there is nothing to worry about. Youth, Doctor, youth!"

"Youth!" The word seemed to depress the Astronomer.

They ate breakfast in silence. The Industrialist said once, "You really think they'll come. The day looks so—*normal*."

The Astronomer said, "They'll come."

That was all.

Afterward the Industrialist said, "You'll pardon me. I can't conceive your playing so elaborate a hoax. You really spoke to them?"

"As I speak to you. At least, in a sense. They can project thoughts."

"I gathered that must be so from your letter. How, I wonder."

"I could not say. I asked them and, of course, they were vague. Or perhaps it was just that I could not understand. It involves a projector for the focussing of thought and, even more than that, conscious attention on the part of both projector and receptor. It was quite a while before I realized they were trying to think at me. Such thought-projectors may be part of the science they will give us."

"Perhaps," said the Industrialist. "Yet think of the changes it would bring to society. A thought-projector!"

"Why not? Change would be good for us."

"I don't think so."

"It is only in old age that change is unwelcome," said the Astronomer, "and races can be old as well as individuals."

The Industrialist pointed out the window. "You see that road. It was built Beforethewars. I don't know exactly when. It is as good now as the day it was built. We couldn't possibly duplicate it now. The race was young when that was built, eh?"

"Then? Yes! At least they weren't afraid of new things."

"No. I wish they had been. Where is the society of Beforethewars? Destroyed, Doctor! What good were youth and new things? We are better off now. The world is peaceful and jogs along. The race goes nowhere but after all, there is nowhere to go. *They* proved that. The men who built the road. I will speak with your visitors as I agreed, if they come. But I think I will only ask them to go."

"The race is not going nowhere," said the Astronomer, earnestly. "It is going toward final destruction. My university has a smaller student body each year. Fewer books are written. Less work is done. An old man sleeps in the sun and his days are peaceful and unchanging, but each day finds him nearer death all the same."

"Well, well," said the Industrialist.

"No, don't dismiss it. Listen. Before I wrote you, I investigated your position in the planetary economy."

"And you found me solvent?" interrupted the Industrialist, smiling.

"Why, yes. Oh, I see, you are joking. And yet —perhaps the joke is not far off. You are less solvent than your father and he was less solvent than his father. Perhaps your son will no longer be solvent. It becomes too troublesome for the planet to support even the industries that still exist, though they are toothpicks to the oak trees of Beforethewars. We will be back to village economy and then to what? The caves?"

"And infusion of fresh technological knowledge will be the changing of all that?"

"Not just the new knowledge. Rather the whole effect of change, of a broadening of horizons. Look, sir, I chose you to approach in this matter not only because you were rich and influential with government officials, but because you had an unusual reputation, for these days, of daring to break with tradition. Our people will resist change and you would know how to handle them, to see to it that—that—"

"That the youth of the race is revived?"

"Yes."

"With its atomic bombs?"

"The atomic bombs," returned the Astronomer, "need not be the end of civilization. These visitors of mine had their atomic bomb, or whatever their equivalent was on their own worlds, and survived it, because they didn't give up. Don't you see? It wasn't the bomb that defeated us, but our own shell shock. This may be the last chance to reverse the process."

"TELL ME," said the Industrialist, "what do these friends from space want in return?"

The Astronomer hesitated. He said, "I will be truthful with you. They come from a denser planet. Ours is richer in the lighter atoms."

"They want magnesium? Aluminum?"

"No, sir. Carbon and hydrogen. They want coal and oil."

"Really?"

The Astronomer said, quickly, "You are going to ask why creatures who have mastered space travel, and therefore atomic power, would want coal and oil. I can't answer that."

The Industrialist smiled. "But I can. This is the best evidence yet of the truth of your story. Superficially, atomic power would seem to preclude the use of coal and oil. However, quite apart from the energy gained by their combustion they remain, and always will remain, the basic raw material for all organic chemistry. Plastics, dyes, pharmaceuticals, solvents. Industry could not exist without them, even in an atomic age. Still, if coal and oil are the low price for which they would sell us the troubles and tortures of racial youth, my answer is that the commodity would be dear if offered gratis."

The Astronomer sighed and said, "There are the boys!"

They were visible through the open window, standing together in the grassy field and lost in animated conversation. The Industrialist's son pointed imperiously and the Astronomer's son nodded and made off at a run toward the house.

The Industrialist said, "There is the Youth you speak of. Our race has as much of it as it ever had."

"Yes, but we age them quickly and pour them into the mold."

Slim scuttled into the room, the door banging behind him.

The Astronomer said, in mild disapproval, "What's this?"

Slim looked up in surprise and came to a halt. "I beg your pardon. I didn't know anyone was here. I am sorry to have interrupted." His enunciation was almost painfully precise.

The Industrialist said, "It's all right, youngster."

But the Astronomer said, "Even if you had been entering an empty room, son, there would be no cause for slamming a door."

"Nonsense," insisted the Industrialist. "The youngster has done no harm. You simply scold him for being young. You, with your views!"

He said to Slim, "Come here, lad."

Slim advanced slowly.

"How do you like the country, eh?"

"Very much, sir, thank you."

"My son has been showing you about the place, has he?"

"Yes, sir. Red—I mean—"

"No, no. Call him Red. I call him that myself. Now tell me, what are you two up to, eh?"

Slim looked away. "Why—just exploring, sir."

The Industrialist turned to the Astronomer. "There you are, youthful curiosity and adventure-lust. The race has not yet lost it."

Slim said, "Sir?"

"Yes, lad."

The youngster took a long time in getting on with it. He said, "Red sent me in for something good to eat, but I don't exactly know what he meant. I didn't like to say so."

"Why, just ask cook. She'll have something good for young'uns to eat."

"Oh, no, sir. I mean for animals."

"For animals?"

"Yes, sir. What do animals eat?"

The Astronomer said, "I am afraid my son is city-bred."

"Well," said the Industrialist, "there's no harm in that. What kind of an animal, lad?"

"A small one, sir."

"Then try grass or leaves, and if they don't want that, nuts or berries would probably do the trick."

"Thank you, sir." Slim ran out again, closing the door gently behind him.

The Astronomer said, "Do you suppose they've trapped an animal alive?" He was obviously perturbed.

"That's common enough. There's no shooting on my estate and it's tame country, full of rodents and small creatures. Red is always coming home with pets of one sort or another. They rarely maintain his interest for long."

He looked at the wall clock. "Your friends should have been here by now, shouldn't they?"

III

THE SWAYING had come to a halt and it was dark. The Explorer was not comfortable in the alien air. It felt as thick as soup and he had to breathe shallowly. Even so—

He reached out in a sudden need for company. The Merchant was warm to the touch. His breathing was rough, he moved in an occasional spasm, and was obviously asleep. The Explorer hesitated and decided not to wake him. It would serve no real purpose.

There would be no rescue, of course. That was the penalty paid for the high profits which unrestrained competition could lead to. The Merchant who opened a new planet could have a ten year monopoly of its trade, which he might hug to himself or, more likely, rent out to all comers at a stiff price. It followed that planets were searched for in secrecy and, preferably, away from the usual trade routes. In a case such as theirs, then, there was little or no chance that another ship would come within range of their sub-etherics except for the most improbable of coincidences. Even if they were in their ship, that is, rather than in this—this—*cage*.

The Explorer grasped the thick bars. Even if they blasted those away, as they could, they would be stuck too high in open air for leaping.

I T WAS too bad. They had landed twice before in the scout-ship. They had established contact with the natives who were grotesquely huge, but mild and unaggressive. It was obvious that they had once owned a flourishing technology, but hadn't faced up to the consequences of such a technology. It would have been a wonderful market.

And it was a tremendous world. The Merchant, especially, had been taken aback. He had known the figures that expressed the planet's diameter, but from a distance of two light-seconds, he had stood at the visi-plate and muttered, "Unbelievable!"

"Oh, there are larger worlds," the Explorer said. It wouldn't do for an Explorer to be too easily impressed.

"Inhabited?"

"Well, no."

"Why, you could drop your planet into that large ocean and drown it."

The Explorer smiled. It was a gentle dig at his Arcturian homeland, which was smaller than most planets. He said, "Not quite."

The Merchant followed along the line of his thoughts. "And the inhabitants are large in proportion to their world?" He sounded as though the news struck him less favorably now.

"Nearly ten times our height."

"Are you sure they are friendly?"

"That is hard to say. Friendship between alien intelligences is an imponderable. They are not dangerous, I think. We've come across other groups that could not maintain equilibrium after the atomic war stage and you know the results. Introversion. Retreat. Gradual decadence and increasing gentleness."

"Even if they are such monsters?"

"The principle remains."

It was about then that the Explorer felt the heavy throbbing of the engines.

He frowned and said, "We are descending a bit too quickly."

There had been some speculation on the dangers of landing some hours before. The planetary target was a huge one for an oxygen-water world. Though it lacked the immense size of the uninhabitable hydrogen-ammonia planets and its low density made its surface gravity fairly normal, its gravitational forces fell off but slowly with distance. In short, its gravitational potential was high and the ship's Calculator was a run-of-the-mill model not designed to plot landing trajectories at that potential range. That meant the Pilot would have to use manual controls.

It would have been wiser to install a more high-powered model, but that would have meant a trip to some outpost of civilization; lost time; perhaps a lost secret. The Merchant demanded an immediate landing.

The Merchant felt it necessary to defend his position now. He said angrily to the Explorer, "Don't you think the Pilot knows his job? He landed you safely twice before."

Yes, thought the Explorer, but in a scout-ship, not in this unmaneuverable freighter. Aloud, he said nothing.

He kept his eye on the visi-plate. They were descending too quickly. There was no room for doubt. Much too quickly.

The Merchant said, peevishly, "Why do you keep silence?"

"Well, then, if you wish me to speak, I would suggest that you strap on your Floater and help me prepare the Ejector."

The Pilot fought a noble fight. He was no beginner. The atmosphere, abnormally high and thick in the gravitational potential of this world whipped and burned about the ship, but to the very last it looked as though he might bring it under control despite that.

He even maintained course, following the extrapolated line to the point on the northern continent toward which they were headed. Under other circumstances, with a shade more luck, the story would eventually have been told and retold as a heroic and masterly reversal of a lost situation. But within sight of victory, tired body and tired nerves clamped a control bar with a shade too much pressure. The ship, which had almost leveled off, dipped down again.

There was no room to retrieve the final error. There was only a mile left to fall. The Pilot remained at his post to the actual landing, his only thought that of breaking the force of the crash, of maintaining the spaceworthiness of the vessel. He did not survive. With the ship bucking madly in a soupy atmosphere, few Ejectors could be mobilized and only one of them in time.

WHEN AFTERWARDS, the Explorer lifted out of unconsciousness and rose to his feet, he had the definite feeling that but for himself and the Merchant, there were no survivors. And perhaps that was an over-calculation. His Floater had burnt out while still sufficiently distant from surface to have the fall stun him. The Merchant might have had less luck, even, than that.

He was surrounded by a world of thick, ropy stalks of grass, and in the distance were trees that reminded him vaguely of similar structures on his native Arcturian world except that their lowest branches were high above what he would consider normal tree-tops.

He called, his voice sounding basso in the thick air and the Merchant answered. The Explorer made his way toward him, thrusting violently at the coarse stalks that barred his path.

"Are you hurt?" he asked.

The Merchant grimaced. "I've sprained something. It hurts to walk."

The Explorer probed gently. "I don't think anything is broken. You'll have to walk despite the pain."

"Can't we rest first?"

"It's important to try to find the ship. If it is spaceworthy or if it can be repaired, we may live. If otherwise, we won't."

"Just a few minutes. Let me catch my breath."

The Explorer was glad enough for those few minutes. The Merchant's eyes were already closed. He allowed his to do the same.

He heard the trampling and his eyes snapped open. Never sleep on a strange planet, he told himself futilely.

The Merchant was awake too and his steady screaming was a rumble of terror.

The Explorer called, "It's only a native of this planet. It won't harm you."

But even as he spoke, the giant had swooped down and in a moment they were in its grasp being lifted closer to its monstrous ugliness.

The Merchant struggled violently and, of course, quite futilely. "Can't you talk to it?" he yelled.

The Explorer could only shake his head. "I can't reach it with the Projector. It won't be listening."

"Then blast it. Blast it down."

"We can't do that." The phrase "you fool" had almost been added. The Explorer struggled to keep his self-control. They were swallowing space as the monster moved purposefully away.

"Why not?" cried the Merchant. "You can reach your blaster. I see it in plain sight. Don't be afraid of falling."

"It's simpler than that. If this monster is killed, you'll never trade with this planet. You'll never even leave it. You probably won't live the day out."

"Why? Why?"

"Because this is one of the young of the species. You should know what happens when a trader kills a native young, even accidentally. What's more, if this is the target-point, then we are on the estate of a powerful native. This might be one of his brood."

That was how they entered their present prison. They had carefully burnt away a portion of the thick, stiff covering and it was obvious that the height from which they were suspended was a killing one.

Now, once again, the prison-cage shuddered and lifted in an upward arc. The Merchant rolled to the lower rim and startled awake. The cover lifted and light flooded in. As was the case the time before, there were two specimens of the young. They were not very different in appearance from adults of the species, reflected the Explorer, though, of course, they were considerably smaller.

A handful of reedy green stalks was stuffed between the bars. Its odor was not unpleasant but it carried clods of soil at its ends.

The Merchant drew away and said, huskily, "What are they doing?"

The Explorer said, "Trying to feed us, I should judge. At least this seems to be the native equivalent of grass."

The cover was replaced and they were set swinging again, alone with their fodder.

IV

SLIM STARTED at hearing the sound of footsteps and brightened when it turned out to be only Red.

He said, "No one's around. I had my eye peeled, you bet."

Red said, "Ssh. Look. You take this stuff and stick it through into the cage. I've got to scoot back to the house."

"What is it?" Slim reached reluctantly.

"Ground meat. Holy Smokes, haven't you ever seen ground meat? That's what you should've got when I sent you to the house instead of coming back with that stupid grass."

Slim was hurt. "How'd I know they don't eat grass. Besides, ground meat doesn't come loose like that. It comes in cellophane and it isn't that color."

"Sure—in the city. Out here we grind our own and it's always this color till it's cooked."

"You mean it isn't cooked?" Slim drew away quickly.

Red looked disgusted. "Do you think animals eat *cooked* food. Come on, take it. It won't hurt you. I tell you there isn't much time."

"Why? What's doing back at the house?"

"I don't know. Dad and your father are walking around. I think maybe they're looking for me. Maybe the cook told them I took the meat. Anyway, we don't want them coming here after me."

"Didn't you ask the cook before you took this stuff?"

"Who? That crab? Shouldn't wonder if she only let me have a drink of water because Dad makes her. Come on. Take it."

Slim took the large glob of meat though his skin crawled at the touch. He turned toward the barn and Red sped away in the direction from which he had come.

He slowed when he approached the two adults, took a few deep breaths to bring himself back to normal, and then carefully and nonchalantly sauntered past. (They were walking in the general direction of the barn, he noticed, but not dead on.)

He said, "Hi, Dad. Hello, sir."

The Industrialist said, "Just a moment, Red. I have a question to ask you?"

Red turned a carefully blank face to his father. "Yes, Dad?"

"Mother tells me that you were out early this morning."

"Not real early, Dad. Just a little bit before breakfast."

"She said you told her it was because you had been awakened during the night and didn't go back to sleep."

Red waited before answering. Should he have told Mom that?

Then he said, "Yes, sir."

"What was it that awakened you?"

Red saw no harm in it. He said, "I don't know, Dad. It sounded like thunder, sort of, and like a collision, sort of."

"Could you tell where it came from?"

"It *sounded* like it was out by the hill." That was truthful, and useful as well, since the direction was almost opposite that in which the barn lay.

The Industrialist looked at his guest. "I suppose it would do no harm to walk toward the hill."

The Astronomer said, "I am ready."

Red watched them walk away and when he turned he saw Slim peering cautiously out from among the briars of a hedge.

Red waved at him. "Come on."

Slim stepped out and approached. "Did they say anything about the meat?"

"No. I guess they don't know about that. They went down to the hill."

"What for?"

"Search me. They kept asking about the noise I heard. Listen, did the animals eat the meat?"

"Well," said Slim, cautiously, "they were sort of *looking* at it and smelling it or something."

"Okay," Red said, "I guess they'll eat it. Holy Smokes, they've got to eat *something*. Let's walk along toward the hill and see what Dad and your father are going to do."

"What about the animals?"

"They'll be all right. A fellow can't spend all his time on them. Did you give them water?"

"Sure. They drank that."

"See. Come on. We'll look at them after lunch. I tell you what. We'll bring them fruit. Anything'll eat fruit."

Together they trotted up the rise, Red, as usual, in the lead.

V

THE ASTRONOMER said, "You think the noise was their ship landing?"

"Don't you think it could be?"

"If it were, they may all be dead."

"Perhaps not." The Industrialist frowned.

"If they have landed, and are still alive, where are they?"

"Think about that for a while." He was still frowning.

The Astronomer said, "I don't understand you."

"They may not be friendly."

"Oh, no. I've spoken with them. They've—"

"You've spoken with them. Call that reconnaissance. What would their next step be? Invasion?"

"But they only have one ship, sir."

"You know that only because they say so. They might have a fleet."

"I've told you about their size. They—"

"Their size would not matter, if they have handweapons that may well be superior to our own artillery."

"That is not what I meant."

"I had this partly in mind from the first." The Industrialist went on. "It is for that reason I agreed to see them after I received your letter. Not to agree to an unsettling and impossible trade, but to judge their real purposes. I did not count on their evading the meeting."

He sighed. "I suppose it isn't our fault. You are right in one thing, at any rate. The world has been at peace too long. We are losing our healthy sense of suspicion."

The Astronomer's mild voice rose to an unusual pitch and he said, "I *will* speak. I tell you that there is no reason to suppose they can possibly be hostile. They are small, yes, but that is only important because it is a reflection of the fact that their native worlds are small. Our world has what is for them a normal gravity, but because of our much higher gravitational potential, our atmosphere is too dense to support them comfortably over sustained periods. For a similar reason the use of the world as a base for interstellar travel, except for trade in certain items, is uneconomical. And there are important differences in chemistry of life due to the basic differences in soils. They couldn't eat our food or we theirs."

"Surely all this can be overcome. They can bring their own food, build domed stations of lowered air pressure, devise specially designed ships."

"They can. And how glibly you can describe feats that are easy to a race in its youth. It is simply that they don't have to do any of that. There are millions of worlds suitable for them in the Galaxy. They don't need this one which isn't."

"How do you know? All this is their information again."

"This I was able to check independently. I am an astronomer, after all."

"That is true. Let me hear what you have to say then, while we walk."

"Then, sir, consider that for a long time our astronomers have believed that two general classes of planetary bodies existed. First, the planets which formed at distances far enough from their stellar nucleus to become cool enough to capture hydrogen. These would be large planets rich in hydrogen, ammonia and methane. We have examples of these in the giant outer planets. The second class would include those planets formed so near the stellar center that the high temperature would make it impossible to capture much hydrogen. These would be smaller planets, comparatively poorer in hydrogen and richer in oxygen. We know that type very well since we live on one. Ours is the only solar system we know in detail, however, and it has been reasonable for us to assume that these were the *only* two planetary classes."

"I take it then that there is another."

"Yes. There is a super-dense class, still smaller, poorer in hydrogen, than the inner planets of the solar system. The ratio of occurrence of hydrogen-ammonia planets and these super-dense water-oxygen worlds of theirs over the entire Galaxy—and remember that they have actually conducted a survey of significant sample volumes of the Galaxy which we, without interstellar travel, cannot do—is about 3 to 1. This leaves them seven million super-dense worlds for exploration and colonization."

T HE INDUSTRIALIST looked at the blue sky and the green-covered trees among which they were making their way. He said, "And worlds like ours?"

The Astronomer said, softly, "Ours is the first solar system they have found which contains them. Apparently the development of our solar system was unique and did not follow the ordinary rules."

The Industrialist considered that. "What it amounts to is that these creatures from space are asteroid-dwellers."

"No, no. The asteroids are something else again. They occur, I was told, in one out of eight stellar systems, but they're completely different from what we've been discussing."

"And how does your being an astronomer change the fact that you are still only quoting their unsupported statements?"

"But they did not restrict themselves to bald items of information. They presented me with a theory of stellar evolution which I had to accept and which is more nearly valid than anything our own astronomy has ever been able to devise, if we except possible lost theories dating from Beforethewars. Mind you, their theory had a rigidly mathematical development and it predicted just such a Galaxy as they describe. So you see, they have all the worlds they wish. They are not land-hungry. Certainly not for our land."

"Reason would say so, if what you say is true. But creatures may be intelligent and not reasonable. Our forefathers were presumably intelligent, yet they were certainly not reasonable. Was it reasonable to destroy almost all their tremendous civilization in atomic warfare over causes our historians can no longer accurately determine?" The Industrialist brooded over it. "From the dropping of the first atom bomb over those islands—I forget the ancient name—there was only one end in sight, and in plain sight. Yet events were allowed to proceed to that end."

He looked up, said briskly, "Well, where are we? I wonder if we are not on a fool's errand after all."

But the Astronomer was a little in advance and his voice came thickly. "No fool's errand, sir. Look there."

VI

RED AND Slim had trailed their elders with the experience of youth, aided by the absorption and anxiety of their fathers. Their view of the final object of the search was somewhat obscured by the underbrush behind which they remained.

Red said, "Holy Smokes. Look at that. It's all shiny silver or something."

But it was Slim who was really excited. He caught at the other. "I know what this is. It's a space-ship. That must be why my father came here. He's one of the biggest astronomers in the world and your father would have to call him if a space-ship landed on his estate."

"What are you talking about? Dad didn't even know that thing was there. He only came here because I told him I heard the thunder from here. Besides, there isn't any such thing as a space-ship."

"Sure, there is. Look at it. See those round things. They are ports. And you can see the rocket tubes."

"How do you know so much?"

Slim was flushed. He said, "I read about them. My father has books about them. Old books. From Beforethewars."

"Huh. Now I know you're making it up. Books from Beforethewars!"

"My father *has* to have them. He teaches at the University. It's his job."

His voice had risen and Red had to pull at him. "You want them to hear us?" he whispered indignantly.

"Well, it is, too, a space-ship."

"Look here, Slim, you mean that's a ship from another world."

"It's *got* to be. Look at my father going round and round it. He wouldn't be so interested if it was anything else."

"Other worlds! Where are there other worlds?"

"Everywhere. How about the planets? They're worlds just like ours, some of them. And other stars probably have planets. There's probably zillions of planets."

Red felt outweighed and outnumbered. He muttered, "You're crazy!"

"All right, then. I'll show you."

"Hey! Where are you going?"

"Down there. I'm going to ask my father. I suppose you'll believe it if *he* tells you. I suppose you'll believe a Professor of Astronomy knows what—"

He had scrambled upright.

Red said, "Hey. You don't want them to see us. We're not supposed to be here. Do you want them to start asking questions and find out about our animals?"

"I don't care. You said I was crazy."

"Snitcher! You promised you wouldn't tell."

"I'm *not* going to tell. But if they find out themselves, it's your fault, for starting an argument and saying I was crazy."

"I take it back, then," grumbled Red.

"Well, all right. You better."

In a way, Slim was disappointed. He wanted to see the space-ship at closer quarters. Still, he could not break his vow of secrecy even in spirit without at least the excuse of personal insult.

Red said, "It's awfully small for a space-ship."

"Sure, because it's probably a scout-ship."

"I'll bet Dad couldn't even get into the old thing."

So much Slim realized to be true. It was a weak point in his argument and he made no answer. His interest was absorbed by the adults.

RED ROSE to his feet; an elaborate attitude of boredom all about him. "Well, I guess we better be going. There's business to do and I can't spend all day here looking at some old space-ship or whatever it is. We've got to take care of the animals if we're going to be circus-folks. That's the first rule with circus-folks. They've got to take care of the animals. And," he finished virtuously, "that's what I aim to do, anyway."

Slim said, "What for, Red? They've got plenty of meat. Let's watch."

"There's no fun in watching. Besides Dad and your father are going away and I guess it's about lunch time."

Red became argumentative. "Look, Slim, we can't start acting suspicious or they're going to start investigating. Holy Smokes, don't you ever read any detective stories? When you're trying to work a big deal without being caught, it's practically the main thing to keep on acting just like always. Then they don't suspect anything. That's the first law—"

"Oh, all right."

Slim rose resentfully. At the moment, the circus appeared to him a rather tawdry and shoddy substitute for the glories of astronomy, and he wondered how he had come to fall in with Red's silly scheme.

Down the slope they went, Slim, as usual, in the rear.

VII

THE INDUSTRIALIST said, "It's the workmanship that gets me. I never saw such construction."

"What good is it now?" said the Astronomer, bitterly. "There's nothing left. There'll be no second landing. This ship detected life on our planet through accident. Other exploring parties would come no closer than necessary to establish the fact that there were no super-dense worlds existing in our solar system."

"Well, there's no quarreling with a crash landing."

"The ship hardly seems damaged. If only some had survived, the ship might have been repaired."

"If they had survived, there would be no trade in any case. They're too different. Too disturbing. In any case—it's over."

They entered the house and the Industrialist greeted his wife calmly. "Lunch about ready, dear."

"I'm afraid not. You see—" She looked hesitantly at the Astronomer.

"Is anything wrong?" asked the Industrialist. "Why not tell me? I'm sure our guest won't mind a little family discussion."

"Pray don't pay any attention whatever to me," muttered the Astronomer. He moved miserably to the other end of the living room.

The woman said, in low, hurried tones, "Really, dear, cook's that upset. I've been soothing her for hours and honestly, I don't know why Red should have done it."

"Done what?" The Industrialist was more amused than otherwise. It had taken the united efforts of himself and his son months to argue his wife into using the name "Red" rather than the perfectly ridiculous (viewed youngster fashion) name which was his real one.

She said, "He's taken most of the chopped meat."

"He's eaten it?"

"Well, I hope not. It was raw."

"Then what would he want it for?"

"I haven't the slightest idea. I haven't seen him since breakfast. Meanwhile cook's just furious. She caught him vanishing out the kitchen door and there was the bowl of chopped meat just about empty and she was going to use it for lunch. Well, you know cook. She had to change the lunch menu and that means she won't be worth living with for a week. You'll just have to speak to Red, dear, and make him promise not to do things in the kitchen any more. And it wouldn't hurt to have him apologize to cook."

"Oh, come. She works for us. If we don't complain about a change in lunch menu, why should she?"

"Because she's the one who has double-work made for her, and she's talking about quitting. Good cooks aren't easy to get. Do you remember the one before her?"

It was a strong argument.

The Industrialist looked about vaguely. He said, "I suppose you're right. He isn't here, I suppose. When he comes in, I'll talk to him."

"You'd better start. Here he comes."

RED WALKED into the house and said cheerfully, "Time for lunch, I guess." He looked from one parent to the other in quick speculation at their fixed stares and said, "Got to clean up first, though," and made for the other door.

The Industrialist said, "One moment, son."

"Sir?"

"Where's your little friend?"

Red said, carelessly, "He's around somewhere. We were just sort of walking and I looked around and he wasn't there." This was perfectly true, and Red felt on safe ground. "I told him it was lunch time. I said, 'I suppose it's about lunch time.' I said, 'We got to be getting back to the house.' And he said, 'Yes.' And I just went on and then when I was about at the creek I looked around and—"

The Astronomer interrupted the voluble story, looking up from a magazine he had been sightlessly rummaging through. "I wouldn't worry about my youngster. He is quite self-reliant. Don't wait lunch for him."

"Lunch isn't ready in any case, Doctor." The Industrialist turned once more to his son. "And talking about that, son, the reason for it is that something happened to the ingredients. Do you have anything to say?"

"Sir?"

"I hate to feel that I have to explain myself more fully. Why did you take the chopped meat?"

"The chopped meat?"

"The chopped meat." He waited patiently.

Red said, "Well, I was sort of—"

"Hungry?" prompted his father. "For raw meat?"

"No, sir. I just sort of needed it."

"For what exactly?"

Red looked miserable and remained silent.

The Astronomer broke in again. "If you don't mind my putting in a few words—You'll remember that just after breakfast my son came in to ask what animals ate."

"Oh, you're right. How stupid of me to forget. Look here, Red, did you take it for an animal pet you've got?"

Red recovered indignant breath. He said, "You mean Slim came in here and said I had an animal? He came in here and said that? He said I had an animal?"

"No, he didn't. He simply asked what animals ate. That's all. Now if he promised he wouldn't tell on you, he didn't. It's your own foolishness in trying to take something without permission that gave you away. That happened to be stealing. Now have you an animal? I ask you a direct question."

"Yes, sir." It was a whisper so low as hardly to be heard.

"All right, you'll have to get rid of it. Do you understand?"

Red's mother intervened. "Do you mean to say you're keeping a meat-eating animal, Red? It might bite you and give you blood-poison."

"They're only small ones," quavered Red. "They hardly budge if you touch them."

"They? How many do you have?"

"Two."

"Where are they?"

The Industrialist touched her arm. "Don't chivvy the child any further," he said, in a low voice. "If he says he'll get rid of them, he will, and that's punishment enough."

He dismissed the matter from his mind.

VIII

LUNCH was half over when Slim dashed into the dining room. For a moment, he stood abashed, and then he said in what was almost hysteria, "I've got to speak to Red. I've got to say something."

Red looked up in fright, but the Astronomer said, "I don't think, son, you're being very polite. You've kept lunch waiting."

"I'm sorry, Father."

"Oh, don't rate the lad," said the Industrialist's wife. "He can speak to Red if he wants to, and there was no damage done to the lunch."

"I've got to speak to Red alone," Slim insisted.

"Now that's enough," said the Astronomer with a kind of gentleness that was obviously manufactured for the benefit of strangers and which had beneath it an easily-recognized edge. "Take your seat."

Slim did so, but he ate only when someone looked directly upon him. Even then he was not very successful.

Red caught his eyes. He made soundless words, "Did the animals get loose?"

Slim shook his head slightly. He whispered, "No, it's—"

The Astronomer looked at him hard and Slim faltered to a stop.

With lunch over, Red slipped out of the room, with a microscopic motion at Slim to follow.

They walked in silence to the creek.

Then Red turned fiercely upon his companion. "Look here, what's the idea of telling my Dad we were feeding animals?"

Slim said, "I didn't. I asked what you feed animals. That's not the same as saying we were doing it. Besides, it's something else, Red."

But Red had not used up his grievances. "And where did you go anyway? I thought you were coming to the house. They acted like it was my fault you weren't there."

"But I'm trying to tell you about that, if you'd only shut *up* a second and let me talk. You don't give a fellow a chance."

"Well, go on and tell me if you've got so much to say."

"I'm *trying* to. I went back to the space-ship. The folks weren't there anymore and I wanted to see what it was like."

"It isn't a space-ship," said Red, sullenly. He had nothing to lose.

"It is, too. I looked inside. You could look through the ports and I looked inside and they were *dead*." He looked sick. "They were dead."

"*Who* were dead."

Slim screeched, "Animals! like *our* animals! Only they *aren't* animals. They're people-things from other planets."

For a moment Red might have been turned to stone. It didn't occur to him to disbelieve Slim at this point. Slim looked too genuinely the bearer of just such tidings. He said, finally, "Oh, my."

"Well, what are we going to do? Golly, will we get a whopping if they find out?" He was shivering.

"We better turn them loose," said Red.

"They'll tell on us."

"They can't talk our language. Not if they're from another planet."

"Yes, they can. Because I remember my father talking about some stuff like that to my mother when he didn't know I was in the room. He was talking about visitors who could talk with the mind. Tele-pathery or something. I thought he was making it up."

"Well, Holy Smokes. I mean—Holy Smokes." Red looked up. "I tell you. My Dad said to get rid of them. Let's sort of bury them somewhere or throw them in the creek."

"He *told* you to do that."

"He made me say I had animals and then he said, 'Get rid of them.' I got to do what he says. Holy Smokes, he's my Dad."

Some of the panic left Slim's heart. It was a thoroughly legalistic way out. "Well, let's do it right now, then, before they find out. Oh, golly, if they find out, will we be in trouble!"

They broke into a run toward the barn, un-speakable visions in their minds.

IX

I T WAS different, looking at them as though they were "people." As animals, they had been interesting; as "people," horrible. Their eyes, which were neutral little objects before, now seemed to watch them with active malevolence.

"They're making noises," said Slim, in a whisper which was barely audible.

"I guess they're talking or something," said Red. Funny that those noises which they had heard before had not had significance earlier. He was making no move toward them. Neither was Slim.

The canvas was off but they were just watching. The ground meat, Slim noticed, hadn't been touched.

Slim said, "Aren't you going to do something?"

"Aren't you?"

"You found them."

"It's your turn, now."

"No, it isn't. You found them. It's your fault, the whole thing. I was watching."

"You joined in, Slim. You know you did."

"I don't care. You found them and that's what I'll say when they come here looking for us."

Red said, "All right for you." But the thought of the consequences inspired him anyway, and he reached for the cage door.

Slim said, "Wait!"

Red was glad to. He said, "Now what's biting you?"

"One of them's got something on him that looks like it might be iron or something."

"Where?"

"Right there. I saw it before but I thought it was just part of him. But if he's 'people,' maybe it's a disintegrator gun."

"What's that?"

"I read about it in the books from Beforethe-wars. Mostly people with space-ships have disinte-grator guns. They point them at you and you get disintegratored."

"They didn't point it at us till now," pointed out Red with his heart not quite in it.

"I don't care. I'm not hanging around here and getting disintegratored. I'm getting my father."

"Cowardy-cat. Yellow cowardy-cat."

"I don't care. You can call all the names you want, but if you bother them now you'll get disinte-gratored. You wait and see, and it'll be all your fault."

He made for the narrow spiral stairs that led to the main floor of the barn, stopped at its head, then backed away.

Red's mother was moving up, panting a little with the exertion and smiling a tight smile for the benefit of Slim in his capacity as guest.

"Red! You, Red! Are you up there? Now don't try to hide. I know this is where you're keeping them. Cook saw where you ran with the meat."

Red quavered, "Hello, ma!"

"Now show me those nasty animals? I'm going to see to it that you get rid of them right away."

It was over! And despite the imminent corporal punishment, Red felt something like a load fall from him. At least the decision was out of his hands.

"Right there, ma. I didn't do anything to them, ma. I didn't know. They just looked like little animals and I thought you'd let me keep them, ma. I wouldn't have taken the meat only they wouldn't eat grass or leaves and we couldn't find good nuts or berries and cook never lets me have anything or I would have asked her and I didn't know it was for lunch and—"

He was speaking on the sheer momentum of terror and did not realize that his mother did not hear him but, with eyes frozen and popping at the cage, was screaming in thin, piercing tones.

X

T HE ASTRONOMER was saying, "A quiet burial is all we can do. There is no point in any publicity now," when they heard the screams.

She had not entirely recovered by the time she reached them, running and running. It was minutes before her husband could extract sense from her.

She was saying, finally, "I tell you they're in the barn. I don't know what they are. No, no—"

She barred the Industrialist's quick movement in that direction. She said, "Don't *you* go. Send one of the hands with a shotgun. I tell you I never saw anything like it. Little horrible beasts with—with—I can't describe it. To think that Red was touching them and trying to feed them. He was *holding* them, and feeding them meat."

Red began, "I only—"

And Slim said, "It was not—"

The Industrialist said, quickly, "Now you boys have done enough harm today. March! Into the house! And not a word; not one word! I'm not interested in anything you have to say. After this is all over, I'll hear you out and as for you, Red, I'll see that you're properly punished."

He turned to his wife. "Now whatever the animals are, we'll have them killed." He added quietly once the youngsters were out of hearing, "Come, come. The children aren't hurt and, after all, they haven't done anything really terrible. They've just found a new pet."

The Astronomer spoke with difficulty. "Pardon me, ma'am, but can you describe these animals?"

She shook her head. She was quite beyond words.

"Can you just tell me if they—"

"I'm sorry," said the Industrialist, apologetically, "but I think I had better take care of her. Will you excuse me?"

"A moment. Please. One moment. She said she had never seen such animals before. Surely it is not usual to find animals that are completely unique on an estate such as this."

"I'm sorry. Let's not discuss that now."

"Except that unique animals might have landed during the night."

The Industrialist stepped away from his wife. "What are you implying?"

"I think we had better go to the barn, sir!"

The Industrialist stared a moment, turned and suddenly and quite uncharacteristically began running. The Astronomer followed and the woman's wail rose unheeded behind them.

XI

THE INDUSTRIALIST stared, looked at the Astronomer, turned to stare again.

"Those?"

"Those," said the Astronomer. "I have no doubt we appear strange and repulsive to them."

"What do they say?"

"Why, that they are uncomfortable and tired and even a little sick, but that they are not seriously damaged, and that the youngsters treated them well."

"Treated them well! Scooping them up, keeping them in a cage, giving them grass and raw meat to eat? Tell me how to speak to them."

"It may take a little time. Think *at* them. Try to listen. It will come to you, but perhaps not right away."

The Industrialist tried. He grimaced with the effort of it, thinking over and over again, "The youngsters were ignorant of your identity."

And the thought was suddenly in his mind: "We were quite aware of it and because we knew they meant well by us according to their own view of the matter, we did not attempt to attack them."

"Attack them?" thought the Industrialist, and said it aloud in his concentration.

"Why, yes," came the answering thought. "We are armed."

One of the revolting little creatures in the cage lifted a metal object and there was a sudden hole in the top of the cage and another in the roof of the barn, each hole rimmed with charred wood.

"We hope," the creatures thought, "it will not be too difficult to make repairs."

The Industrialist found it impossible to organize himself to the point of directed thought. He turned to the Astronomer. "And with that weapon in their possession they let themselves be handled and caged? I don't understand it."

But the calm thought came, "We would not harm the young of an intelligent species."

XII

I T WAS twilight. The Industrialist had entirely missed the evening meal and remained unaware of the fact.

He said, "Do you really think the ship will fly?"

"If they say so," said the Astronomer, "I'm sure it will. They'll be back, I hope, before too long."

"And when they do," said the Industrialist, energetically, "I will keep my part of the agreement. What is more I will move sky and earth to have the world accept them. I was entirely wrong, Doctor. Creatures that would refuse to harm children, under such provocation as they received, are admirable. But you know—I almost hate to say this—"

"Say what?"

"The kids. Yours and mine. I'm almost proud of them. Imagine seizing these creatures, feeding them or trying to, and keeping them hidden. The amazing gall of it. Red told me it was his idea to get a job in a circus on the strength of them. Imagine!"

The Astronomer said, "Youth!"

XIII

THE MERCHANT said, "Will we be taking off soon?"

"Half an hour," said the Explorer.

It was going to be a lonely trip back. All the remaining seventeen of the crew were dead and their ashes were to be left on a strange planet. Back they would go with a limping ship and the burden of the controls entirely on himself.

The Merchant said, "It was a good business stroke, not harming the young ones. We will get very good terms; *very* good terms."

The Explorer thought: Business!

The Merchant then said, "They've lined up to see us off. All of them. You don't think they're too close, do you? It would be bad to burn any of them with the rocket blast at this stage of the game."

"They're safe."

"Horrible-looking things, aren't they?"

"Pleasant enough, inside. Their thoughts are perfectly friendly."

"You wouldn't believe it of them. That immature one, the one that first picked us up—"

"They call him Red," provided the Explorer.

"That's a queer name for a monster. Makes me laugh. He actually feels *bad* that we're leaving. Only I can't make out exactly why. The nearest I can come to it is something about a lost opportunity with some organization or other that I can't quite interpret."

"A circus," said the Explorer, briefly.

"What? Why, the impertinent monstrosity."

"Why not? What would you have done if you had found *him* wandering on *your* native world; found him sleeping on a field on Earth, red tentacles, six legs, pseudopods and all?"

XIV

R ED WATCHED the ship leave. His red tentacles, which gave him his nickname, quivered their regret at lost opportunity to the very last, and the eyes at their tips filled with drifting yellowish crystals that were the equivalent of Earthly tears.

Idle
Winter
Press

www.ingramcontent.com/pod-product-compliance
Lightning Source LLC
Chambersburg PA
CBHW071232250626
47163CB00001B/152